Living Consequences

Living Consequences

Brittney Holmes

www.urbanchristianonline.net

Urban Books
10 Brennan Place
Deer Park, NY 11729

ISBN-13: 978-1-60162-981-4
ISBN-10: 1-60162-981-8

First Trade Printing February 2007
First Mass Market Printing February 2009
Printed in the United States of America

10 9 8 7 6 5 4 3 2 1

Submit Wholesale Orders to:
Kensington Publishing Corp.
C/O Penguin Group (USA) Inc.
Attention: Order Processing
405 Murray Hill Parkway
East Rutherford, NJ 07073-2316
Phone: 1-800-526-0275
Fax: 1-800-227-9604

Acknowledgments

First and foremost, I would like to thank the Man who is the center of my life—God. Thank You for blessing me with the gift to put Your words to paper so that Your people may have the chance to hear You throughout the pages of this book.

To my parents, Jonathan Bellamy and Kendra Norman-Bellamy, thank you for supporting and believing in me. Thank you, also, for raising me to be a God-fearing young lady. I pray that I've made you proud. I love you guys very much. Crystal, my baby sister, I thank you for letting me hog the computer. Even though I don't say it very often, I love you, also.

To my grandparents, Bishop and Mrs. H.H. Norman, Mr. Jesse and Mrs. Dorothy Holmes, and the late Elder Clinton and Mrs. Willie Mae Bellamy, and the rest of my extended family (uncles, aunts, and cousins): whether you're here with me physically or spiritually, I carry you in my heart always.

Terrance, my cousin and publicist, you've done so much for me (reading my manuscripts, telling me, honestly, if they were good or not, and just hanging out with me and making me laugh until I cry), and words could not express how much I appreciate you.

Mr. Jamill, Ms. Shunda, and the entire Booking Matters family, thank you for believing in me.

To my best friends, Alexandria, Inonege, and Gabrielle—I love you guys to death. I hope we'll always be friends even if we end up living on opposite ends of the country. To all of my other classmates and educators at Redan High School, and especially to the Class of 2008 (I wish I could name you all, but time and space will not permit it)—thank you all for your support.

All of my love to my spiritual family at my home church, Revival Church Ministries, and my home away from home church, Church of God by Faith Ministries—you all have been by my side from the very beginning and I plan on taking you all the way to the end.

To my publishers, Urban Books (Urban Christian), I thank you for making all my dreams come true. A special thanks to my editor, Ms. Joylynn, thank you for everything.

And finally, to my readers, this book will make you laugh and cry; you might even get angry, but I hope entertainment is not all you get out of it. I pray that you will learn what it means to put your faith and trust in God so that no matter what you go through in life, you'll always know that He is with you.

Living Consequences

Chapter 1

December 16
Last day of First Semester

The last period bell sounded as students rushed into the hallway. It was the last bell they would hear for almost two weeks. The Christmas holiday had been a long-time coming for the students at Frederick Douglass High School.

Nevaeh rushed out of her creative writing class, almost knocking down a girl in the process. "Oh . . . I'm sorry," she said.

"No, the word is *excuse me!*" the girl snapped.

It was Sierra Monroe, a girl who had a reputation for catching an attitude quick, fast, and in a hurry. Nevaeh was constantly trying to steer clear of the girl, but Sierra somehow always managed to pop up in her face.

Trying to be as polite as she could, Nevaeh managed a weak, "Excuse me," as she rushed around the corner and almost bumped into her best friend, Shimone.

"Girl, where's the fire?" Shimone laughed. "You look like you've just seen a ghost."

"No ghost, just a witch with a deadly attitude," Nevaeh responded, using the phrase they coined to describe Sierra.

"You lettin' that . . . that *girl* get to you again?" Shimone rolled her eyes at her friend, who never let her forget that she didn't care how mean or obnoxious someone was, profane words were not allowed around her. "Well, you know all you got to do is say the word and I'll take care of that chick," Shimone added, cracking her knuckles for emphasis.

"No, it's cool," Nevaeh responded, not wanting to start any unnecessary drama.

Shimone shrugged. "Well, c'mon. Let's go 'fore our men leave us stranded here."

As Shimone and Nevaeh made their way out to the parking lot, Shimone talked about her plans with her boyfriend, Marques, that night. Nevaeh wondered why her friend was so caught up in Marques' rap. He used it on every girl he came in contact with. He was a playa, a bona fide dog, as far as Nevaeh was concerned, and she wished Shimone would somehow see him for who he really was.

"Hey, baby." The voice of Nevaeh's boyfriend, Ronald, broke into her thoughts as she climbed into his 2004 Toyota Camry. He picked up the red roses that lay in the back seat and handed them to her.

"Thank you, Ronald," Nevaeh said, giving him a quick kiss on the lips before closing the door and putting on her seatbelt.

"Wassup, sexy?" Marques said to Shimone as she settled into the car.

Nevaeh rolled her eyes while Shimone giggled at Marques' nickname for any girl he thought looked halfway decent.

"What's wrong?" Ronald asked Nevaeh, noting her grim attitude when Shimone and Marques started kissing one another as if they were the only two people in the vehicle.

"Nothing," Nevaeh said, trying to sound cheerful.

"You sure?" Using his hand, Ronald forced her to face him so she'd be looking directly into his dark eyes.

Lord, please help me, Nevaeh thought as he searched her face for the truth. She gave Ronald her best smile and offered him another peck on the lips to assure him she was fine. She also wanted him to stop looking at her in the manner that he was. He had the most hypnotic eyes. They were so dark that when she looked in them, she either wanted to search them for whatever secret they hid, or look away before she got lost in them.

Ronald Jaheem McAfee was six-foot-two, a solid 190 pounds, all packed in smooth, dark chocolate skin, with a goatee that surrounded his full lips. When he spoke or smiled, his cheeks displayed deep dimples that made any girl weak. Being the quarterback on Douglass' football team was an added bonus to his massive appeal.

He and Nevaeh Keion Madison made the perfect couple. At five-feet-five and 125 pounds, Nevaeh's mocha brown skin and shoulder-length sandy brown hair, with a face that belonged on a Cover Girl magazine, complemented everything that was Ronald McAfee. Being cheerleading captain made them an even better combination.

Nevaeh's best friend, Shimone LaNia Johnson,

stood at five-foot-two and 153 pounds. It was no secret that Shimone felt very comfortable in her bira-
cial skin. Being half white never fazed her, and as
captain of the dance team, she was never afraid to remind someone she could out-dance them in a hot
second. Nevaeh and Shimone were as different as
they were alike. The major difference between the
friends, however, was their view on abstinence.

While Nevaeh and her boyfriend of two years believed that a couple should be married before they
shared that level of intimacy, Shimone had no qualms
about showing her guy how she felt about him. Nevaeh
had tried to convince Shimone to change her views
on the matter, but had made no progress. Shimone
had been sexually active since the second semester of
their sophomore year.

Nevaeh often recalled the day that they returned
to school after spring break. Shimone had spent her
time in Daytona Beach, Florida, and when she met
up with Nevaeh, she was all smiles.

"Girl, you must've had some real fun for you to be
cheesin' like that," Nevaeh had said to her friend at
their lockers on the first day back.

"Girl, I'm so much in love that *love* doesn't even
describe how I'm feeling!" Shimone squealed.

"That doesn't even make any sense," Nevaeh said
with a laugh. "So, who is this Romeo?"

"His name is Julio Montana, and he worked at the
hotel we stayed in."

"And y'all just met and hung out for the whole
week?"

"No, we just met and stayed in for the whole week,
if you know what I mean."

Nevaeh remembered her jaw dropping in surprise. "You lost your virginity to a complete stranger?" she questioned.

"He wasn't no *stranger*. I knew everything I needed to know about him," Shimone responded with an attitude.

"I can't believe you . . ."

"You know what?" Shimone's hand in the air cut short Nevaeh's rebuke. Accompanying her hand was a rolling neck and a wagging finger. "I can't believe *you*! All up in my face tryin' to judge me like you some kinda angel!"

"But Shimone . . ."

"Save it! I'm out. Call me when you get over it, 'cause it's done!"

When Shimone walked off, leaving Nevaeh's mouth wide open, standing speechless, she knew that wouldn't be the end of that argument. And she had been right. Every chance she got, Nevaeh tried to convince Shimone that what she was doing was not right. As hard as Nevaeh tried, Shimone continued to have sexual relationships with several other guys, including her current boyfriend, Marques.

Marques Tyrone Anderson had been dubbed "King Playa" in the ninth grade by his friends, who continuously praised him for all the girls he had relationships with. He was known to "drop a chick" in a split second if she got too clingy, and pick up two more to compensate for the one lost.

At five-feet-eleven with a caramel complexion and clean-shaven head, he weighed in at 178 pounds. As the star point guard on the basketball team for Douglass, he had already been offered full basketball scholarships to several different universities throughout the states of Georgia, South Carolina, and Florida.

Marques never stayed with any girl for longer than three weeks; four at the max. Even he wondered why he hadn't gotten rid of Shimone yet. They'd been going out for more than three months. Next week would mark month four, and he couldn't understand why he hadn't made up any excuses to try to dump her, or at least find another girl to hang out with when she was not around.

Shimone had his heart open, but he couldn't admit it to himself, let alone to his friends who questioned his prolonged relationship. She was so beautiful and confident with herself and she didn't take anyone's smack, not even his. She had such an effect on Marques that he'd even gone as far as introducing her to his parents, and that was something he'd always steered clear of when dating, but Shimone had changed that too. He really liked her, but her girl, Nevaeh, was another story.

Marques had tried getting with Nevaeh when they were freshmen, but found himself being dismissed every time. Once he started going out with her best friend at the beginning of their senior year, he found out just what she really thought of him. Marques knew Nevaeh thought he was no good, and he wasn't. But the more time he spent with Shimone, the more he felt his old ways dispersing.

As Ronald pulled into Marques' driveway, Shimone asked Marques, "What time are you picking me up tonight?"

"'Round eight, 'cause I gotta get my car out the shop," Marques responded. "And you know that could take forever, 'cause they don't never have it ready when I get there."

"Okay, I'll be ready when you are," she said with a smile.

As Marques leaned in to kiss Shimone, he could see Nevaeh rolling her eyes and so could Ronald. Pulling out of the driveway, after Marques was in the house, Ronald gave Nevaeh a look that said *we need to talk*. The car was quiet for most of the five-minute drive to Shimone's house.

"Nevaeh, are you going to do my hair tonight?" Shimone asked, breaking the silence that loomed throughout the car.

"Yeah, as long as you come over before five," Nevaeh answered.

"Alright," she said as Ronald pulled up to her duplex home. "I'll have my mom drop me off."

"Okay," Nevaeh said as Shimone got out of the car. "Bye."

"See ya," Shimone said as she disappeared into her house.

The car was once again quiet as Nevaeh and Ronald drove down the traffic-filled streets. It normally took a little under ten minutes to get to Nevaeh's neighborhood from Shimone's, but it was rush hour and Nevaeh knew that today the ride would seem extra long.

"What's wrong with you? I saw the way you kept giving Marq them ugly looks," Ronald said, finally cutting into the silence. "What's the deal?"

"I told you I was fine," Nevaeh responded with a tad bit of an attitude.

"Okay, look at me and tell me you are not upset about something," he said, trying to steer the car and look in her direction without causing an accident.

"I am *not* upset," she said, looking at the smooth waves of hair on his head.

"No," he said calmly, but with a hint of annoyance. "Look into my eyes and tell me you are not upset."

The stop sign allowed for Ronald to give Nevaeh his complete attention. His deep, dark brown eyes bore into hers. She couldn't lie to him now, and he knew it. The cars behind them began to honk.

"I'm not moving until you say something," he said. She knew he was serious.

"Okay, I'm upset." Another car honked. "But can we talk about it at my house, please?"

A small smile crept across his face and she could see a hint of his left dimple as he made a left turn onto her street. They drove into Nevaeh's neighborhood and Ronald tried to maneuver his way around the elementary school children who were outside playing.

"Okay," Ronald said after pulling into her driveway. "Talk."

"I just don't like him!" Nevaeh blurted out after a moment of hesitation.

Ronald was confused. "Why? Marq is cool."

"He's a dog with no collar!" she said. "He treats girls like toys. When he gets tired of one, he gets another, using them up in the process."

"I know, but that's just how he is," Ronald tried to defend his friend. "But can't you see that he's changing?"

"I see him changing girls and that's about it."

"No. He's been with Shimone for almost *four* months. He usually dumps a girl after two or three weeks of going out with her."

"That's because she's having sex with him!"

"So did some of those other girls, but I don't think that has anything to do with it," Ronald said, shaking his head. "He is really feelin' her. I can see something in his eyes when he looks at her."

Getting tired of the conversation, Nevaeh asked, "What can you see that I can't?"

Ronald grabbed her hand and kissed the back of it. Looking directly into her eyes, he unconsciously sent shivers through her body.

Trying to shake off the feeling, she asked, "What do you see in his eyes when he looks at her?"

"Love," Ronald answered softly.

"*Love?*" Nevaeh repeated with disgust. "How do you know?"

He smiled. "'Cause it's the same look we give each other when we look into each other's eyes."

She tried to hide it, but the smile made its way across her face anyway. Ronald smiled, too, showing even white teeth and his deep dimples.

"I love you, Nevaeh."

"I love you, too," she said as she reached up and affectionately rubbed her thumb across his right dimple. She leaned over and kissed him with passion he'd never known her to have.

She pulled away from him and looked into his eyes, which held the surprise she felt from her own actions. "I'll see you tomorrow," Nevaeh said, getting out of the car.

"Yeah," Ronald said, literally breathless.

"Bye."

He watched her walk to her front door, unlock it, and go inside the house. *Yes,* he thought as he pulled out of the driveway. *Tomorrow will be a day of new beginnings . . . and experiences.*

Even the traffic lights were synchronized in his favor. Smiling, Ronald drove all the way home without being stopped by a single one.

Chapter 2

"It's 'bout time you got here!" Nevaeh said as she opened the door to let Shimone inside of her house.

"Dang! I'm only like fifteen minutes late," Shimone said, sucking her teeth. "My mom just got home."

"You're over a half-hour late. You know it takes like two hours to do your hair."

"What's your problem?"

"Nothing! Why does everyone keep asking me that?" She saw the questions in Shimone's eyes. "Never mind," Nevaeh said through a heavy sigh. "C'mon."

After washing and shampooing Shimone's long, light brown hair, Nevaeh put in a leave-in conditioner that would repair her split ends. Nevaeh turned on the radio, and then took a pair of scissors and began to trim Shimone's locks. She turned up the radio when her favorite song began to play. Shimone began to sing along to Mary J. Blige's "Be Without You" while Nevaeh blow-dried her hair. Soon, Nevaeh joined in, harmonizing.

"I forgot how well you could sing," Nevaeh said, smiling after the song ended.

"Me? You the one who be holding those high notes for, like, forever." Shimone laughed.

Soon silence became a third person in the room as Nevaeh started putting twists in Shimone's hair. Fantasia's "Baby Mama" began to play through the speakers on the stereo and Nevaeh could tell something was on her friend's mind because she became very fidgety. She knew that the fact that Shimone was tender-headed wasn't the only reason.

"Is there something you need to talk about?" Nevaeh asked.

"Huh? I mean . . . why would you ask me that?" Shimone stammered.

"Well, for one, you are really jumpy." Nevaeh put her hands on Shimone's shoulders. "And you're pulling your ears," she noted Shimone's nervous habit. "What's up?"

"Nothing. I'm cool," Shimone answered, nervously toying with her fingers.

"No, you're not cool. You're visibly trembling."

Shimone was silent for a moment and then she burst into tears and her body began to shake even more. With her shoulders heaving, she fell off the chair and onto the floor. Not knowing what else to do, Nevaeh turned off the radio and joined her emotional friend in a kneeling position on the floor as she began to pray.

"Lord, I come to You right now asking that You please help my friend," Nevaeh said. "She seems to be hurting and I have no clue as to why. I ask that You guide my tongue as I try to help her through whatever it is that is bothering her."

Shimone's cries began to subside as Nevaeh continued. "Your Word says that You'll never put more on us than we can bear, and I thank You in advance for helping her through this. In Your name I pray. Amen."

Coming to her feet, Nevaeh brought a now calmer Shimone up with her. Still a little shaky, Shimone hugged her best friend with all that was in her.

"Thanks, girl," Shimone said, wiping her lingering tears.

"You're welcome," Nevaeh said. "Now, what's wrong?"

"I'm not even sure I should tell you," Shimone said with a look of apprehension, adding more worry lines to Nevaeh's forehead. "But I need to tell someone before I start showing," she said as more tears began to stream down her face.

"Showing?" Nevaeh asked in confusion before her mouth dropped open in realization and shock. "Shimone," she said calmly, trying hard not to upset her friend, who was already beginning to return to her earlier hysterical state. "Shimone, please look at me."

As Shimone's wet, red eyes met Nevaeh's questioning ones, Nevaeh asked, "Are . . . are you . . ."

"Pregnant?" they both said in barely audible whispers.

All Nevaeh could do was hold Shimone and cry with her. It was such a shock, although not completely unbelievable. Nevaeh thought for sure that if she was not smart enough to abstain, her friend would have at least had enough common sense to use protection. Nevaeh had a million questions running through her mind, but two stood out the most: *How far along is she? Who is the father?*

Nevaeh knew Shimone had never slept with anyone she was not in a relationship with, except for Julio. And since she already knew that Shimone and Marques were together, there shouldn't have been any question in Nevaeh's mind about who the child's father was. But she still needed to be sure.

"I'm three months pregnant with Marques' baby," Shimone said as if she'd read Nevaeh's thoughts.

Breaking free from their embrace, Shimone walked over to and sat on the queen-sized bed. Nevaeh decided to continue standing. Although concern showed on her face, the overwhelming emotion that Nevaeh felt on the inside was extreme disappointment.

"I don't know what happened," Shimone continued. "We used protection all the time. I mean, we had sex after two weeks of dating." A dry chuckle escaped from her lips, but no laughter showed on her face. "But I guess that's no surprise. I slept with that Julio guy after just a few of days of talking to him." A look of regret appeared in her eyes as she looked up at Nevaeh, who had silent tears streaming down her cheeks.

"On our one-month anniversary, Marques took me out. Treated me like a queen—not like I've seen him treat his other girlfriends; like play-things that meant nothing to him. He was really attentive and romantic that night. We went to a movie, and then out to dinner. A simple, but sweet date. Afterwards, Marques took me home and he was about to leave, like he should have, but I invited him in. My mom was out of town that weekend. I had it all planned out," Shimone said as she recalled her anniversary gift to Marques. "My cycle was scheduled to start a few days after our anniversary and I didn't want to miss the opportunity. I didn't feel like we needed protection, especially since he didn't have any. I didn't want to ruin everything by asking him to go out and get some. I should have known better."

Nevaeh offered nothing to the conversation, so Shimone continued. "I missed my period the next month, but I didn't think much of it." She started to cry again. "Then I missed it the month after that. I got real worried, so I went and got *three different* pregnancy tests. They *all* came back positive!"

Nevaeh could only stand in her place as Shimone's shoulders began to heave again. She had nothing to say. She had known that her friend's promiscuity would someday catch up with her, just not now and not in this way. And what about Mr. Marques? Did he know about this? *Apparently not, since he's still hanging around*, Nevaeh thought.

"I plan on telling him tonight," Shimone said, cutting into Nevaeh's thoughts. "I'm just afraid of how he'll take it."

Nevaeh's eyes moved to the digital clock on her nightstand. She had an hour to finish Shimone's hair if she wanted to be home by the time Marques got to her house to pick her up. Nevaeh motioned for Shimone to sit in the chair so she could finish her hair.

"Have you told Ms. Misty?" Nevaeh asked, referring to Shimone's mother.

"Did you see me come over here with a duffle bag?" Shimone said sarcastically.

"You should tell her before she finds out from someone else."

"I know. I plan to, but I need to tell Marq first." She took a deep breath. "Nev, I know you don't like him, but I really do. I think I may love him."

Nevaeh laughed softly, remembering her conversation with Ronald.

"I know that what I just said wasn't funny, so why are you laughing?" Shimone asked.

"Oh, I'm just thinking about this talk I had with Ron after we dropped you off. He was getting on me for giving your man nasty looks." Nevaeh laughed again. "It seems funny because he was talking to me like I was his child. But seriously, he said that while I only see Marq changing girls every other week, he could see him changing as a person. And Ron said that when Marq looks at you, he has love in his eyes."

"I don't really know how he could tell that." Shimone sounded as dispirited as she felt.

"He said he knows because it is the same look that me and him give each other."

"That is so sweet. Girl, I hope Ronald is right, 'cause I really do love Marq."

"Well, Ron is positive that Marques loves you." Nevaeh hesitated. "And it's not totally . . . unbelievable."

"Why you got to say it like that? Like it's choking you?" Shimone laughed in spite of the nerves that still jittered in her stomach at the thought of revealing her secret to Marques and her mother.

Nevaeh laughed along as she plugged in the hot curlers so she could put candy curls in Shimone's hair. She decided not to answer the question that had been posed to her. Doing so would do nothing to make her friend feel better. For a few moments, both girls allowed the silence that had crept in to envelop them as their minds became occupied by their thoughts.

How is Shimone going to take care of a baby? Nevaeh thought. *We still have five months of high school to finish. And what about college? I don't know how she is going to be able to handle it all.*

God, please don't let Marq leave me with this child, Shimone cried on the inside. *I don't want to be a single mother. I definitely don't want to give it up for adoption. And abortion . . . well, that's completely out of the question.*

"So, how do you plan to tell him?" Nevaeh asked as she patted the iron to see if it was hot enough for her to proceed.

"I really don't know," Shimone answered, shrugging her shoulders.

"What if he asked you to . . . you know, get rid of it?" Nevaeh said, curling a strand of Shimone's hair.

"An abortion?" Shimone said, shuddering at the mention of the word. "If he loves me like you guys think he does, then maybe . . ." She stopped. "Who am I kidding? Even if he really likes me, he's only seventeen. What is he gonna want with a fat, pregnant girlfriend? Even worse, a baby whose gonna take up his time and money!"

"Oh, girl . . . since when do you care about being big?"

"Since I'm going to be big *and* pregnant! That's like an added fifty pounds." Shimone wiped invisible tears. "Don't get me wrong. You know I love being a big, beautiful woman, 'cause . . ."

". . . a big, beautiful woman is hard to resist!" Nevaeh helped Shimone finish her authentic quote.

"But being a big and beautiful one hundred and fifty pounds is nowhere near being a fat and ugly two hundred pounds, or even more." Shimone closed her eyes as Nevaeh sprayed her hair with oil sheen to add shine and body. "I know I plan to keep my baby, though." She half-smiled and touched her stomach. "I can't believe there is actually a small human being growing *inside* of me."

"Well, I know this is a lot for you to handle, but if it

helps, I think you're going to be a good mother," Nevaeh said, adding the finishing touches on Shimone's hair.

"You think so?"

"You may not be ready, but I know you can get through it."

Hearing a car's horn honk outside, Shimone looked at her watch; it was 7:15 p.m. She needed to go home and get ready. She looked out of the window and saw her mother sitting in Nevaeh's driveway.

"I guess I need to go," Shimone said. "It's now or never."

She gave Nevaeh a hug that thanked her for more than doing her hair. As Shimone walked out of the house into her mother's old Buick, Nevaeh stood at the door and whispered, "Lord, I thank You for saving me. Now, I ask that You show Your grace and mercy to Shimone. I ask that You forgive her and wash away her guilt. Thanks for getting her through this slowly, but surely. I love You. Amen."

Nevaeh waved as Shimone's mother backed out of the driveway. She went inside the house and locked the door before going upstairs to put away the hair supplies in her room. *I really hope that everything works out,* she thought. *I hope Marques will take responsibility.*

Chapter 3

"**D**ad!" Sierra yelled as she walked in her condo. "Daddy!"

Walking into the kitchen, she saw an all too familiar note on the refrigerator.

Sierra, I have a date tonight. I will be going straight from work and probably won't be back until late. I left some cash on the table if you get hungry.

Dad

Sierra balled up the letter and threw it into the trash can. She really didn't have to read it; it was the same thing every weekend. Her dad was never home. Either he was working around the clock at Monroe & Associates law firm, or he was out with some woman who Sierra would never meet.

"I'm sick of this crap!" Sierra yelled at nothing in particular. It always seemed like she was alone.

When her mother died in a car accident involving a drunken truck driver, Sierra was just two years old.

As a result, Christopher Monroe dealt with his broken heart in an ironically harmful way. It started with a drink here and there, and then he became a full-fledged alcoholic, causing Sierra's aunt to take temporary custody of her when she was five.

After six years of counseling and taking part in a twelve-step recovery program, Christopher was allowed, with court approval, to take full responsibility for his daughter. But being absent for such a long period of his daughter's life, Christopher had a lot of time to catch up on. He knew that with only memories of an intoxicated father and a deceased mother, Sierra had no idea as to who she was or where she came from.

Over the next couple of years, Christopher spent a lot of time with his daughter, trying to get to know her again. They spent hours of each day together. He'd even call in to work, pretending to be sick, just so he could spend quality time with his "baby girl." They would go to the park, bike riding, skating, and horseback riding. Anything that Sierra wanted to do, they did.

But during the year of Sierra's thirteenth birthday, everything changed. Christopher thought it was time to begin going out and dating again. Leaving after Sierra went to sleep for the night, he wouldn't be seen until after working hours the next evening. When Sierra wanted to go somewhere or do something with her father, he'd always have something important to take care of. After all of her attempts to get her father's attention, Sierra began getting attention from strange guys she'd meet at parties, when she went to the movies, or hung out at the mall.

At fifteen, Sierra found out she was pregnant. Neither she nor the father wanted to take responsibility, so she asked the father of her best friend, LaToya Thomas, to perform an abortion on her for 150 dollars, which was nothing compared to the usual fee. Getting the money was no problem. After Sierra asked her dad for the money to go shopping, she headed straight to the abortion clinic where Alonzo Thomas worked.

Sierra didn't know much about the joys of pregnancy, and she knew even less about the emotional pains of abortion. So, it surprised her when she'd find herself up late at night crying and moaning for her baby, whom she hadn't realized she'd fallen in love with. She couldn't eat or sleep, and when friends asked about her distant behavior, she just shrugged it off while trying to fight off threatening tears. After some time and a few sessions with her school counselor, Sierra was finally able to stop letting her guilt control her life.

The following year, she ended up pregnant again. Knowing the pain her abortion caused her, Sierra decided she wanted to have the baby. When she told her father, Christopher lost his temper, and in his uncontrollable wrath, made the mistake of hitting her right in the stomach. A miscarriage followed, and Sierra was sure that it was the enraged blow that caused it.

Although she knew she was not ready to be a mother, Sierra felt empty inside. But instead of withdrawing from everyone, like she had done in the past, she started having sex with any guy who wanted her and met her "qualifications." With her father always gone, Sierra had multiple opportunities to spend time with her "guy friends."

Even though Sierra could get just about any guy she wanted, she was never happy. She didn't feel loved or even cared about. Not like Nevaeh, who, in Sierra's opinion, had the most perfect guy in the world. Ronald was sweet, romantic, and needless to say, one of the finest boys she knew.

At five-feet-seven, 130 pounds, and a flawless face, Sierra couldn't understand why Ronald would never ask her out. Yes, he had a girlfriend who was sweet and beautiful, but that didn't seem to matter to the other guys she'd been with.

Sierra had made it obvious to Ronald that all he had to do was say the word and she'd come running, but he had not shown one bit of interest in her.

She had seen on many occasions how Ronald showed affection to Nevaeh. He brought her flowers almost every Friday, and every year on Valentine's Day since they were freshmen, he brought her gifts that ranged from chocolates and stuffed animals to flowers and jewelry.

Nevaeh was just as affectionate. She held his hand, rubbed his cheeks, and when she was trying to make Ronald feel better before a football game, she was known to massage his back as a sign of support. She had even sung a song she wrote just for him at their school's annual talent competition.

Sierra was aware of all of this, but she knew that if she could get Ronald to go out with her, just to spend one night with her, she could get to see what it was like to be in the arms of the most popular boy at Douglass High.

Sierra had nothing against Nevaeh. It was just that everything she wanted, Nevaeh got. When the school had tryouts for the dance team, they only had one more spot for a freshman. She and Nevaeh were the only ones to compete, and Nevaeh won. When cheerleading tryouts for their junior year came around,

Nevaeh got the last Varsity spot, and Sierra had to take the position of captain of the Junior Varsity squad. As if that weren't enough, she and Nevaeh competed for captain of the Varsity squad for their senior year, and it was no surprise when Nevaeh beat her out for that also. Even though Nevaeh, being her usual sweet self, offered her the position of co-captain, Sierra rudely declined, saying that there was no way she'd ever get along with, let alone work with, Nevaeh even if she was the last person on earth.

That was probably the reason Nevaeh always tried to be as kind as she possibly could, but Sierra never acknowledged it. Like earlier today, when Nevaeh almost knocked her down and Sierra rudely dismissed her apology, she never intended to be so mean. It just made her so angry to see that someone like Nevaeh got almost everything she wanted just because she was smart, kind, and beautiful.

As she fixed herself a ham and cheese sandwich, she dialed her best friend's number.

"Hello?" LaToya answered in a sing-song voice.

"Hey, girl. It's me," Sierra said in a deflated tone.

"What's up?" LaToya asked, noticing her friend's depression.

"Nothing much." Sierra sighed. "My dad's gone out again."

"You wanna come over then? We could watch a movie and give each other manicures or something."

Sierra thought for a moment. It wasn't the best plan in the world, but it beat being home by herself. "Okay, I'll be there in ten minutes," she said just before hanging up the phone.

As she finished her sandwich, she ran upstairs to pack an overnight bag. She made sure she packed

her sexiest piece of lingerie as she thought about La-
Toya's brother, Corey Thomas. He was a sophomore
at Missouri College in Saint Louis. He'd been home
for the past week for the Christmas holiday. He had
always been like an older brother to her, especially
because she and LaToya had been friends since elementary school.

When Sierra was fifteen, right before she found out
she was pregnant, she had tried to take her relationship with Corey a little further, but he'd denied her,
saying she was too young. As she got older and more
developed, he'd been dropping hints that said if she
asked again, he'd take her up on her offer.

Better pack a T-shirt in case my plan doesn't work out,
she thought.

Setting the alarm system and locking the door,
Sierra walked out of the house and got into the brand
new Mazda 6 that her father had given her for her
seventeenth birthday a few months ago. She turned
up the volume on her favorite Destiny's Child CD and
pulled out of her driveway. As she neared her best
friend's home, Sierra began to get nervous; she had
no idea how Corey would respond when she went to
his room that night.

When she pulled up in front of the two-story town-
house, she noticed that LaToya's Altima was not
there, but Corey's used Navigator was sitting right in
front of the two-car garage. Sierra rang the doorbell
and wasn't surprised when he opened the door to let
her inside.

"Wassup? I didn't know you were coming over
here," Corey said.

Sierra loved his St. Louis accent. "Well, there are a
lot of things you don't know about me that you will

by the end of the night," Sierra said as she winked. She was amused by the mixture of confusion and interest that crossed his face.

"Well, Toya left like five minutes ago, so she should be back soon."

"Okay, I'll just sit *here* and wait for her to come back," she said, mimicking the way he said "here."

His laugh was deep and mellow. "You think you're funny."

"No, but the way you talk is."

He laughed again. "You want something to drink?"

"No, I'm fine."

Corey sat down on the love seat opposite Sierra and looked at her. She could see the look of approval in his eyes, but she asked anyway.

"Why are you looking at me like that?" she said, playing coy.

Corey sat back and chuckled. "You've just grown up. That's all."

"Is that a good thing or not?"

"It's good, but I remember when you and my sister were playing in the sandbox and eating mud pies."

"Whatever. We were not that young." She laughed and gave him her best smile.

Corey knew exactly what Sierra was thinking as he looked directly in her eyes. She could see it and she knew tonight was their night.

Hearing the door being unlocked, Corey excused himself and went to the kitchen for a drink. When he returned, LaToya and Sierra were heading upstairs. Sierra looked down at him and winked again. He smiled, shook his head and waited until he heard his sister's bedroom door close before he went up to his own room.

* * *

Looking into the mirror on the wall in her bedroom, Shimone straightened out the straps on her red spaghetti-strapped dress for the fifth time. With the way Nevaeh had done her hair earlier, and with her recent visit to the nail shop, Shimone knew she looked good. Now if she could just get the butterflies out of her stomach.

She had been practicing the way she was going to tell Marques about her pregnancy. She'd even thought about not telling him, but she knew that wasn't an option. She was going to need his help raising this baby. Shimone knew that Marques wasn't going to take it well. No guy was going to take well the fact that he was about to be a teen father. If Marques denied this baby, Shimone didn't know what she was going to do. But what reason would he have to deny it? Since they became an official couple, she hadn't been with anyone except him, and Marques knew that.

It was 7:55 p.m.; Shimone needed to get herself together. Marques was always on time. Rubbing her stomach, which had now become a habit that she tried to hide, Shimone said a silent prayer that everything would go well. The sudden appearance of shining headlights through her curtains made her aware that Marques' Toyota Rav 4 had pulled into her driveway. Shimone grabbed her red purse and shawl and slipped her feet in her red stilettos.

"Ma, I'm leaving," Shimone said as she stuck her head into her mother's room.

"Okay, have fun," her mother replied.

Shimone's mind had been so preoccupied with how she was going to tell Marques about her pregnancy, that she hadn't even considered what her mother's reaction would be. Shimone knew that she had not been conceived under the best circumstances, but it hadn't been the worst either. Her mother, Misty Johnson, had her at the age of sixteen, and her father, who happened to be white, denied her from the beginning.

Her mother and father dated for a few months when they were in high school. Shimone had heard the story more than a few times. Being that Misty went to an upscale private school in North Carolina, most of the students there were white, but for some reason, she had never felt like an outsider. Every time Misty would mention the name of the man who'd impregnated her, she had a bittersweet smile on her face. Shimone never really knew the reason for that.

Tyler Calhoun. Tyler Calhoun. Tyler. Calhoun. When her mother first said his name, Shimone knew he was a white man. To her, the name just didn't fit a black man.

Tyler and Misty had been a couple for about eight months, but he dumped her after she told him she was expecting and that she was not getting the abortion that he'd suggested. Afraid to tell her parents, Misty began to wear big clothes and eat more so it would seem as if she was gaining weight, in order to hide her pregnancy.

Rumors went around school that Misty had gotten pregnant on purpose to keep a hold on one of the most popular guys in school. Soon she became an outcast. The students would chase her home after school and throw rocks at her while they yelled racial slurs. After several weeks of the abuse and being on public display, she broke down and told her parents about her pregnancy and the effect it was having on her life. They withdrew her from the school and enrolled her in a nearby public school, where her condition wasn't an unusual sight. Although she was not proud of her circumstance, at the new school, Misty didn't feel nearly as alone.

Because of that chain of events, Shimone never knew her father, and after learning what he'd done, she'd rather have it that way. Shimone always said that if she ever got to meet the man who denied her, she'd tell him exactly what she thought of him for leaving her and her mother out in the cold to fend for themselves.

When Shimone got to the stairs, she heard the doorbell ring. The butterflies got worse with each step she took toward the door. By the time she reached the last step, Marques had rung the doorbell twice already. She opened the door and was very surprised to see a large bouquet of red roses.

"Oh my goodness," she gasped. "They're beautiful!"

"Not as beautiful as you." Marques seemed to surprise himself with that statement.

"Thank you." Shimone blushed. "You look good, too." It was an understatement. The black tail-less tux he was wearing looked as if it were custom made for him.

Taking the flowers, she went to the kitchen to put them in water.

"Ready?" he asked when she returned.

She knew his question only required a simple answer, but to her, it caused mixed feelings.

"As ready as I'll ever be," she said as they walked out of the house.

"So, what movies did you get?" Sierra asked LaToya.

"Does it matter? They all have Denzel in them,"
LaToya said with a laugh.

"That's true."

Sierra put *John Q* into the VCR and opened a bag
of Doritos. As they sat on LaToya's bed, Sierra tried
her best to concentrate on the movie's handsome
leading man, but she couldn't help but to think
about her life and how she'd chosen to live it. She
knew that some of the choices she had made weren't
always the best ones. She also knew that she could
only look out for herself because no one else cared,
including her father and all of the boys she'd given
herself to.

Sierra never asked anyone for anything because
she knew she'd have to give up something to get it.
All she ever asked for was to be loved, and as bad as it
sounded, if she thought she could get what she
needed from just one night of meaningless pleasure,
she'd do what she had to do. One by one, Sierra reminisced about all the guys she'd had sexual relationships with, and none of them had satisfied her to the
point of happiness. And now, as she thought about
the many guys she'd been with and how they never
called the next day, she realized that she was tired of
the one night stands with guys whose last names she
could barely remember or never knew in the first
place.

"Sierra?" She heard LaToya calling her name.

"Huh?"

"The movie is over."

"Oh." Sierra laughed softly. "I guess I just zoned
out for a minute."

"On a Denzel Washington movie?" LaToya said
with total disbelief. "Something's wrong. And don't
try to lie, 'cause Denzel to you is like Usher to me;

and for *you* to 'just zone out for a minute' is not even gonna sit right with me until I know what had your mind so occupied."

Sierra knew it was coming. She didn't know why she didn't just try to play it off. If she told LaToya what she had just been thinking about, Sierra knew she'd hear the same lecture she'd just gotten from her friend last week after a spontaneous rendezvous with a new student at their school. Although Sierra's head told her to keep it to herself and save herself from the oncoming lecture she was sure to get, her heart said she needed someone to confide in, and LaToya was the only person she knew she could do that with.

Chapter 4

They'd been sitting in silence for almost five minutes.

"You know you want to tell me, so go ahead," LaToya urged.

Sierra hesitated, but decided that this time was as good as any to release her frustrations and get all of it off her chest. "I'm just tired of being loved part-time," she confessed.

"What are you talking about?"

"You know, just letting any and every guy get with me with no effort on their part."

LaToya took this as her cue to begin her lecture. "You see? I knew it was going to start getting to you. I don't understand why you would put yourself in a position where you know that the only person getting something out of it is the guy. Can't you see that?"

Sierra had gotten LaToya started, and there was nothing she could do to stop her. Not even the tears that started to slowly stream down her face would make a difference.

"You always said that you would never ask a guy for anything 'cause you thought he'd want you to do something for him in return, but that's what you're doing. You may not be asking them for anything, but you are certainly giving them something that you don't want them to have."

"But *I'm* the one using *them*. I want to be loved, and I get my satisfaction from being with them." Sierra tried wiping the tears, but new ones continued to flood her eyes.

"But don't you see that it is not satisfying you? You just said that you were tired of being loved temporarily, and you are not benefiting from this at all. You are worth so much more than a few meaningless nights, Sierra Celeste Monroe," LaToya said while using her own hands to wipe Sierra's tears. "I know that you lost two babies, but maybe it was a sign for you to stop doing what you are doing. But instead, you continue to do whatever you want, and you feel even emptier than you did after you had that abortion and miscarriage."

Sierra moved LaToya's hands from her face and forcefully wiped away the tears that refused to stop. "I don't need you to remind me of the murder that I committed. I know how empty I felt, and I know how I dealt with it, and I don't need to be reminded of that terrible time in my life," she said through clenched teeth. "Yes, I blocked out the world by trying to ignore the emotions that I went through after your dad used that cold piece of metal to scrape that baby out of me. And I know that I tried to do the same by sleeping with guys I knew didn't care about me after my dad literally beat the life out of the baby in my stomach." Sierra's voice rose with each statement. "I don't need you to remind me of it."

Hearing a light knock on the bedroom door, the girls tried, unsuccessfully, to dry their tears as Corey walked into the room.

As he drove, Marques wondered why Shimone was so quiet. She was never at a loss for words when they were together. He was already nervous, and her silence was making it worse.

He'd been trying to figure out how he was going to tell Shimone how he felt about her. It took him from the time Ronald dropped him off at his house to when he got to Shimone's home to figure out that he loved her. At first he had his doubts. How could he, the "King Playa," be in love? But when she'd opened her front door, he knew all uncertainties he had about his feelings for her were gone. She looked so beautiful that he had to literally catch his breath before he could get out his first word. He knew tonight was as good a time as any to tell her how he felt.

When they arrived at the City Grill, the restaurant where they'd had their first date, Marques got out and walked around the car to open Shimone's door. As they walked through the crowded restaurant, they attracted looks of approval from all sides of the building. Marques was relieved that he thought to make reservations the night before.

"Reservations for two," he said to the hostess, who seemed to think Marques was alone as she fluttered her false eyelashes in his direction.

"Name please?" The hostess said the words in a manner that made her sound like her second job was as a 1-900 telephone operator.

"Marques Anderson," he responded as Shimone gave the hostess a look that said *this one's taken.*

"Right this way, please," she said, quickly getting the hint.

Walking them to a secluded part of the restaurant, the hostess watched as Marques pulled out Shimone's seat for her before taking his own.

"Your waiter will be here to serve you momentarily," she said in a more professional tone.

"Thank you," they responded in unison.

Handing Shimone her menu and then picking up his own, Marques was confused about why Shimone hadn't said anything to him since they walked out her front door. He was about to question her silence when the waiter approached the table.

"Hi, my name is George and I'll be your server this evening," he said just before asking for their drink orders.

Marques smiled in Shimone's direction. "Could we get a bottle of your non-alcoholic Ariel, please?"

"I'll get that right out to you all. Would you like any appetizers while you wait?"

Marques looked at Shimone, who shook her head. "No, thank you. We'll be ready to order soon," he said. Consciously, he waited until the waiter left the table before he asked, "Shimone, are you okay?"

"Uh . . . yeah, I'm fine," she lied.

"Are you sure? You look nervous." He put his hands over hers so she would stop picking at the fibers of the tablecloth.

"Yeah, I'm sure."

The waiter returned with their drinks and asked for their orders.

"I would like the roasted chicken breast," Shimone requested.

"Good selection. What about you, sir?" the waiter asked.

"I'll have the same."

"Your wait shouldn't be too long. If you all need anything else, just ask."

"Thank you," Marques responded.

They sat in silence for a few minutes, but to them it seemed like hours. Their food arrived fifteen minutes later, and before Shimone could pick up her fork, Marques took her hands in his.

Looking into her eyes, he said, "I have something to tell you."

Pulling her hands out of his grasp, she averted her eyes. "I have something I need to tell you, too."

Corey looked from his sister to her friend, in curiosity. "Dad's home. He wants you." He said the words to LaToya, but directed his attention to Sierra, who was still crying.

"Okay, tell him I'll be down in a minute," LaToya said as she got up to go to the bathroom to wash her face.

Still standing in the doorway, Corey asked Sierra, "Are you all right?"

"Yeah, I'm fine. Everything's cool," Sierra said, still sniffling.

"You know if you need to talk, I'm here."

She smiled and said, "I can see you, Corey. I know you're *here*, and I appreciate it."

"You *really* think you're funny," he said, laughing.

"I know I am," she said.

Corey walked over to the bed, leaned down and placed a soft kiss against Sierra's lips. Though his lips barely touched hers, Sierra couldn't help but feel the surge of warmth that shot through her body. When he stood up, her eyes were still closed. He reached down and wiped the lingering tears with his finger-tips. When she opened her eyes, he smiled and walked out of the room.

Still in her daze, Sierra wondered if she should still make tonight special for her. She really liked Corey, and what he did just proved that the feeling was mutual. Or was he just another one of those guys who would use her to get what he wanted during her moment of vulnerability? No, he couldn't be; she'd known him for too long. And he must have just heard her revelation. She was sure that he hadn't all of a sudden come to the door after her talk with La-Toya ended. He must have been standing out there for some time. He had to hear about her abortion and miscarriage and about the guys.

But what about her mission to get Ronald? Should she just put it on the back burner for now until she could figure out what was going on between her and Corey? Maybe it was time for her to stop living life the way she had been.

"Hey," LaToya said as she walked into the room.

"Hey." Sierra saw the look of apprehension in La-Toya's eyes. "Don't worry. I'm fine."

"I know, and I'm sorry. I didn't mean to bring that up. I know it's a sore spot for you, and I should have thought about that before I opened my mouth to even say anything."

"It's cool. And I apologize for going off like that."

"How about I go get that big carton of cookie dough ice cream and we watch another Denzel movie," LaToya suggested.

"Okay, I'll put in the movie."

When LaToya returned, Sierra had already for-warded past the previews of *Man on Fire*. By the time the movie ended, both girls were in tears, and the only thing left in the ice cream carton was melted ice.

"I don't see why they had to let a man that fine die," LaToya said, wiping her tears.

"Well, I guess they didn't think that we could take all that fineness for much longer, so they better had done something," Sierra reasoned.

LaToya yawned. "Well, after all that action, I'm tired. I'm going to bed."

"Okay. I want to take a shower," Sierra said while gathering her bag with her shower gel and other moisturizers and her clothes.

When Sierra finished her shower and moisturized her body, she put on her T-shirt, deciding not to put her plan into action, and headed back into LaToya's room. With her friend already knocked out, Sierra climbed onto the queen-sized bed and turned off the lamp.

An hour later, sleep eluded Sierra, so she decided that maybe she should go to the room further down the hall. Getting out of the bed as easily as she could so as not to wake her snoring friend, Sierra tiptoed down the hall and stopped right outside the room. She could hear soft jazz being played from the stereo that she knew sat adjacent to the window in the corner of the room. She knocked softly on the closed door three times. When the door opened, she knew this is where she wanted to be.

He smiled slightly. "I knew you were coming," he said as he stepped aside and let her in, closing the door behind her.

Chapter 5

When Shimone took her hands out of his grasp and placed them in her lap, Marques began to rethink telling her how he felt. Then, when she began to cry, he didn't know what to do.

"Shimone, what's wrong?" he asked in confusion and fear.

"Nothing . . . everything," she said, confusing him even more.

He took her hands again. "Just tell me."

She looked away. "I'm not sure if I should. It could ruin everything." She bit down on her bottom lip so hard Marques thought it would bleed. "I just don't want you to leave me."

"Baby, I love you."

When he said those words, Shimone's head turned in his direction and she looked directly in his eyes. "I'm pregnant."

She said the words so softy that Marques wasn't sure if he'd heard her correctly, but the way Shimone looked at him told him that what he heard was what she'd really said.

Sierra walked inside Corey's bedroom and watched as he closed the door behind her. She knew that this was going to be like all the other times with all the other guys.

She sat on his king-sized bed, but he remained standing by the closed door.

After a few minutes of silence, Sierra finally said, "If you're gonna stand by the door, I'm going back to bed."

With a slight smile, Corey sat on the bed next to her. Sierra didn't waste any time as she quickly made her intentions clear by forwardly leaning in to kiss him. At first, Corey returned her advances, and then he suddenly stopped.

"Sierra, I don't want to be one of *those* guys," Corey said as he got up from the bed.

"What?" Sierra was obviously confused.

"I really care about you, but I think you have the wrong idea here. I don't want you to think that what I want from you is sex."

All Sierra could do was sit on his bed and stare at him in disbelief. She had never before heard the words "I care" directed toward her; never from a guy, not even her dad. Corey's words left her feeling utterly confused. She didn't know what to say or do next. Should she just walk out? Should she tell him her story? Should she just continue to sit there and look dumbfounded?

Corey got up from the bed and repositioned himself in a seated position on the floor. "When you got here, you said there were a lot of things that I didn't know about you, that I would by the end of the night," he said as she continued to stare down at him. "I know how you meant it, and I was tempted to consider your proposal, but now that statement has a different meaning. And to be honest, I don't know much about *you* as a person." He motioned for her to join him on the floor. "I'm listening."

Pregnant, pregnant, pregnant. The word had been swirling around in Marques' head for the past ten minutes.

"Pregnant?" he said aloud as Shimone continued to cry. "Are you sure?"

"Yes. I missed my period the past two months, and I took three pregnancy tests."

"Okay," he said, choosing his next words carefully. "Are you sure it's mine?"

Shimone couldn't believe he'd actually said the words, but he had. "Yes, I'm sure it's yours! I ain't been with nobody else!" She cried harder.

"Okay," Marques said, trying to calm her down as the people at nearby tables turned and looked in their direction. "I'm sorry. I . . . I just . . . man," he said as he ran his hand across his bald head.

"I'm sorry, too." she said. "But I plan to have this baby, so if you gonna leave, then go, 'cause I don't believe in abortion."

"What?" he said in confusion. "Girl, did you not just hear what I said? I . . . love . . . you. I ain't going nowhere," he said, kissing her hands. "And even if you wanted an abortion, I wouldn't let you. I take care of mine."

Relieved and overwhelmed, Shimone leaned across the table and kissed Marques on the lips. "I love you, too."

Coming out of her initial shock, Sierra eased down onto the floor and rested her back against the wall where Corey sat. She began to tell him about her mother's death and the effect her father's drinking habit had on her. He listened as she told him about the many men she had given herself to in order to compensate for her father's absence in her life, and how they only used her to satisfy their personal desires. He listened as she cried over her abortion and miscarriage. He held and consoled her until she had no tears left.

When she was finished, Corey began to share his personal story.

"When my mom left me, my sister, and my dad in St. Louis after she found out that she was pregnant by another man," Corey started, "I became emotionally unstable. I cried every night, praying that my mom would come back just to hold me and assure me that she still loved me." His voice slightly cracked, and Sierra looked up to see a single tear trailing down his face. "I got even worse after my dad sent La-Toya down here to stay with our grandparents. She was just three years old at the time, so she probably had no idea what was going on, except that she couldn't stay with me and Dad anymore because Dad was having a hard time trying to take care of both of us and work. I hardly ever got to see LaToya unless it was Thanksgiving or Christmas or Dad just felt like driving down here for a visit."

Sierra remained quiet as she allowed Corey to reminisce. She took comfort in his embrace as she shed tears on his behalf.

Corey's voice became slightly cheerful. "I was happy when Dad finally quit his job and opened up his own practice down here. When we moved, La-Toya was able to come stay with us. Things went well for a while. Even though we still missed my mom a lot, we were starting to become the happy family that we used to be before drama entered our lives." His face became stiff as his story took a turn.

"Mom's boyfriend was crazy," he confessed. "We didn't know it until the police found her and the brother I'd never gotten to know, dead in their apartment, almost a year and a half after Dad had moved us down here." Corey's tears came faster, but his voice remained steady. "Dad wanted to kill the man for what he'd done, but he never really had the strength to do it because of his grief."

He sighed. "Then the guy had the nerve to show up to the double funeral that Dad had for my mom and her son. When the police came and arrested him, the man refused to leave without viewing the bodies of his *loved ones.*"

Sierra could clearly see the anger that Corey held for his mother's boyfriend. She held his hand and continued to sit silently as Corey's tears flowed like a river. Even though Sierra had heard bits and pieces of this story from LaToya, she'd never known the entire truth, nor had she ever known the effect it had on Corey. She felt herself drawing nearer to him, knowing that they had shared similar experiences, but Sierra couldn't help but feel a twinge of jealousy from the fact that Corey's father had not once abandoned him or LaToya during the tragic events in their lives. Sierra could only wish that her father had been that selfless.

After several long minutes of silence, Corey's tears had subsided and he'd explained to Sierra how special she was and how much she was loved and cared about by him, his sister, their father and her own father, even if she didn't know it. With all the guys she had been sleeping with, he told her that she could have gotten a disease.

"Why would you say that?" Sierra asked, getting a little fearful.

"I'm just being real," Corey replied. "The world ain't as safe as it used to be."

"So, you're saying I should go get tested for some disease that I know I don't have?"

"I didn't say it, you did. But it's not such a bad idea." He wrapped his arms around her waist. "Better safe than sorry, right?"

Sierra knew she didn't have anything to worry about. Corey was just speaking hypothetically. It's not like he thought she had any diseases. He just wanted her to be safe. But deep down in her spirit, Sierra knew she needed to get tested. *Just so I'll know,* she thought. *Just so I'll know I'm right.*

After leaving the restaurant, Marques decided to drive down to his and Shimone's favorite spot, Heartstone Park, a place where couples went to enjoy each other's company. He parked his car in the parking lot that was occupied by only one other vehicle, and shut off the engine so that the only noise was the soulful sounds of Jagged Edge coming through the speakers. They sat in silence for a few moments, and then Shimone began to sing along to the words of "Good Luck Charm." When the song ended, Marques shut off the engine and stared at Shimone through the darkness.

"What?" she said, getting scared.

Marques' stare continued. He seemed trapped in his own body, unable to immediately move.

"What did I do? Why are you looking at me like that?" Shimone continued to question him as he looked at her in bewilderment.

"I'm mad at that," he finally said.

"What?" Shimone said, getting annoyed.

"We been goin' out for four months and this is the first time I've ever heard you sing."

"Oh . . . well, I just never had a reason to sing around you."

"Why not?" He thought for a moment and then said, "People usually sing when they're happy. You're not happy around me?"

"No, it's not that. It's just that I've never had a reason to sing around you . . . until now."

"Well, I plan to give you many reasons to sing from now on," he said as he leaned over to kiss her.

Shimone savored his sweet kiss before pushing him back a little. "You know, this is all we can do from now on," she said, referring to the kissing she just interrupted.

"Why?" Marques asked, offended.

"'Cause I ain't tryin' to get pregnant again."

Marques, at first, was disappointed, but after a moment of thought he said, "Well, if you're three months, that means that it was that night on our one-month anniversary, right?"

"Yeah, but what does that have to do with anything?"

"Well, we didn't use protection that night. So, all we got to do is make sure we're using it from now on."

Shimone was shaking her head before Marques could finish his statement. "You aren't comprehending this, are you?" she asked as he looked at her like she was the one who didn't understand. "I don't want to have sex anymore, because I know that there is a possibility that we will forget to use protection and *I* will be the one to end up pregnant. We're already having one baby. We still have a semester of school to finish, and then college. Now, it's going to be tough with one. Do you want to make it even more difficult with two?" She stared at him for a long moment as she awaited his response.

After some thought and a lot of hesitation, Marques agreed that it probably was best. "Well, when are you due?" he asked after turning on the car so the music would once again fill the car, taking the place of the two-minute silence that sat between them.

"I don't know. I have to go to the doctor, but I don't know how I'm gonna get there 'cause I ain't even told my momma yet."

"Well, I can take you tomorrow. I ain't got to be to work until five. I'll have to take you somewhere where they take walk-ins 'cause it's probably too late to make an appointment anywhere."

"We can go see my regular doctor," Shimone suggested. "She's not usually open for appointments on Saturdays, but we have a pretty close relationship where she'll see me if I tell her it's an emergency," she explained.

"A'ight, well, call me and tell me what time we need to be there and I'll come pick you up."

"I can't believe that I am going to be a mother," Shimone said as if speaking to herself.

"Yep, and my li'l man is gonna be a baller like me," Marques said proudly, shooting an imaginary ball into the air.

"Please," Shimone laughed. "And what makes you think we're having a boy? If I *got* to have a baby, I want a girl."

"Well, whatever we have, I promise I'll take good care of it and you," he said, kissing her once more for added assurance.

Chapter 6

Waking up with the sun's rays peeking though her window, Nevaeh stretched out her body as she got up to take her Saturday morning shower. As she prepared for her shower, all she could think about was how much sleep she'd lost last night because she was so worried about her best friend. She didn't know how in the world Shimone was going to take care of a child. And if Marques denied this baby, Nevaeh knew she would lose her mind. If he thought he knew how Nevaeh felt about him now, he'd have another thought coming when she'd finished telling him off. And Nevaeh knew Shimone would be right behind her. But she also knew that she didn't need to get involved in anything that didn't concern her, unless her friend came to her first.

She walked into the bathroom and was completely engulfed. This was her favorite room in the house. With its plush deep purple-carpeted floor and wallpaper with ivory-colored flowers, it completely calmed her every time she walked into it. This was her place to come and take a relaxing shower; or if she was stressed, she could use the Jacuzzi and allow its powerful jets to massage away all of her anxieties.

As she stepped into the steaming hot water, Nevaeh's mind once again became occupied with thoughts of Shimone. *How in God's name is she going to take care of a baby? She's just a baby herself. And what if Marques wanted her to get an abortion? Would Shimone change her mind and have one "in the name of love"? And if she did not change her mind and he left her to take care of it herself, would she be able to handle being a single mother?*

Using her lavender body scrub to try to cleanse herself of the hounding negative thoughts, Nevaeh said a silent prayer that everything would be all right. After washing her hair and body, she turned off the shower and wrapped a purple towel around her body and a matching one around her wet tresses. As she opened the bathroom door, she heard her telephone ringing. By the time she got to her room, her answering machine had already picked up the call.

"You've reached Nevaeh Keion Madison. I'm not in right now, but if you leave your name, number and a brief message, I promise I'll return your call as soon as I can. Have a wonderful, blessed day," was Nevaeh's recorded message.

When the phone beeped, the caller's voice made her smile. "Now that's a voice I'd love waking up to in the morning," Ronald said.

Nevaeh thought about picking up the phone, but decided to just listen to his voice.

"Hey, beautiful," he continued. "I was just calling to see what you have planned tonight. If you are free, I'd love to take you out to dinner. I have to go, but call me when you get this. I love you. Bye."

When she and Ronald began dating in their fresh-

man year, Nevaeh never thought it would last for two
years, but it had. In two months, they'd be celebrating their three-year anniversary. When Ronald asked
her to be his steady girlfriend a few days before Valentine's Day, she had her doubts, especially since they
had been friends since the seventh grade and she'd
seen how he talked about the different girls he wanted
to "get with," as if he were a grown man. He was never
the type to cheat or play games, but he sometimes
talked like the boys who did.

But as Nevaeh began to hang around him more,
she began to see him for the true person he was, and
after giving his request some thought, she finally accepted on February 14. And she had been very surprised when Ronald left a huge teddy bear and a box
of chocolates on her desk in her homeroom class
without even knowing if she'd agree to be his girlfriend.

Although Nevaeh continued to have her doubts
about Ronald, he continually proved himself to her
as each month passed and he remained by her side.
They did, however, have their share of problems.

During the summer before their junior year, Ronald
thought they needed "space to see other people."
Nevaeh was never one to force someone to do something he didn't want to do, so she solemnly agreed
with the guy she felt already had her heart. But what
she didn't know was that Ronald felt the same way
and was afraid of the feelings he knew he had developed for Nevaeh. He didn't want to hurt her, but he
had no idea how to deal with those feelings.

That whole summer, they both felt miserable.
Each was too afraid to call the other, so they nearly
drowned in their sorrows. When Shimone wanted to
go hang out at the mall, Nevaeh wanted to mope

around in her room. And when Marques or one of Ronald's other friends wanted to go play ball at the park, all he wanted to do was reread letters that Nevaeh had stuck in his locker during the months that they were together.

When their junior year began, Ronald walked into Douglass with a mission: to apologize to Nevaeh and to get her back. As soon as he saw her, he ran to her and kissed her right in front of all the students and teachers who stood in the hallway. As they embraced, those around them laughed, applauded, and some were even disgusted. Ronald repeatedly apologized and told her, for the first time, that he loved her. She returned the sentiment as the teachers tried to clear the hallways.

Since then, they'd always been by each other's side. But Nevaeh had to tighten her grip on him as his football status grew. Other girls had begun letting her know that they had no problems taking her place if Ronald grew tired of her again; specifically, Sierra Monroe. Nevaeh had no idea what the girl's problem was, and frankly, she didn't care. All she was worried about was keeping her man away from Sierra.

She remembered a recent incident when Sierra ran up to Ronald after their football team had just won the championship game, and kissed him square on the lips. He didn't pull away immediately, which made Nevaeh even angrier. When he finally did pull her off of him, it didn't matter anymore because Nevaeh had already left.

Calling her all day the next day, Ronald wished a million times over that he had handled the situation better. He had no idea what had come over him. Sierra was nowhere near his type. Although she was appealing to the eye, she was much too aggressive.

After finally getting in touch with Nevaeh and arguing about the situation, he apologized and was eventually forgiven. Since then, they'd disagreed and argued on other issues, but their love for each other had not changed.

After blow-drying her hair, Nevaeh pulled it into a ponytail and put on a pair of boot cut jeans and a long-sleeved orange sweater. As soon as she was about to settle down and return Ronald's phone call, she heard her mother calling her downstairs.

"Coming!" she yelled, placing the phone back on its hook.

When she got downstairs, she saw the most beautiful arrangement of roses. There were dozens of them; some were red, others were white, and a few were pink. All Nevaeh could do was stare at them, afraid that if she touched them, they would be ruined.

"Don't you want to read the card?" her mother asked, amused at the look on her daughter's face.

Nevaeh walked over to the dining room table and picked up the card, careful not to touch the arrangement. Slowly, she opened the card and read it silently.

Just looking at these flowers made me think of you. Although their beauty is nothing compared to yours, I thought you'd love them anyway. I hope I was right.

I love you,
Ronald

She folded the card and placed it back in its envelope.

"So . . . ?" her mother inquired.

Nevaeh couldn't help but smile. "They're from Ronald," she said.

"That's it?" her mother asked. "What did the card say?"

"Nothing much," Nevaeh replied, although the words meant everything to her.

"Fine, you don't have to tell me," her mother said, walking into the kitchen. "Breakfast will be ready soon, and your dad is taking your sister to her dance lesson. If you want to go, you can."

"Okay."

Nevaeh took the flowers up to her room and placed them on her nightstand next to the ones Ronald had given her just yesterday. She picked up the phone and dialed her boyfriend's number.

"Hello?" he answered on the third ring.

"Hey. It's me," she said.

"Hey, babe," Ronald greeted cheerfully. "What's up?"

"I got the flowers. They're very beautiful, and so is the card. Thank you."

"Well, you're welcome."

"And I got your message. I'd love dinner, but I have to ask my dad first. I'd ask my mom, but all she's gonna say is, 'It's fine with me if it's fine with your dad.'"

"That's cool." He laughed at the way she mimicked her mother.

"Oh, did you talk to Marques this morning?" she asked, trying to see if he knew about Shimone's situation.

"Yeah, he's supposed to be taking Shimone to the doctor this morning, like at eleven or somewhere around that time."

I guess Marques told him, Nevaeh thought. She was surprised. "You mean he's actually taking responsibility?"

"Why do you sound so surprised? I told you he loved her, and *he* told her that last night."

"Are you serious?"

"Yes," Ronald laughed. "Why is it so hard to believe? I thought women were supposed to have some type of sixth sense where this kind of stuff was concerned."

"Well, I kinda knew it was true. I guess I just didn't want it to be."

"Why?"

"I just don't want her to get hurt, you know?"

"I see what you mean, but let's just focus on the positive right now. They are about to have a baby, and we need to be there for them if they need us to be."

"Okay."

"Well, I hope I'll see you later. Call me on my cell after you ask your dad about tonight. I'm gonna be out most of the day with Jeremy," he said, speaking of his eight-year-old brother.

"Okay, that's cool because I plan to go to Imani's dance lesson, and you know how long those last. Hey, if your sister wants a ride, tell her that my dad wouldn't mind."

"A'ight, I'll tell her to be ready, 'cause that'll save me some gas money."

Nevaeh laughed. "Whatever, you know you love spending time with Nikki."

"I do, but every time we go somewhere, she spends all my cash."

"It ain't like you never have money, though. I know those flowers cost a fortune. There had to be *at least* two dozen of them."

"Well, they were for you, and when it comes to you, money's no object."

"Aww . . . that is so sweet."

"Well . . . sometimes it is," he said with a laugh.

"That's not even funny," she said, although she laughed along with him.

"You know I'm just playin'," he teased, still laughing. "Well, I got to go 'fore Jeremy hangs up for me."

Nevaeh laughed. "Okay, don't forget to tell Nikki to be ready in the next hour or so, and tell everybody I said hey."

"Okay," he said as she was about to hang up. "Oh, and Nevaeh?"

"Yeah?"

"I love you." He could feel her smile.

"I love you, too," she responded.

Nevaeh was smiling so hard by the time the call ended, that when she went downstairs to eat breakfast, her sister asked her if her face hurt. Nevaeh just sat at the table as her mother placed a plate of buttered grits, eggs, bacon, and biscuits in front of her.

Michelle Madison stood by and looked at her daughters as they blessed their food and began to eat. She and James, her husband of twenty-one years, had raised their girls to be respectable, God-fearing young women. She was proud of both her daughters, but mostly with Nevaeh.

Nevaeh had been a handful when she was a little girl. Whoever created the term "terrible two" must have had Nevaeh in mind. But she wasn't just a terrible two; she had been a terrible three and four. She would blatantly disobey her parents and practically tear up the house. No matter how many times she got a whipping and her toys were taken away, she would go back and do the same thing over again.

By the time she was five, she had settled into the role of big sister. She helped feed and take care of her little sister, Imani. When she turned ten, she became more independent and spent most of her time by herself in her room, writing poetry and songs that she would sing at any chance she got.

At the age of thirteen, the same day she accepted Christ into her life, she and her father attended a seminar on sexual purity. After the seminar, a ceremony was held for anyone who wanted to commit to abstinence, and she vowed to her father and to God that she would remain pure until marriage. Her father gave her a silver band to wear on her left ring finger as a constant reminder of the promise that she made.

While Imani wasn't involved in any type of relationship just yet, Nevaeh would soon be celebrating her three-year anniversary with Ronald, and Michelle was afraid that Ronald's view on abstinence would change any day now. Just the fact that he was a handsome young man made her wonder what he did when he wasn't around her daughter. Michelle had been a teenager once, and knew how some girls could be. She couldn't help worrying what Ronald would do if the time came that he found himself ready to take the relationship to the next level and Nevaeh was not. What would he do?

Nevaeh had never shown any interest in giving up her virginity, and that was just fine with Michelle. Both her daughters made a promise, and she planned to make sure both of them kept it.

Nevaeh was very strong in her faith, and sometimes Michelle wondered if she should have given Nevaeh the name that she had saved for her second child, Imani. But she knew when Nevaeh was born that God had sent her straight from heaven, so she simply reversed the letters and came up with the name. She knew Nevaeh would, somehow, be used by the Lord, and she wanted a name that reflected her beliefs. As each day passed, Nevaeh grew more in the Lord, and Michelle hoped the trend would continue.

"So, is Daddy ready?" Imani asked as she got up to take her plate to the sink.

"He will be as soon as he gets a plate of this delicious-smelling food," James said from the doorway of the dining room.

"Good morning, Daddy," Nevaeh and Imani said in unison.

"How are my princesses doing this morning?"

"Fine," they answered.

He turned toward his wife. "And what about my queen?"

"Just fine, my king," Michelle said as she kissed him.

"Some people are trying to eat here," Imani said, making a disgusted grimace.

"Girl, you're done eatin'," her father said.

"Let me fix you a plate, Daddy," Nevaeh offered as she got up and took her plate to the sink.

James eyed his eldest daughter as she rushed to prepare his breakfast. "Uh-oh. How much is this gonna cost me?" he said, taking out his wallet.

"Nothing. All I need is your approval."

"Okay," he said with hesitation.

Nevaeh began to pile his plate with grits. "Ronald wants to take me out tonight." She knew her father loved Ronald like a son, but she also knew that James could be overprotective of her at times, and she wasn't getting out of the house without his permission.

"And . . . ?"

"And I just need you to say yes," she said, putting eggs and bacon on the plate.

"Where is he taking you?"

"He said dinner, but he didn't name a place, so I am guessing it's a surprise." She placed the plate on the table in front of him.

James bowed his head and said grace. Nevaeh knew he was giving it some thought as he prayed, but she wished he'd just give an answer.

"Okay, you can go," he said when he finished praying.

"Really?"

"Yes, but make sure that you are back before ten. We got church tomorrow."

"Thank you so much, Daddy!" Nevaeh hugged him and followed up with a kiss to his cheek.

"You're welcome."

Nevaeh suddenly remembered. "Oh, I have something else to ask you."

"And what's that?"

"I *kinda* told Ron that you wouldn't mind picking up his sister for the lessons, so . . ."

"It's fine, baby girl. I can get her."

"Thanks."

"Nikki is coming?" Imani asked.

"Yeah. Why?" Nevaeh asked.

"I don't like that girl. She thinks she's *all* that just 'cause she gets all the leads in the recitals. She makes me sick!"

"That is enough, young lady," Michelle scolded. "Now, you know we don't have that type of talk in *this* house."

"I'm sorry," Imani said as she returned to her task of washing the dishes.

"Now, haven't you been the lead in plenty of recitals?" her mother asked.

"Yes, but she's been in more," Imani said.

"Why don't y'all work on something together?" Nevaeh suggested.

"Why would I want to do that?" Imani crinkled her nose at the idea.

"So you can become friends. She really likes you, Imani, and I know you like her. I've seen you guys laughing like best friends at rehearsals," her father pointed out.

"Well, I do *kind of* like her, and she's cool most of the time." Imani gave it some thought. "I guess it wouldn't hurt for me to teach her a thing or two." Her mother gave her a look that said her joke was not funny. "Or . . . maybe we can work together and help each other out?" she added as if the suggestion was an Imani original.

"That's more like it," Michelle said.

"Well, c'mon, let's hit the road," James said a few minutes later as he got up from the table and Imani had placed his plate in the sink to be washed. "We've got a dance rehearsal to get to."

Chapter 7

Both Shimone and Marques had been sitting nervously for over an hour in the waiting room of the doctor's office. Despite the fact that it had been almost midnight, Shimone called her doctor at home as soon as Marques dropped her off at her house the night before. When Shimone told her that it was a very important situation, Dr. Anther said she could see her at noon because she had a few Saturday morning errands to run.

When Marques came to pick Shimone up at eleven, Shimone's mother had a ton of questions about why her daughter was leaving the house so early on a Saturday morning, but none of them got answered as Shimone rushed out of the house. The car was totally silent as they rode into downtown Atlanta. When they reached the doctor's office, a receptionist was waiting for them in the waiting area. The woman informed them that Dr. Anther had not come into the office yet, but she would be there soon. So, Shimone and Marques sat down and waited.

"Will you stop shaking? You are making me nervous," Shimone said to Marques.

"Sorry, I just don't like being here," Marques said as he placed his hands on his knees in an unsuccessful attempt to stop their bouncing motion.

"Well, I don't either, especially for this situation," she said as she rubbed her bare arms.

"Where is your doctor? We've been sitting here for almost an hour and a half."

"Dr. Anther said she would be here at twelve."

"Well, it's 1:10 now and I'm tired of waiting," he said as he got up and walked over to the receptionist's desk.

"May I help you?" the receptionist asked.

"Yes, you can," Marques replied. "Can you please tell me when the doctor can see my girlfriend? We've been sitting over there for over an hour, and the doctor said that our appointment was at twelve."

On cue, Dr. Anther rushed through the entrance and offered her special appointees an apologetic smile. "I'm sorry I'm late. A patient of mine went into labor early this morning and I had to go to the hospital to deliver her baby. I didn't even get to run any of my errands before coming here," she explained as she slipped out of her winter coat, revealing that she was already dressed in her scrubs. She motioned for them to follow her through a door that led to the examination rooms.

Shimone got up and walked toward the door, with Marques following close behind. Dr. Anther led them to a room at the far end of the hall. To Shimone, the walk seemed to take hours.

"So, how are you today, Shimone?" the doctor asked.

"Okay, I guess. I'm really not here for a routine check-up," Shimone replied.

"I kind of figured that when you called my house last night and said it was an emergency," Dr. Anther said as she motioned for Shimone to sit down in one of the chairs. "So, what's the problem?"

Shimone looked at Marques for assurance. When he nodded, she said, "I'm pregnant."

"Really?" Dr. Anther asked. She sounded surprised, but her facial expression remained professional. Shimone now had her full attention.

"Yes, I think I'm about three months, and all I need to know is if my baby is okay, and the due date."

Shimone knew that Dr. Anther was not going to offer an opinionated comment on the predicament she'd gotten herself into. The woman was always professional when it came to her job.

"Is this the father?" Dr. Anther asked, nodding in Marques' direction.

"Yes," Shimone answered.

"Well, I take it that the fact that you're here means that you plan on taking care of her and this baby," the doctor said to Marques.

"Yes, I do," Marques said.

"Well now, isn't that a good change of pace?" The doctor smiled as she motioned for Shimone to stand on the scale so she could check her weight. "Most of the girls that come in here don't have someone with them who plans on sticking by their side."

"I'm going to try to do the best I can to be there for her, Doctor," Marques stated.

"That's good to hear," she said as she checked Shimone's heartbeat.

After Dr. Anther recorded the information on her chart, she told Shimone to put on a hospital gown and wait for the nurse. When Shimone came out of the bathroom, a woman, who'd apparently been called in to help Dr. Anther with her special patient, came in and led them to a room with an ultrasound machine. Marques helped her onto the bed. While they waited for Dr. Anther to come into the room, Marques held Shimone's hand and looked into her eyes. He knew he had to be there for her; he loved her too much not to.

When Dr. Anther rejoined them, she sat on a stool next to the bed and told Shimone exactly what she was going to do. "Shimone, I am going to rub some of this gel on your stomach so that I will be able to see what's going on in there, and we'll also hear the heartbeat on the monitor. If there's something pertinent for you to see, I'll let you know, okay?"

"Okay," Shimone said as she held Marques' hand tighter.

The gel was cold and made Shimone squirm, but when she heard her baby's beating heart through the speakers, she could not hold back the tears that pressed against her eyes. Seeing the small movements that his baby made, Marques turned his head in an effort to hide his emotions. When Shimone gently squeezed his hand, he knew that his attempts were unsuccessful.

While Dr. Anther wiped the excess gel from her stomach, Shimone asked the doctor about the due date.

"When was your last cycle?" Dr. Anther asked as she made notes on her chart.

"Umm . . . the week of August fifteenth. And I believe we conceived on September tenth," Shimone answered.

Dr. Anther made notes and took out a chart that indicated a baby's approximate birth date from the day it was conceived. After studying the information, she concluded, "You are going to be due around June twelfth, and now that you are about to enter your second trimester, I need for you to schedule regular appointments with me."

"Okay," Shimone nodded. "Could I get dressed now?" she asked, squirming from the draft she felt from wearing the paper gown.

Dr. Anther laughed. "Sure," she said as she led them back into the room where Shimone had earlier undressed, and then left to record Shimone's condition.

Marques settled in one of the chairs by the window and laughed as Shimone grabbed the back of her gown in an attempt to cover her behind.

He continued to laugh. "It ain't like I ain't ever seen it before."

"And you not gon' ever see it again," Shimone said as she went into the bathroom.

"See, now you ain't right," he said, even though he knew she was serious.

As Shimone changed, Marques sat nervously in a chair in the corner of the room. He could hardly stop shaking. When Dr. Anther was speaking to him, he had to use everything that was in him to keep his voice steady. He wasn't ready to be a father, but he had to be there for Shimone. He couldn't just do this to her and leave her by herself. *I just hope I'll be a good father,* he thought. *I just want to be a good father.*

Ever since Shimone told him last night that she was not going to have sex with him anymore, Marques had been thinking of ways to get her to change her mind. He knew that would be a tough job. Although he had agreed with her, he only did it so there wouldn't be an argument. He'd thought about calling some of his old girlfriends to see if they wanted to hang out. He knew all he had to do was ask and they'd come, but he couldn't get up enough nerve to pick up the phone. He knew he couldn't do something like that after he told Shimone how he felt about her and after he told her he'd be there for her and their baby.

Marques also realized that he couldn't do something like that because he wouldn't feel right. It had everything to do with Shimone. If he didn't love her so much, he would be able to do whatever he wanted. If she hadn't changed him by being herself instead of being fake like most of the girls he dated, he would be able to call up any girl right now and do whatever he wanted with her. But Shimone had been herself with him, and she didn't play games. Marques liked that. In fact, he *loved* it. She even had him thinking about his future with her and their baby.

"What's that saying?" Shimone probed as she walked out of the bathroom. "A penny for your thoughts." She laughed then stopped when he didn't join in. "What's got you deep in thought?"

"You," he said to her surprise.

"Good things, I hope."

"Mostly," he said as he sat up in the chair. "I need to tell you something."

Shimone braced herself. She knew last night was too good to be true. It was all too perfect, especially on Marques' part.

"I was so tempted last night to call up some of my old girls." He saw Shimone's nose flare, and he quickly added, "But I couldn't do it."

Shimone relaxed. "Okay?"

"I really love you, and I meant everything I said last night about being here for you and the baby. I want to be with you and you only, but I have to tell you now that it is going to be hard, on my part." He took a deep breath. "But I plan on being faithful to you and my baby boy."

"You mean girl," Shimone said, smiling as she sat in the chair next to him. "I know it's gonna be hard for you, and probably hard for me, too," she paused. "But I don't want to be in this position again, where I have to go home and tell my mom that I am pregnant. Do you know how hard that is going to be for me? She is going to *kill* me." Her voice cracked as tears began to well in her eyes.

Marques got up and pulled her up with him. "Okay, I'm sorry. I didn't mean to bring it up. Don't cry," he said as he hugged her.

She wiped her eyes. "You know these next six months are going to be crazy. I may be a burden, you know, with the mood swings and stuff."

He dismissed her comment with a wave of his hand. "I already know. My older sister went through all of this with both her babies, and I think I can handle it." He looked into her eyes. "Shimone, I don't know if I am ready to be a father," he said, "but I really want to be there for you. I just don't know how."

Shimone reached up and touched his cheek. She brought his face to hers and kissed him lightly on the lips. "Just don't leave me," she said softly. "All you have to do is stay here with me."

A few moments later, Dr. Anther came back into the room with a small bottle of prenatal vitamins and a prescription for a refill. "I want you to take one of these vitamins every day for the next six months, starting today," Dr. Anther said.

"Okay," Shimone said as she took the bottle and

the paper with the scribbled writing that was barely legible.

"And I have made an appointment for you to see me in four weeks. If you have any problems before then, call my office." She made some notes on her chart. "I've also taken the liberty to set you both up with a counselor and enroll you all into a teen parenting and child birthing preparation class. They can be of great assistance in the long run."

"Thank you," Marques said as he took the paper with the name and phone number of the counselor and the location of the parenting class.

"You're quite welcome. I want to see you *both* back here in four weeks."

"You will," he said as he helped Shimone put on her coat.

"Bye," Shimone said.

"Bye, sweetie. The next time I see you, I hope your mother will be here, too."

"I'll see what I can do." Shimone sighed as she and Marques headed out the door.

I'll see what I can do, she thought as the cold December air surrounded her.

Chapter 8

"Will everyone get into your positions for *Lookin'
4 U*?" Misty said as she walked over to the
stereo and inserted Kirk Franklin's *Hero* CD.

The students walked to the center of the room and
lined up in three rows of five, while Nicole McAfee,
Ronald's fourteen-year-old sister, stood in the front,
preparing to lead the dance. When the music started,
all of the students began to move their feet. The
music seemed to take control of their bodies. They'd
been taught to allow the energy to flow from their
souls and into the audience. The routines they performed were so rousing that only paralysis would prevent their audience from getting out of their seats in
applause at the end of each performance.

Misty Johnson bought the studio seven years ago
when she inherited more than twenty thousand dollars from her grandmother, who had just passed. After
she paid all her debts, she had more than enough
money to buy the abandoned building and turn it into
Misty J's Dance Studio, a place designed for neighbor-

hood children. She'd always had a passion for dance, but after giving birth to Shimone, she never made her dreams of becoming a dancer a reality.

When the studio first opened, Misty's services were free to the public, but only five members consistently took advantage of that offering. Nevaeh was one of her first students. She and Shimone became instant friends when they met during one of the lessons. Misty taught them jazz, hip-hop, and inspirational dance, which they did the most. They performed in all of the talent shows at school, and when they entered high school, they used the skills they learned in Misty's dance classes to obtain spots on cheer squads and dance teams.

As Misty's reputation grew, so did her class roster. More and more kids wanted to perform and be a part of the parades and shows the studio sponsored at local churches and schools. Soon the demands became costly. Misty's first imposed fee was a meager five dollars per class, but as her classes began to multiply, her price increased to twenty dollars a class, which afforded her almost twenty-four hundred dollars at the end of each month, just enough to keep the roof over her and her daughter's heads, their utilities running, and food on the table. Her classes were now so full that she held four every other Saturday, and each class had a maximum of fifteen students, so she and her student-volunteer dance instructors from Clark Atlanta University were able to provide individual attention to the students. She often received requests for her students to perform for various organizations throughout metro Atlanta.

As the routine ended, the visitors stood and clapped as each of the dancers struck her own individual pose in concurrence with the last beat of the song.

"Ms. Misty, can me and Nikki perform our routine now?" Imani asked after the applause had died down.

"Yes, you can," Misty said.

Nicole handed Misty Fred Hammond & Radical for Christ's *Pages of Life Chapter I* CD. "Number six, please," she requested.

While waiting for the music to start, Imani stood with her head lifted high and her palms toward the ceiling, and Nicole kneeled with her head down and her hands in prayer position. When the music began to play, both girls moved as if they were butterflies emerging from a cocoon.

Nevaeh was amazed as she watched her little sister and Nicole gracefully dance, across the floor of the studio. She had forgotten how well her sister could dance, and Nicole was just as good. It amazed her that they had come up with this routine in just thirty minutes. Imani and Nicole danced like they'd been practicing for months. They had a chemistry that was undeniable to anyone watching.

As "Your Steps Are Ordered" came to an end, the girls kneeled on the floor with their hands in prayer position, facing each other with their heads toward heaven. When the last note of the song ended, everyone in the room stood and applauded.

"Encore, encore!" Misty yelled as she got up and hugged each girl. "That was wonderful!"

"Thank you, Ms. Misty. We have to add more to it," Imani said, "but Nikki came up with most of it."

"Yeah, but you know it was Mani who came in with all the at-ti-tude," Nicole said, snapping her finger with each syllable of the word "attitude."

"Well, I want you both to perform that routine in

February's recital. Do you girls think you can do that?" Misty asked.

"Yes," they responded.

"Good," Misty said, and then gave the rest of the class her full attention. "Now, we are all to meet here next Saturday at noon. Have a great rest of the day."

Parents chatted with each other as they waited for their children to get all of their things together. James walked over to Imani and Nicole to help them get their belongings.

"You were great, princess," he said to his daughter. "You too, Nicole."

"Thanks, Daddy," Imani said as Nicole showed her appreciation of his compliment with a wide smile.

"Thank you, Mr. Madison," Nicole said.

"How is your brother?" James asked Nicole.

"He's fine. He talks about Nevaeh all the time," Nicole answered.

"Oh, he does, huh?"

"Yes, and all good things, too."

"Well, you be sure to tell Nevaeh that, okay?"

"Okay."

Nevaeh had been thinking about Shimone again as she watched Misty teaching the dance class. She wondered if Shimone had told her mother about her pregnancy. She was so tempted to ask, but didn't want to get her friend in deeper trouble than she was in already.

"Hi, Nevaeh. How are you?" Misty said, breaking into Nevaeh's thoughts.

"Hi, Ms. Misty," Nevaeh said, hugging her. "I'm fine. How are you?"

"A little worried about my baby," Misty said. "Do you notice anything *different* about her?"

"No . . . no, I . . . I'm not sure if I know what you mean," Nevaeh stammered, knowing Misty was prying for information.

"Well, she's been kind of distant from me all of a sudden." Misty had the most worried look on her face Nevaeh had ever seen. "We haven't had one of our girl talks in a while."

"Well, I am sure you will have one really soon," Nevaeh said mostly to herself. She tried to choose her words carefully. "Umm . . . well, I haven't noticed anything different, but I'm sure if something's wrong, she will talk to you about it."

"I know she's been hanging out with that Marques boy a lot lately, but I don't think it would have anything to do with him, do you?"

"Oh . . . well . . . umm . . . if it does, she can handle it, trust me." Nevaeh needed a way out of the conversation before she said something that might cost her her friendship with Shimone. "I think my dad is ready to go. If Shimone needs to talk, I know she will come to you. Bye, Ms. Misty."

"Bye, Nevaeh," Misty replied as James and the girls got ready to leave.

As Nevaeh walked out of the building, she wondered if Misty had picked up on her uneasiness. She hoped that Shimone would tell her mother what was going on soon, because she hated lying, especially to someone who was like a second mother to her.

Shimone hadn't called Nevaeh all day, and Nevaeh was getting worried. She had left a message at her home and on her cell for Shimone to call her after her doctor's appointment, but she hadn't heard a word.

"Oh, Nevaeh, Ronald wanted to know if going to

Ruby Tuesday was okay for you guys' date tonight?" Nicole asked from the backseat of the SUV.

"Sure," she said, barely hearing the girl's question.

"Hey, Nicole, did you tell her what you said about Ronald?" James asked with a grin.

"Oh, yeah." Nicole laughed. "My brother talks about you all the time. He tells my little brother that if he is lucky, one day he will be able to get a girl-friend as *beautiful* and *loving* as you."

"He said that? Seriously?" Nevaeh couldn't help but smile.

"Nevaeh, are you blushing?" Imani laughed from the back seat.

"No! I think it is hot in this car." She covered her cheeks. "Daddy, turn on the AC."

"Girl, it is thirty-five degrees outside. Ain't no AC comin' on in this car," he said with a laugh. "And you *are* blushing."

The girls laughed as Nevaeh tried to change the subject. "Nikki, you and Mani did a good job today. I had no idea how good of a dancer you were."

"Thanks," Nicole said, still laughing. "It was no big deal."

"No big deal?" Imani said. "Girl, we were off the chain."

"Okay, we were hot," Nicole said, giving Imani a high-five.

Nevaeh jumped as her phone vibrated. She looked at the caller ID and answered, "Hey, Ron."

"*Hey, Ron,*" the girls mimicked.

Without greeting, Ronald said, "Tell my sister I said she better quit, 'cause she knows she got to come home," just loud enough so Nevaeh didn't really have to repeat it.

"Whatever. He ain't gon' do nothin'," Nicole challenged.

"Anyway," Ronald said, ignoring her comment. "Where are you guys?"

"We're about to drop Nikki off. We should be there in about ten minutes," Nevaeh informed him.

"All right. Did she tell you where I was taking you tonight? Is it okay?"

"Yes, and she told me how you talk about me to Jeremy." Nevaeh could tell that Ronald was smiling.

"She did?" he said quietly, as if someone would be listening.

"Yes, she did."

"Well, did she tell you how I tell him how much I love and care about you?"

Nevaeh was smiling, and she knew that her father was listening, but she didn't care. "I love you, too, Ron."

Imani and Nicole burst into laughter while James just smiled.

Ronald cleared his throat. "Well, I'ma let you go since they're laughing. Boy, I'm glad I ain't in that car," Ronald joked.

"Lucky me." Nevaeh laughed with him. "Bye, Ronald."

"Bye, baby."

When she hung up the phone, the girls began to mimic the conversation.

"Hi, Ron," Imani said.

"Oh, Nevaeh, I love you," Nicole dramatized.

"I love you, too." Imani laughed.

"Y'all just need to shut up," Nevaeh said.

"We not the ones acting like an old married couple," Imani said.

"What's wrong with being an old married couple?" James asked as he turned onto Nicole's street.

"Nothing, if you are *actually* old and married," Imani said.

"The boys at our school don't act like y'all do," Nicole said.

"That's because they are immature little eighth graders, while we are mature seniors who know how to express our feelings without caring what our friends will say," Nevaeh retorted.

"Well, I hope we don't ever get like that," Nicole said with a laugh as James pulled up to her house.

While she was getting her stuff out of the trunk, Ronald came out to the car with a wife beater shirt on. It took all that was in Nevaeh not to stare at his muscled arms.

"Ain't you cold, boy? It's almost below freezin'," Nicole said as she closed the trunk. "You know you need to go put on some clothes."

"Mind your business," he said as she scrunched up her nose at his attire. "Hey, Mr. Madison," he said when he got to the car.

"Hey, Ronald. How you doing, son?" James said.

"Just fine, sir. And you?"

"As long as my daughter's happy, I'm happy."

"Well, you're going to be happy for a long time."

"I'm glad to hear it."

Realizing that he hadn't asked James to take Nevaeh out this evening, Ronald posed the question, and James gave his daughter's boyfriend his permission.

"Hey, Imani," Ronald greeted, looking toward the back seat.

"Hi, *Ronald*," Imani responded, to her sister's embarrassment.

He gave her a deep-dimpled smile and a wink. It was her turn to blush while Nevaeh laughed.

"And how are you doing?" Ronald spoke to Nevaeh as he leaned into her window and placed a quick kiss on her cheek.

"Fine," Nevaeh said in a low voice.

"Well," Ronald said, clearing his throat and standing to go in the house, "I'll pick you up at seven?"

"Yes." She nodded.

"Have a nice day, Mr. Madison. And you too, *Mani,*" he said, making Imani blush again.

"Bye, y'all," Nicole said as James backed out of the driveway.

While James drove home, Nevaeh couldn't help but think that tonight would change her life. She couldn't tell if it was for better or worse, but something inside of her made her believe that when she came home from her date that night, she wouldn't be the same.

Chapter 9

When Shimone walked into her bedroom, she noticed the blinking light on her answering machine. Walking over to the nightstand, she turned on the speakerphone and dialed her voicemail number to see who had called her while she was out.

"Hey, Shimone, it's me, Nevaeh," she heard her best friend speak. "I was just calling to see if your appointment went well. I want to hear all about your night, so call as soon as you get this 'cause I am going out with Ron tonight. Love ya, girl. Bye."

Shimone deleted the message and picked up the phone to call her friend. Speed dialing Nevaeh, she waited for her to answer.

"Hello," Nevaeh answered the phone.

"Wassup?" Shimone said, sitting on the bed and taking off her shoes.

"Nothing much. Did you get my message?"

"Yeah. Last night was the best night of my life." Shimone smiled, remembering her date with Marques.

"So, what happened? Ron told me that Marques told you that he loved you."

Shimone was more than happy to recap the happenings of her latest date with the boy she now knew loved her as much as she loved him. Nevaeh was quiet as Shimone gave the play-by-play review. She didn't leave out any details, and telling the story made her relive the joy that she felt the night before. Even to herself, she sounded as if she was bursting with happiness.

"And he was cool with it? I mean he didn't deny being the father or anything like that?" Nevaeh asked, still finding it hard to believe that everything had gone as perfectly as Ronald had told her earlier and her friend was now validating.

"At first he just sat there with his mouth open, looking at me like he was in a dream and nothing I had just said was reality," Shimone said. "Then he had the nerve to ask me if I was sure he was the father. Girl, I almost cussed him out. When I raised my voice at him and those people in the restaurant started looking at us, he knew I was for real. He believed me then."

Nevaeh laughed and imagined Shimone yelling like she was in a deserted parking lot. When the laughter calmed, Shimone went on to tell her the rest of the story, including Marques' reaction when she took her stance against the idea of aborting the child. She felt herself blushing when she told Nevaeh that Marques told her that he wouldn't allow her to do it even if she wanted to. The part that seemed to surprise her best friend the most was Shimone's revelation that Marques had agreed to use abstinence as their birth control from now on.

"Well, I guess that I underestimated Mr. Anderson. He really *has* changed," Nevaeh said. "So, how was the doctor's visit?"

"We had a long wait, but once I was seen, we found out that everything was fine."

"So, did you get to see the baby?"

"Yeah. It didn't look like much, but when I saw my baby on the monitor, all I could do was cry. Marq tried to hide it, but I saw him fighting tears too."

"Marques Anderson cried? Well, I guess things like hearing your baby's heartbeat can break any man down no matter how tough they try to act."

"Yeah, I think he is going to be a good dad. When we left, Dr. Anther said for me to be there with my mom the next time. I was like, that is going to be impossible."

"Oh . . . I spoke to your mother after practice today," Nevaeh informed.

"Nevaeh, please don't tell me you told her," Shimone said, sounding like she was already in panicky tears.

"No, I didn't. But she knows something is wrong 'cause she approached me and asked me if I thought something was different about you."

"Man, I hate that mother's intuition thing." Shimone sighed. "Well, did you tell her you thought something was different about me?"

"No, I told her that if something was wrong that you would come to her for sure. Shimone, you really need to tell her. She is even thinking it has something to do with Marques," Nevaeh stressed.

"Are you for real? Nev, please be lying."

"No, I'm not lying now, but I hated lying to your mother for you earlier. You need to tell her *today*."

Shimone was near tears. "Okay, I'll tell her when she gets home. I promise."

Nevaeh took a deep breath and softened her tone. "Good, and try to be strong for her, 'cause if you break down, she is gonna break down too."

"I'll try. Well, I'm going to let you get ready for your date tonight."

"Yeah, okay," Nevaeh said as if she was dreading the upcoming date.

"You don't sound too excited."

"I am, really. It's just that I feel like something big is going to happen, and I'm just nervous. I feel like my whole life is about to change," Nevaeh said.

"Well, maybe it's for the better."

"Maybe," Nevaeh mumbled. "Okay, I got to go. I'll talk to you later."

"Bye." Shimone hung up the phone and remained seated on the side of her bed.

The last time she was this afraid of her mother coming home was in the eighth grade. She had gotten into a huge fight at school, and she knew that her mom had gotten a call at her job about her daughter's ten-day suspension.

When Shimone got home that day, she was glad that her mother had to work late. The whole time she was home, she tried to come up with a good excuse for why she had been fighting in the first place. She couldn't tell her mother that it was because she'd seen the girl pinned up against the wall with her boyfriend. That version of events would get her the beat down that she gave both the girl and her boyfriend, who had the nerve to stand there and laugh while the two girls fought.

By the time her mother arrived at home, Shimone was a wreck. When Misty came into her daughter's room, Shimone was already in tears. The belt Misty held in her hand seemed larger than any Shimone had ever seen. She had not gotten a whipping since she was in the fourth grade. When Shimone entered middle school, Misty thought she was old enough to be just put on punishment. But Shimone had never been suspended before, and Misty always said that if her daughter ever got suspended, she would get a whipping every day she was on suspension.

Although she didn't get a whipping every day of her suspension, the pain from the one she did get seemed like it lasted the whole ten days, especially since all she could do was stay in her room unless it was to go to the bathroom or to eat. She couldn't talk on the phone, watch television, hang out with friends, or anything else that required contact with the outside world. That had been the longest punishment Shimone had ever received, and although she was now eighteen, she still lived with her mother, by her mother's rules, so she tried hard to stay out of trouble.

Shimone had been pacing in her room for more than a half-hour. She felt like she was back in the eighth grade, trying to figure out a way to get out of the trouble she knew she was in. She sat on her bed and got her manicure set. She always painted her toenails when she was upset or anxious. She rummaged through the different colors and decided on the firecracker red, seeing it as a symbol of courage, something she definitely needed right now.

When she heard the garage door opening, she nearly knocked over the polish. She had only done one foot, but she couldn't concern herself with that now, especially once she heard her mother coming up the stairs. Shimone ran to her bedroom door and opened it.

"Hey, Ma," she said, standing in the doorway.

"Hey, baby," Misty replied right before she went into her room.

"Can I talk to you in the living room?"

"Sure, just let me take off these shoes," Misty said as she went into her room. "Lord, have mercy. Those kids 'bout wore me out today, but I think they are almost ready for the show in February." She came out of the room and noted the distressed look on her daughter's face. She looked down at Shimone's half-painted toes. "Baby, what's wrong?"

Shimone was already close to tears as she unconsciously reached up and pulled at her left earlobe. "Mama, can we please talk . . . downstairs? I have something I really need to tell you."

"Okay," Misty said, looking as worried as she felt.

Misty dreaded the walk down to the living room as she thought of all the possible things her daughter had to tell her. Was she in some type of trouble? Was she using drugs? Was she pregnant? Did she have some kind of disease? All the questions that swirled around in Misty's head made the walk seem even longer. She knew her daughter was sexually active, having found an open box of condoms in Shimone's underwear drawer nearly a year ago. Although Misty had taught her daughter to have religious beliefs and convictions, Misty knew Shimone would be stubborn and do whatever she wanted.

When they finally reached their destination, Shimone had already begun to cry. She sat in the loveseat and watched as her mother stood in the entranceway.

"Could you please sit?" Shimone asked.

"I don't think I want to," Misty said, becoming extremely nervous. "What do you have to tell me?"

"Mama, I'm so sorry. I'm really sorry," Shimone

cried. "I didn't do it on purpose. I never want to hurt you, Mama. I really am so, so sorry."

"Shimone, what are you apologizing for? Why are you crying? What have you done?"

With every question her mother asked, Shimone's body rocked faster and faster. She could tell her mother was near tears and she hated herself because she knew she was the cause of them. Shimone wanted to just come out and say it, but she was afraid of her mother's reaction.

"Nia, baby, please tell me. What is wrong?"

Shimone almost jumped when her mother called her the shortened version of her middle name. Misty had not called Shimone that since she was a little girl. The last time she referred to her by "Nia," Misty had explained to her why she didn't have a father.

Shimone raised her head and looked into her mother's eyes, full of unshed tears. "Mama, I'm . . . I'm . . . I am . . . pregnant."

It was like a slap in the face. Misty's eyes released the tears that they could hold back no longer. She turned away and went upstairs. Shimone's head jerked when she heard the door slam. With nothing else to do, she buried her head in her hands and re-leased a flood of tears.

Chapter 10

Nevaeh had taken her shower and was now in her closet searching for something to wear when she heard a knock on her door. When she opened it, she was surprised to see Imani standing before her.

"Oh, so you *do* know how to knock before barging in," Nevaeh teased as Imani brushed past her and sat on the bed.

"I just came to apologize for the immature way me and Nikki acted in the car," Imani stated. "I know that we are just fourteen-year-old eighth graders, but the truth is that I am jealous."

"Jealous of what?" Nevaeh asked, tightening the belt on her silk bathrobe.

"Of you and Ronald's relationship. He is so cute, and I think that I have a crush on him," Imani said in a tone that sounded apologetic.

Nevaeh waved her hand in the air. "I already knew that, girl. Ron knows you like him, too."

"How do you know?"

"For one thing, he wouldn't mess with you like he

does if he didn't know. And we've talked about it before."

"Hold up. Y'all be talkin' 'bout me?" Imani questioned defensively.

"A few times," Nevaeh answered. "It's not hard to see, especially since you blush at anything he says to you. Like today when he said 'hi,' your face went completely red." They both laughed.

"Well, consider yourself lucky, 'cause I know a lot of girls at my school who want him," Imani stated matter-of-factly.

"When have they even seen him?" Nevaeh asked.

"You remember those pictures you gave me that y'all took at the junior prom?" Imani asked and Nevaeh nodded. "Well, a few of my friends have seen them. There are guys who like you, too."

"Please," Nevaeh spat as if she were disgusted. "I do not have time for little middle school boys who don't do anything except worry about what other people think of them."

"Well, excuse me. I'm sorry that everybody ain't a mature high school *senior* like you." Imani playfully rolled her eyes. "So, are you ready for your date with Ronald?"

"If I can find something to wear, I will be," Nevaeh said as she walked back into the closet. Looking through her slacks, jeans, dresses, blouses, and sweaters, Nevaeh couldn't find one thing that seemed suitable.

Imani got off of the bed and joined her sister in the closet. "Girl, all these clothes you got in here and you can't find nothing to wear. I'm just looking and I see about fifty combinations for an outfit. You're acting like you're going to the Oscars or something. You're just going to dinner at *Ruby Tuesday*," Imani said with so much attitude that Nevaeh felt, for a moment,

that she was with Shimone. "Just put on some jeans.
If you want to look a little dressier, then wear a pair
of slacks or a skirt. But trust me, whatever you wear,
Ronald is going to like it."

Nevaeh sighed as she took out a pair of black silk
pants and a red blouse.

"Something's wrong with you. I can tell. You are
not just stressin' over some dumb clothes," Imani said.
"What's wrong?"

Nevaeh sank into one of the beanbag chairs that
sat in the corner across from the television. She
rarely confided in her younger sister. The years between them prevented her from seeing Imani as
someone who would understand the problems of a
high school senior. But at the moment, Imani's ears
seemed as good as any.

"I don't know about this date tonight," Nevaeh
said. "I mean, I've been on a million dates with Ron
before, but I have never felt this way before any of
them."

"What are you talking about?" Imani asked as she
plopped into the other beanbag chair.

"It just feels like something big is about to happen.
I felt it when he kissed me after we dropped Nikki
off. I couldn't tell if it was a good or bad feeling, but
the closer I get to going on this date, the worse I feel.
I think that something bad *is* going to happen."

Nevaeh was sure that she shouldn't go on this
date, at least not tonight. But she didn't want to call
Ronald an hour before he was supposed to pick her
up and say she didn't want to go out.

"I just think you need to pray before you leave,
and everything will be all right," Imani said. "What's
that thing Dad says all the time? Put it all in God's
hands . . ."

"And He'll make it all right," Nevaeh finished the saying. She got up and smiled as she helped Imani up also. "You know you are pretty smart for a fourteen-year-old."

"You can learn a lot from the young and wise," Imani teased.

"C'mon, pray with me," Nevaeh said as she held out her hands for Imani to take them.

"Dear Lord, I thank You for this day and for my little sister, who is here to remind me that I am not alone, especially when I am carrying a burden. I just pray that whatever this feeling is, it will go away. I want to enjoy this night with one of Your very own. I just pray that everything will go well tonight. Thank You for my sister and her wisdom, and I pray that she is right about my doubt. In Your name I pray." She squeezed Imani's hands for her to continue.

"Heavenly Father, I just want You to help my sister to give all of her problems to You and let You take control. I just hope that I am right also, and that nothing bad will happen tonight, with Nev, Ron, or anyone else. All we can do is believe in You and Your Word, and we do. In Jesus' name I pray."

"Amen," they said together.

Nevaeh hugged Imani. When she released her, Imani smiled.

"So, this is what you are wearing?" Imani said as she went into her sister's closet.

"What are you doing?" Nevaeh asked as Imani went through boxes of shoes.

"Trying to find you some shoes that match. I know I said that Ronald likes whatever you wear, but those silver pumps ain't gonna work this time," she said as she came out of the closet holding a pair of red heels.

"I was not about to put on those silver shoes and you know it. I know how to color coordinate, thank *you* very much," Nevaeh said as she took the shoes.

"So, what are you going to do with your hair?"

"It's already in a bun," Nevaeh said, getting annoyed.

"How many times has Ronald seen you in that bun this week?" Imani asked with her hands on her hips.

Nevaeh sighed and rolled her eyes without answering.

"Take it down," Imani instructed.

"Well, what am I supposed to do with my hair?" Nevaeh asked.

Imani could tell her sister was stressed. "Nev, you're the hair stylist. Hook it up."

"Since when did you become my personal advisor? You were the one who said that I was just going to dinner at Ruby Tuesday and—"

"Not the Oscars. I know, but you still need to look nice. Ronald is probably tired of that bun. I know I am."

"Okay, now that you have picked out my clothes, shoes, *and* told me how to wear my hair, can you leave so I can dress *myself*?" Nevaeh said, pushing Imani out of the door.

"Fine, but if you need my help, I am right across the hall." Imani laughed as she turned around and walked to her room.

As Nevaeh got dressed, she noticed that the bad feeling she had earlier was not as bothersome as it was before the prayer. "Thank you, Jesus," she whispered as she walked to the bathroom to turn on her flat iron.

She went back into her room and looked at the clock; it was 6:35 p.m. She finished putting on her clothes and placed her robe over them while she went back to the bathroom to do her hair. As she flat-ironed her tresses, she began to hum the melody of "Your Steps Are Ordered." The song had been on her mind since leaving the dance studio. She had heard it before, but she never really paid attention to the words. Her favorite part of the song was the vamp. It talked about how God's people's steps were ordered by Him before the world was even made, and anything that a Christian went through in life didn't change the fact that his steps would still be ordered by God. She felt blessed knowing that.

When she finished her hair, Nevaeh was glad that she had taken her sister's advice. She went back to her room and noticed that it was ten minutes before seven. She quickly slipped into her shoes, put on a pair of dangling earrings, and adjusted the silver band on her finger. She brushed her face lightly with a loose powder and sprayed on a little perfume.

Just as she grabbed her purse, the doorbell rang. She heard Imani's door open, and laughed as her sister ran downstairs like she was in a marathon. Nevaeh knew she needed to rush now because it was her mom who had answered the door, and if she didn't get downstairs now, she and Ronald would be eating dinner with the rest of her family.

As she walked downstairs, Nevaeh saw Imani standing next to Ronald while Nicole was sitting on the couch, talking with her mother. She wondered why Ronald would bring his sister over.

"Hi," Nevaeh greeted as she reached the last step.

Ronald looked at her and smiled. "You look beautiful." He took her hand and led her down the rest of the steps.

"Thank you," she said as she walked over to the couch. "Hey, Nikki. What are you doing here?"

"I called earlier and asked if I could spend the night," Nicole explained, pointing to her book bag.

"Mom said it was cool," Imani jumped in. If Imani's smile was any indication, she was pleased to have her friend with her.

"We should go." Ronald said, grabbing Nevaeh's hand as he made the suggestion.

"You two have fun," Michelle said.

"Bye, Ron," Imani said.

"Bye, Mani," Ronald laughed. "Nikki, you better be good," he warned as his sister rolled her eyes in response.

"Don't worry about her," Michelle said. "You two go on now."

"Bye, Mama," Nevaeh said, giving Michelle a kiss on the cheek.

As he helped Nevaeh into the car, Ronald hoped that all his efforts to make tonight special would not be unsuccessful. Hopping into the driver's seat, he turned on the car and turned up the volume as the John Legend CD that he was listening to on the way to Nevaeh's house continued to play. Ronald smiled when she started to sing along to "Ordinary People." He loved to hear her sing, and hoped to give her many more reasons to do so by the end of the night.

Fifteen minutes later, Ronald pulled into the driveway of his ranch-style home. He was amused by the puzzled look on her face.

"I thought we were going to Ruby Tuesday," Nevaeh said as she noticed that his parents' car was not out front as it usually was.

"Change of plans," he said as he helped her out of the car and led her to his front door.

As Ronald unlocked the door, the bad feeling, which Nevaeh thought had left her alone, reappeared.

She knew she should tell him to take her home, or at least try to persuade him to go to the restaurant, but with her heart and his strong hand on her back, leading her in the other direction, she was outnumbered.

She gasped as she stepped into the living room that was lit only by strategically placed candles. She was even more impressed with the smell of seafood and pasta coming from the kitchen.

"Did you make dinner by yourself?" she asked.

"Yes, I did," he stated proudly as he turned on the stereo and allowed Tevin Campbell's voice to stream through the speakers.

Nevaeh looked around the quiet house. "So, where is everybody?"

"Well, Dad decided to take Mom out tonight. And Jeremy is at a friend's, and you know where Nikki is," Ronald said as he looked into her eyes.

Usually it was hard for Nevaeh to hold a steady gaze with Ronald, but tonight she knew there was a mystery behind his dark eyes, and she wanted to find out what it was. "So, we are here . . . alone." Her statement sounded more like a question.

Ronald smiled and went into the kitchen to put the final touches on the dinner. When he was done, he went back into the living room and led Nevaeh to the dinner table. As she prayed over the shrimp alfredo, she also said a silent prayer that she had not made a mistake by allowing her boyfriend to treat her to this unexpected in-house date.

As they ate, Ronald wished over and over again that this night would not be a total disappointment. He loved Nevaeh so much that he would do anything for her, but this whole abstinence thing was getting old. Being almost eighteen and still a virgin was not something he liked to brag about.

When he met Nevaeh, he was happy he was not alone, but he was tired of hearing his friends' weekend stories and not having a story of his own to share. Becoming intimate with Nevaeh would only make their relationship stronger; he was sure of it. And he was sure that tonight was the night to make all of his dreams a reality.

Chapter 11

Shimone had no idea how long she had been on the living room floor in a fetal position, and she really did not care. All that was on her mind was how her mother had left her after she told her she was pregnant. The image of the tears uncontrollably overflowing in Misty's eyes caused Shimone to feel guiltier and cry even harder. She knew her mother was reliving her past, and Shimone knew that she had just ruined the dreams Misty had for her daughter's future.

When Shimone heard her mother's door open, she quickly dried her tears, but new ones replaced them. She stood when her mother entered the room. The once fragile look that covered her mother's face was now replaced with an unyielding one. Shimone wanted to say something, anything, but she was afraid to even move.

"Sit," Misty said through lips that barely moved.

Knowing that she was better off being quiet, Shimone quickly did as she was told, sitting on the sofa nearest her. Misty continued standing in the doorway and boldly stared into Shimone's eyes, daring her to return the stance. When Shimone turned her head, Misty walked over and sat on the chair opposite her daughter, satisfied that she was still in control.

"Why?" Misty asked as she continued to stare at Shimone. When she didn't answer right away, Misty grew aggravated. "Shimone LaNia Johnson, if you do not answer me right now, you gonna have to explain to all your little friends why you got whip marks all over your body at the age of eighteen!" She had Shimone's full attention. "Now, I asked you a question and I want an answer. Why would you go and do something like this when you know all that I been through?"

"I don't know. I wasn't thinking. I wasn't thinking 'bout getting pregnant. I wasn't thinking 'bout nothin' or nobody, except for myself," Shimone said through mounting tears. "I don't know why I did it, Mama, but I promise I'm not doing it no more. I promise."

"Girl, how many times you done made me that promise? I done heard that one so many times that you sound like a song on a CD, playing in a stereo that's set on repeat. So how I'm 'posed to know that you ain't gonna do it again? Huh?" She stared at her daughter. "Oh . . . I see." Misty got out of the chair and paused for dramatization. "Just 'cause you're reaping the consequences mean you gonna change? I'm 'posed to believe just 'cause you done up and got yourself pregnant that you ain't gon' up and lay with some other li'l knucklehead boy. All he got to do is

say come, and you go to runnnin'." She was now pacing the living room floor.

"Oh . . . and I can just guess who the baby daddy
is! Who is it, Shimone, huh?" Misty asked as she put
her face close to her daughter's. "You know how
hard it was for me to take care of you while I still had
three years of high school to finish?" she continued,
not giving Shimone a chance to answer the first question. "I ain't have hardly no help from your grandparents. They were already outdone with me when I
told them I was pregnant, so they sho' didn't help
none while I was strugglin'. Yeah, they gave us the
shelter that we needed, but after I dropped out in
the middle of my junior year, I was out on my own, in
the streets.

"You wanna know how I survived?" Misty said
through tears. "I ain't never told nobody this except
your great granny, and I never planned on telling
you, but you need to know before you end up in the
same position." She took a deep breath to calm herself. "I prostituted."

Shimone's eyes bulged and her mouth dropped
open in surprise.

"I couldn't get no job 'cause I had you," Misty continued. "I ain't have a penny to my name, so I did
what I had to do. I left you with your great grandmother and told her that I would be back for you
once I made enough money to take care of you. She
tried to get me to stay by telling me that she'd take
care of everything, but I wanted to prove that I
could do things on my own. So, I went out and took
care of business. You was 'bout two, but you probably don't remember anything way back then, do
you?"

Shimone shook her head slowly from side to side as the tears continued to fall.

"And that's how I wanted it," Misty continued. "I'd still be out on the streets if it wasn't for this one man. I'll never forget him." She closed her eyes as she told the story. "He was a fine man, too. Had the nicest clothes and could buy anything he wanted. I saw an opportunity and I acted on it. We got together, and he said he didn't pay women for sex. I thought I was getting nothing, but then he started buying me things; jewelry and shoes and the most gorgeous clothes I had ever seen.

"Then things took a sharp turn. He didn't tell me he was a dealer. I knew he had money, but I didn't know where it all was coming from. That is, until he started having me run packages for him. When he first asked me, I said no. You know what he did? He hit me! Slapped me dead across my face. Then he literally kicked me out the door and told me not to come back until I sold what he gave me.

"I thought about running, but then I thought about all those beautiful minks that hung in the closet of his beautiful apartment. I can't tell you how many times I found myself at Big Mama's doorstep crying. She'd let me in and take care of my wounds. She never asked me what I was doing out on the streets. She'd just hum and let me cry on her lap like a little baby. Then, the next morning, I'd be back out on the street running packages for that abusive dog. I sold his dope for six months. And in between my dope sales, I was beaten and kicked around like a slave.

"Well, I had decided that I didn't want to live that type of lifestyle anymore, so I went down to the police station one night after he had beat me. I walked into the place, bruises and all, and turned his sorry behind in." Misty wiped tears from her eyes. "After that, I moved in with you and Big Mama, who was all too happy to open her doors to me. By then, you were four, and you still had no clue as to what I had been through. And you still wouldn't if you had not gotten yourself in a position like this," Misty said as her eyes bore into Shimone's.

Shimone was crying so hard that she could not see anything.

"Who is the father?" Misty asked through clenched teeth.

"Mar-Mar-Marques Anderson," Shimone stuttered.

"Marques Anderson? This is the guy you've been seeing for the last few months?"

"Yes, ma'am."

Misty walked back over to the chair she had earlier vacated. She stood in place for a while before sinking down into the cushions. Shimone sat in silence as she watched her mother mutter what she hoped was a prayer to keep from hitting her. Misty took a deep breath and then sat up straight in the chair as if she was about to make a legal negotiation.

"How far along are you?" Misty asked.

"About three months," Shimone whispered.

"Does he know?"

"Yes, ma'am. I told him last night."

"Does he plan to take responsibility?"

"Yes, ma'am. He even took me to see Dr. Anther. We got to see the baby and everything. She said I would be due around the fifteenth of June."

"That's where you were running off to this morning?" Misty asked.

"Yes, ma'am."

Misty seemed to be calming with each question that was answered truthfully. She stood up once more and looked Shimone square in the eyes and said, "Well, it seems that you have taken the necessary precautions to make sure everyone involved was informed." She walked out of the room, but turned back to her daughter, who was still sitting in the same position she had been for the past forty-five minutes. "I just hope that you are ready to live with the consequences." Misty turned and walked up to her room, closing the door more gently than she had before.

Nevaeh sat in the living room as Ronald washed their dinner dishes. *What are you doing here?* Nevaeh's conscience reprimanded her. *You know nothing good can come from this. You need to go home.*

"Nothing's going to happen," she whispered aloud, trying to believe that she was right, but the knotting in her stomach told her otherwise. She jumped as she heard the soft, sensual melodies of Brian McKnight replace the less polished voice of Tevin Campbell.

"Are you okay?" Ronald asked as he noticed the expression on her face.

She tried to smile. "Yes."

He reached for her hand and led her to the middle of the room. Gently pulling her into his chest, Ronald inhaled her perfume. He loved the way she held onto his neck as they danced. It seemed as if she'd fall if she released the hold she had on him; he liked that. He was her protection, and he kept her from all harm and danger. If someone wanted to get to her, they'd have to go through him first. He knew he wanted to spend the rest of his life protecting and loving her.

"Nevaeh?" Ronald said as he pulled back slightly.

"Yes?" Nevaeh said as she looked into his eyes.

"I love you so much."

She could see the passion in his eyes, and the level of it made her want to run out of the front door. When he leaned down to kiss her, she pulled away. "Ronald, I—"

He gently pulled her to him and caressed her mouth with his. When she didn't offer resistance, he released all the passion that was built up inside of him. Nevaeh gave in to the feeling. She knew where she was headed, but she didn't want to stop. Before she knew it, she was lying on the couch and Ronald was on top of her. While he kissed her, he fumbled with her bra strap.

Marriage is honorable, and the bed undefiled; but fornicators and adulterers God will judge.

It was like God was in the room, whispering in her ear. Nevaeh froze when she saw what she thought was a man in the corner of the room. He was a rugged-looking man holding a huge cross on his back, and he was shaking his head sadly as he turned, trudged away slowly and disappeared. Quickly, Nevaeh pushed Ronald off of her and began to fix her clothes.

"Nevaeh, what's wrong?" he asked.

"Everything!" she cried. "I cannot believe what I almost allowed to happen! How could you? How could I? How could we? Oh my God!"

Ronald couldn't believe it. He had been so close. "What is your problem?" he asked.

"What?" Nevaeh yelled. "I can't believe you have the audacity to sit there and ask me that after what just almost happened! What happened to our commitment?" she asked, fighting off threatening tears. "*We*," she said, pointing to herself and then to him, "don't believe in sex before marriage, remember?" She was really mad at herself for letting it go as far as it had. She looked down at the silver band that rested on her ring finger. *What would my daddy think?* she thought as she twisted the band around her finger.

"Baby, that was over two years ago. It's hard, Nevaeh. No one says anything when girls say that they are virgins. It's like they should get a gold medal because of it. But guys . . ." he said, getting angry. "You *cannot* expect for me to keep that dumb promise."

"Actually, I *do*, and so does God!"

"I didn't make any promises to God. I made one to you, and I never had any intentions on keeping it, especially when I have girls tryna get with me every second of the day!" The words escaped his lips before he had a chance to stop them.

Nevaeh felt like he'd just slapped her in the face. "Really!" she said as she picked up her purse and coat. "Well, how 'bout you call one of them after you take me home."

"Baby, I didn't—".

"I don't even want to hear it," she said, flashing the palm of her hand in his face. "Just take me home."

"But I—"

"Ronald, take me home, *now*!" she screamed at the top of her lungs.

Ronald was tired, and arguing with Nevaeh was not an option at this point. "Fine!"

Nevaeh walked out of the house, slamming the door behind her, and climbed into the back seat of the car and slammed that door also. When Ronald got in, he didn't even acknowledge the fact that Nevaeh was not on the passenger side of his car as she usually was. The silence was deafening, and it was killing him. He turned on the radio, but the last thing he wanted to hear was a sappy love song, so he turned it off. At first, Ronald drove as if his life depended on it, but as he neared her home, he began to slow down as if keeping her in the car longer than necessary would somehow calm her attitude and get her to open up to him.

Nevaeh wanted to tell him to speed up because she wanted to get as far away from him as possible, but that would require speaking to him, and that was the last thing she wanted to do right now.

When he pulled into her driveway, Nevaeh didn't even wait for him to turn off the engine before she jumped out of the car. Ronald followed her to the front door and stepped in front of it before she could open it.

"Baby, I'm sorry," he said, hoping she'd see the apology in his eyes.

"You know what?" she said as she took her house key out of her purse. "Before you came to pick me up, I had this bad feeling that something wasn't right. I felt it when we dropped your sister off earlier this afternoon, too." She wiped a lone tear from her cheek. "But you know, I prayed that everything would be all right. After I prayed, I felt better, but as soon as you pulled up to your house, the feeling came back."

Nevaeh hated herself for crying, but she knew what she had to do. "All the warning signs were there, but love kept me from believing something was wrong. We are not in the same place in our lives. We're unequally yoked, and it's not pleasing to God. I'm trying to be the Christian that He wants me to be, but you don't seem to be putting forth the same effort that I am," she said, looking into the eyes that usually made her weak. "So, I have to get rid of those who hinder me from doing God's will. Goodbye, Ronald," she said as she unlocked the door and stepped inside the house, leaving Ronald outside in disbelief.

Chapter 12

Nevaeh ran up the stairs and into her room, locking the door to prevent anyone from coming in without knocking first. She sprawled across her bed and released a flood of tears. She had never wanted to break up with Ronald, and she was sure he wasn't expecting it, but it had to be done. If this was the first time intimacy had been an issue in their relationship, maybe she would have reconsidered her decision, but this was the umpteenth time Ronald had shown that he was not interested in keeping his commitment to her or God.

Ronald always made sure he never put too much pressure on her. He'd bring up the subject and they'd spend hours talking about it. Nevaeh was always able to stand her ground, but being with Ronald seemed like the most wonderful thing in the world. She could envision him touching and caressing her. But while her vision was that of her wedding night, his was much sooner than that.

The first time he'd really tried to get Nevaeh to go

against their commitment was just a few months earlier. They were at a party that some of the soon-to-be
seniors were throwing to celebrate the upcoming
school year. Nevaeh had begged the whole day before finally convincing her parents to allow her to go.
When they finally agreed, she was happy. Celebrating
the beginning of her senior year with the man she
loved seemed like the makings of a perfect evening.

Nevaeh and Shimone rode together, and were
going to meet Ronald at the party, but as soon as they
got there, she found herself alone when Shimone
started talking to Marques. Nevaeh looked all around
for Ronald and found him in the kitchen. He was
drunk after consuming several glasses of punch that
had been spiked with alcohol, and was making a scene
of himself while others stood around and encour-
aged him.

"Ronald, what are you doing?" Nevaeh said as she
took a half-empty glass from his hand just as he was
about to take another drink. It looked like punch,
but just from his behavior, she knew better.

"What's wrong, baby?" Ronald said. "It's just Kool-
Aid, and I only had one," he said, holding up three
fingers.

"Come on," she said as she helped him to his feet.
"I need to get you home." Nevaeh tried to help him
walk, but her 125-pound frame was no match for his
nearly 200-pound one.

When she fell against the counter and tried to get
up, she was held down by him while he clumsily tried
to kiss and fondle her.

"Ronald, get off me!" she yelled as some of the
football players cheered him on.

"Yeah, man. Get some of dat!" They laughed.

"Let . . . let's go upstairs, baby" Ronald suggested as he grabbed her by the forearm.

"No!" Nevaeh yanked her arm from his grasp. "We are going home, now!" she said while trying to get a grip on his arm and tug him toward the door.

"Girl, you ain't my mama," he said, pushing her off of him with more force than he intended, causing her to fall backward and hit her head on the counter.

"Ouch!" Nevaeh immediately felt the back of her head begin to swell.

"Oh, baby, I'm so sorry," Ronald said, obviously sober enough to try to help her stand.

"Leave me alone," she said, pushing him away. "Find yourself a ride before you don't even live to see your senior year." She walked out of the kitchen with as much dignity as she could muster.

"I'll make sure he gets home, Nevaeh. Don't worry." The assurance came from Darnell Parker, one of the few sensible football players and a member of her church.

"Thanks," Nevaeh said just as she spotted Shimone in a corner, still talking to Marques. "I'm about to go," she said as she approached her friend. "If you want a ride, then you need to come now."

"Naw, I'm cool," Shimone said, barely acknowledging Nevaeh's presence. "Marques will give me a ride."

"Fine," Nevaeh said as she stomped out of the house.

Now that Nevaeh thought about it, it seemed like Ronald's signature statement was "Baby, I'm sorry" and she was tired of hearing it. He'd said it on their first day back to school their junior year, and they got back together. He'd said it after he kissed Sierra, and she forgave him. He'd said it at least a million times the day after the party, and she took him back then, too. But when Ronald said it again tonight, Nevaeh realized that he sounded like a broken record and she was sick of it. If she stayed with him, their life together would be just one apology after another.

Hearing a knock on her door, Nevaeh quickly got up and wiped her face. She opened the door just as her mother was about to knock again.

"Hey, sweetheart, I was just coming to check on you. I heard you come in, but after that it was silent," Michelle said.

"Mom, it's late and I'm kinda tired, so I'm going to just get a shower and settle for the night, okay?" Nevaeh said, hoping her mother couldn't sense her uneasiness. She knew there was no such luck when her mother began to search her eyes.

"Nevaeh, what's wrong? You look like you've been crying."

"Mama, I'm fine." Nevaeh fought the onset of more tears.

"Girl, don't lie to me. Your eyes are bloodshot red, so either you been drinking or you been crying," Michelle said with her hands on her slender hips. "Now, which is it?"

Nevaeh fell into her mother's arms and openly wept. Michelle held her daughter while she tried to step inside the room and close the door. All of her fumbling caused Imani and Nicole to come out of the room across the hall and see Nevaeh in Michelle's arms.

"Mama, what's wrong with Nevaeh?" Imani asked.

"Did Ronald do something to you?" Nicole demanded.

Michelle wanted to ask the same question, but

when she saw how hard her daughter was crying, she opted not to pry. "Everything's fine," Michelle said to the girls as she rubbed Nevaeh's back. "Now close this door and go back to your room. You all need to get ready for bed. We got church tomorrow."

"Yes, ma'am," Imani said as she closed Nevaeh's door and they walked back to the room.

Michelle sat Nevaeh on the bed and did something she hadn't done in years. She held her oldest daughter in her arms and rocked her until Nevaeh cried herself to sleep.

After standing on Nevaeh's front porch for almost twenty minutes, Ronald finally realized that she was not coming back out to say that she had just been kidding. Dejected, he walked back to his car and got in the driver's seat.

What am I going to do without you? he thought. "What am I going to do?" he said aloud.

How could he have messed up all that they had in one night? Why couldn't he just have stuck to his promise? He had plans to spend the rest of his life loving Nevaeh, but now that dream would never become reality.

After sitting in the car for a few more minutes, Ronald finally got enough strength to pull out of the driveway. As he rode down the street, he reminisced about all the good times they'd shared—the day he finally got up enough nerve to ask Nevaeh out; their first kiss and the first time he told her that he loved her; the many solo dates they'd gone on, as well as the group ones they'd gone on with friends; the time she sang to him at their school talent show, and the times she'd cheered just for him at the football games; when she would give him a congratulatory kiss after they had just won a game. Every moment with her had made him feel special.

Then Ronald's mind became crowded with memories of all the times he'd consciously and unconsciously pressured her to do things she didn't want to. Like that time at the party when he got drunk and embarrassed them both in front of his teammates and friends. Or like tonight, when he sent Jeremy to spend the evening with a school friend who lived across the street and made his sister call and ask to stay at Nevaeh's house, just so he could make tonight "special." He definitely made it a night Nevaeh would not forget, but it wasn't quite what he'd had in mind.

When Ronald finally made it back to his house, he was glad to see that his parents were not home yet. He parked the car outside of the garage and walked up the steps to the house. When he walked inside and looked around, what once felt romantic now felt like a slap in the face. He stood in the middle of the living room floor as the candles reminded him of the night's events. As they cast dancing shadows on the wall, it seemed as if they were taunting him. They laughed and teased him, knowing how he'd planned this special evening and got nothing out of it except a broken heart.

Moving as quickly as he could, Ronald ran around the room and blew out each of the candles, letting the darkness of the room surround him. He somberly went up the stairs and walked into the black-and-gold bathroom. Turning the gold knob to its hottest temperature, he stepped out of his clothes and dimmed the lights as he stepped into the steaming hot water. He turned the shower radio to V-103; Joyce Littel's voice would be very soothing at this point.

"It's time to let the day go," the sultry voice said, "so release and relax to the Quiet Storm, guaranteed to be soft and warm."

As the water hit his face, Ronald released the tears that he'd held all through Nevaeh's break-up speech and on the drive home. He was glad that no one was home to hear his sobs and the sounds of his fists banging against the shower walls.

"Nevaeh, how could you do this to me?" he screamed.

His cries came to a halt when he heard Boyz II Men's "Doing Just Fine" come through the speakers of the radio. Ronald quickly turned off the radio. That song definitely had not been written with him in mind, because he knew nothing would ever be fine without Nevaeh in his life.

Chapter 13

Shimone awoke to the clanking sounds of pots and pans being used in the kitchen. She looked at her clock and noticed that it was nearly two o'clock in the afternoon. Her mother had come home from church and was finishing up Sunday dinner. Shimone swung her feet over the right side of her bed. Sitting on the side of her bed, she unconsciously rubbed her stomach.

Being that she was already full-figured, she knew she could hide her pregnancy for a while. But that time was quickly coming to an end as she noticed her stomach was slightly bigger than it was a few weeks ago.

Reaching over to her dresser, she pulled out a pair of baggy jeans and a large shirt that sported the words "Douglass' Astro Dancers" on the front. As she walked down the stairs, she could smell the fried catfish her mother was preparing. Shimone loved her mother's cooking and blamed it for being partially responsible for why she was overweight. But her body's makeup was never an issue with Shimone. She knew her figure was genetic, and when she looked at her mother, she knew where she had inherited it. Shimone loved being a big, beautiful woman. She always told people that her role model was Toccara, the full-sized beauty that outlasted many of the skinny girls who competed against her in the third season of UPN's *America's Next Top Model*. Shimone wasn't as heavy as Toccara, but the model's self-confidence had inspired her to feel good about herself.

"Hey, Mama," she said as she walked into the kitchen.

"Morning," Misty said as she continued to flour the rest of the catfish. "Have you talked to Nevaeh today?"

"No," Shimone responded. "Why?"

"Well, all of her family was in church today, except for her."

"Maybe she didn't feel like going this morning," Shimone suggested, although she knew nothing kept Nevaeh from attending Sunday services.

I wonder what kept her away. Shimone shook off the negative thoughts that began to enter her mind. She watched as her mother placed the catfish in the frying pan. "Mama, why didn't you wake me for church?"

"I thought you could use the rest," Misty said as she turned toward her daughter. "How you feelin'?"

"Fine," Shimone said, looking down at her toes, which she had finished painting late last night. "Mama, I know it may take a while to get used to, but I'm gonna have this baby, and—"

Misty put her hand in the air to stop Shimone's next words. She walked over and hugged Shimone, who didn't resist the motherly love. "I want you to have this baby. I know you're gonna be a good mother, even if you're not ready," Misty said as she walked back to the stove and stirred the collard greens that sat in a hug pot on one of the back burners. "And I don't want any more apologies, okay?"

"Yes, ma'am." Shimone walked over to the dining table and sat in one of the navy blue chairs. "Mama?"

"Yes, baby?"

"Dr. Anther wants you to come to my next appointment. It's in four weeks."

"Okay."

"Really? You'll come?" Shimone was surprised.

"Don't sound so shocked. I've been through it before, so I don't mind being there for support."

"Thank you," Shimone said as she got up to hug her mother. She looked at the stovetop. "Mama, why are you cookin' so much food?"

Misty smiled and wiped her hands on her apron. "'Cause we're having a few dinner guests. And speaking of which, I think you should go upstairs and put on something a little bit cuter than what you got on," Misty said as the doorbell rang.

"I'll get it," Shimone said.

"Oh, no you don't," Misty said, pushing her daughter in the other direction. "You go upstairs and put on something nice."

Shimone ran upstairs, all the while wondering what her mother was up to. She looked through her closet and pulled out a long wrap skirt. While searching for her favorite pink sweater, she could have sworn she heard Marques' voice downstairs. "Oh, no she didn't," she said to herself. She looked out of her bedroom window. "Oh, *yes* she *did*!" she responded aloud, spotting Marques' parents' BMW.

Locating her sweater, she put it on. She fluffed out the candy curls that were still in her hair and sprayed a little hair sheen for shine. Grabbing two pairs of stud earrings, she placed them in her double-pierced ears. Walking toward the stairs, she saw Marques' parents sitting on the couch, and wondered if they knew.

"Hi, Ms. Shundra, Mr. Robert," she said when she reached the living room.

"Hi, Shimone," Shundra said, getting up and hugging her. When she pulled back, Shimone's eyes asked her the question she was afraid to speak. "It's okay, sweetie. We know," Shundra whispered.

Shimone hugged the woman again and apologized over and over. "I never meant for this to happen." She was beginning to cry.

"You don't have to apologize," Robert said, patting Shimone on her shoulder. "We know the whole story, and it ain't like our son didn't play a role in it."

"This baby is not a mistake," Shundra said, helping her husband to calm Shimone. "What you and my son did to get in this position may have been wrong and against everything that God commands, but *this*," she said, placing her hand on Shimone's stomach, "this is not a mistake, and don't ever think that. You understand me?"

"Yes, ma'am," Shimone said, wiping her face.

Shundra gave Shimone's back a supportive pat and said, "Now come, so we can eat."

When Marques saw Shimone, he walked over to her and gave her a hug and a kiss on the forehead. Looking into her eyes, he noticed that they were red. "Are you okay?" he asked her.

"Yeah, I'm fine," Shimone assured, smiling.

"Okay, let's eat," Misty said.

After blessing the meal, they passed bowls of food around the table. Shimone couldn't help but think that her mother had cooked enough food to feed an army. Fish, rice, macaroni and cheese, greens, lima beans, and cornbread lined the table, and even more was still on the stove.

"Ms. Johnson, this is good," Marques said while piling his third helping of greens onto his plate, and then stuffing a forkful into his mouth.

"Boy, you ain't the only person that has to eat," Shundra warned, pointing at her son. "You too, Rob," she said, noticing that her husband had two more pieces of fish on his plate than before.

"Well, Mama did cook like we were feeding *all* the homeless people in Atlanta," Shimone said.

"Girl, hush. You need to eat, too," Misty said. "You didn't eat last night, and there's a little somebody in you who I know is hungry."

"I know, I know," Shimone said, stuffing a fork full of rice in her mouth.

"Speaking of the baby," Marques said while finishing off his second piece of fish and grabbing another at the same time, "I've decided that after graduation, me and Shimone and the baby should get an apartment."

The table grew silent as all eyes rested on Marques. He didn't seem to notice as he picked up the bowl of lima beans to add to the pile already on his plate.

"What about school?" Robert finally asked, taking the bowl from his son and adding more food to his plate also.

"Well, you know that Clark Atlanta offered me a basketball scholarship," Marques said, looking at his father, and then directing his attention to Shimone. "I was thinking that maybe you would come with me?" he suggested as he chewed the macaroni he'd just placed into his mouth.

"I haven't even applied to CAU. This is kinda short notice, don't you think?" Shimone replied, at the same time looking at both sets of parents for backup. She only received silent stares that were broken by Shundra's voice.

"Forget school," Shundra said. "What do you mean the two of you are getting an apartment? Are you talking about living together . . . *shacking*?" she whispered the word as if doing so would make it less bitter on her tongue.

"I already spoke to the Dean of Admission and the athletic director yesterday and told them about you and the baby," Marques said to Shimone, purposefully avoiding his mother's statement. "They said that if you apply, they could offer you a two-year academic scholarship, but we would have to get an off-campus apartment."

"My grades are not good enough for an academic scholarship. And what about the other two years of college?" she questioned. "And how are we going to pay for an apartment?"

"Yes, your grades are," he insisted. "You're an A/B student. That's good enough to get in, and you could get a dance scholarship, but if you don't want to dance, you could get the HOPE scholarship," he said matter-of-factly. "You got a 1750 on your SATs." He took a sip of his drink in order to wash down all of the food he'd eaten.

Shimone thought about it. "Mama, what do you think?" she asked her mother.

Misty quietly eased her fork into her plate and used her napkin to wipe her mouth. "What do I think?" she said in a voice that was just above a whisper. "I think the two of you done went and lost your minds."

"My thoughts exactly," Shundra added. "You sitting up here talking like you got it all worked out," she said to Marques. "Now, when your daddy and me talked to you last night and said that we respected you for stepping up to the plate and taking care of your responsibilities, we didn't mean that we were going to support the idea of you living with Shimone and playing house."

"But this is my baby, Ma," Marques said. "I gotta do what I gotta do. Tell her, Dad." He looked to his father for support.

As soon as Robert opened his mouth, Shundra gave him a look that seared into his flesh like a hot iron. Her eyes dared him to side with his son.

"Put the knife away, woman," he said to his wife. "I'm on your side. This ain't our way, and it sure ain't God's will. But let's be real," he added. "These ain't no little children no more. Once they get out of high school and move out, we got to rely on our prayers and our teachings to steer them in the right direction. God said that you teach them when they're young and they won't depart from it. We can tell this knot-headed boy that he can't bring a woman up in our house, but we can't tell him what he can't bring in his own."

Shundra sighed and turned her eyes to her plate. It was a hard pill to swallow, but she knew her husband was right.

Misty looked at her daughter, at Marques, then back at her daughter before shaking her head. "Well, you know how I feel about couples who ain't married living together," Misty said, "but Robert's right. I think that this is the first decision you guys are going to have to make on your own as adults and parents. But you should consider this baby also." She looked at Marques again. "Like, where is the baby going to be while you two are in school?"

"I've already looked into that," Marques said. "There's a daycare center near campus that is affordable. I can pay for it and for the apartment by working nights and weekends."

"When did you have time to set all this up?" Robert asked his son as he placed a hefty spoon of rice into his mouth.

"Yesterday," Marques said. "I wanted to take care of all of this before I told you guys. I called the athletic director, and he's the one who told me about the center. He said lots of students send their children to this daycare, so I called them yesterday afternoon and asked about the price and the environment."

"And you have a job lined up already?" Shundra asked, not believing that her son could be both this responsible and this irresponsible at the same time. His decision was foolish, but well thought out.

"Yes, ma'am," he said and reached for another piece of cornbread. "I have an interview next weekend, which was set up way before this, and I still have that job waiting for me at Uncle Percy's company this summer."

"Well, the baby is supposed to be due before we go off to college," Shimone said slowly, watching her mother's face for her reaction before turning back to Marques. "And I have to work this summer to pay for clothes and food and stuff for the baby. And you are going to be working too."

"I know, and I was thinking that you guys could help us for a few months?" Marques said, looking at the adults with a pleading look.

The silence that had set up camp in the room earlier now lingered again. This time, it was Misty who spoke first.

"I'll be the first to say that I think you all are making a foolish decision," Misty stated. "However, I ain't gonna take it out on my grandbaby. I don't mind keeping the baby as long as I don't feel like you all are taking advantage of me. This baby is yours, and you are going to raise it like responsible parents do."

"We will, Ms. Johnson," Marques promised.

"I don't mind either," Shundra said, shrugging her shoulders. "I could use the extra company while Robert's at work, and the boys would love the baby," she said referring to her two grandsons.

"Thanks," Shimone said to both women.

"I don't like this planned arrangement," Robert said as he resumed eating, "but I'm glad that you're serious about taking care of this baby."

"I'm dead serious. I want my son to have the best that I can give him, which isn't much, considering." Marques shrugged, biting into a piece of cornbread and looking at Shimone. "So, are you coming?" he asked with his mouth full.

Shimone looked at Misty and then at Shundra and Robert before turning her attention to Marques. Knowing they were going against their parents' beliefs was hurtful, but she had a baby to consider. "Sure, I don't see why I shouldn't. I want the best for our *daughter* too," Shimone added, rolling her eyes at Marques, who stuck out his tongue at her, breaking the thick tension in the room.

"I know y'all are not fighting over what this baby is

gonna turn out to be," Robert said over the laughter of the mothers.

"Yes," Shimone said. "Marq has been claiming a son, but I want a girl."

"What's wrong with a boy?" Robert asked before eating several forkfuls of the beans on his plate.

"I've always wanted a granddaughter," Shundra said. "Our daughter has given us two grandsons, so a girl would be a nice change."

"I wouldn't mind a granddaughter, either," Misty agreed.

"Man, I can't believe y'all are taking her side," Marques said, looking at his dad, for help.

"I'm with you, son. Ain't nothing wrong with a little man," Robert said while taking a drink of water to wash down the beans he'd just eaten.

"Thanks, Dad," Marques said, shaking his head at his mother. "Figures . . . all women stick together."

"Boy, shut up," his mother said, taking the bowl of rice out of his hands.

"Ma, whatchu doin'?" he asked, settling for the bowl of greens.

"Why are y'all acting like you ain't ate in centuries?" Shundra said, looking at her husband and son in disgust. "Y'all don't ever eat my food like this."

"Well, you don't cook like this," Robert said.

"No, you didn't," Shundra said, reeling back her neck as if she were about to snap.

"Girl, let them eat. I think I did overdo it with all this food," Misty said as she pointed toward the pots of food still on the stovetop.

"Think?" Shimone said. "Ms. Shundra, you might as well let them take a few plates home, and you get some, too. If you don't, I'll have to finish the rest. It'll take the rest of this year and then some."

"I don't mind taking a plate," Marques said, still piling his plate with more food.

"Me neither," Robert said, his mouth full of macaroni.

"Well, what you don't take, we can finish on Christmas," Misty said, extending an invitation.

"We'd love to," Marques and Robert said simultaneously.

When they finished eating, Shimone, Shundra, and Robert relaxed in the den while Marques volunteered to help Misty in the kitchen. It was a quiet task at first, but Marques knew that he needed to have a heart-to-heart with Shimone's mother.

"Ms. Johnson?" Marques said as he dried the dishes she'd just rinsed.

"Call me Ms. Misty. All of Shimone's high school friends call me that."

"Okay, Ms. Misty. I hope you believe me when I say that I am going to take care of this baby."

"I believe you," Misty assured him. "But I really want you to take care of my baby girl, too. I know she loves you, and from what I can see, the feeling is mutual." She looked at him. "Am I right?"

"Yes, I do love Shimone," he said honestly. "But I am not gonna lie to you, Ms. Misty. At Douglass, I'm known as King Playa," he said, using his fingers to make invisible quotations when he mentioned his famous nickname. "Well, I used to be, but your daughter has a way of changing people."

Misty smiled. "She's always been that way, but maybe some part of you wanted to change yourself."

Marques thought about it for a minute. He loved being a ladies' man, but Shimone made him want to be one lady's man; specifically, her man. "I guess you are right," he said, drying another dish. "Having a lot of female admirers is cool, but it gets old after a while."

"Do you see yourself having a long-term relationship with Shimone?" Misty asked him. "I know you're still young, but now that y'all are about to have a child, and you've already planned to *move in together*," she struggled to say the words, "I figure you've been giving some thought to what the future holds for you two . . . and the baby."

"Actually, I have. I know you don't agree with the living arrangements, Ms. Misty, but I think it'll only be for a little while that we'll be sharing the same house without being married. Shimone has me thinking about life after college with her. And not just because of the baby," he quickly added. "I been thinking 'bout things like this for a while now."

"I see," Misty said, handing him the last dish. "Well, that's good to hear. Welcome to our family," she said, giving him a motherly hug. "And I say that in the faith that you'll not only take care of my daughter and grandbaby, but you'll do the right thing . . . and *soon.*"

"Thank you," he said, bending down to return the embrace.

When Misty and Marques went into the den, Shimone looked up at her mother.

"Don't worry, I didn't grill him too much," Misty said to Shimone.

"Well, we better get going," Robert said, getting off of the couch.

"Wait, I gotta get the takeout," Marques said, running back into the kitchen as if the food would disappear if he didn't get to it fast enough.

- Shundra shook her head in embarrassment and said, "I can't take that boy nowhere." They all shared a laugh.

When he came back into the den, Marques held five plates of food wrapped in foil. While Robert helped Shundra put on her coat, Marques pulled Shimone up off of the couch then leaned down and kissed her on the lips.

"I'll call you later on tonight," he said.

"Okay." She smiled.

Robert delivered a harmless whack to his son's head, resulting in laughter from the mothers. "C'mon, boy," he said. "Ain't you done enough damage for one night?"

Chapter 14

Sierra and LaToya had been out all Sunday after-noon spending their fathers' money. Walking from store to store at Stonecrest Mall, the girls, between the two of them, had bags from Sears, Parisian's, Macy's, JC Penney, Dillard's and many other stores that were housed in the two-story mall.

As they walked along the perimeter of the shop-ping center, they received looks of admiration from almost every guy they passed. LaToya had several dif-ferent phone numbers in her purse that had been of-fered to her, but Sierra was not interested in any of them. Her mind was still on the events that had oc-curred on Friday night.

She still couldn't believe that Corey had kissed her. He had the softest lips that had ever touched hers. Then when he turned down her obvious sexual advances, she was even more amazed. Except for the times when she'd approached Ronald, Sierra had never been turned down before.

She had been even more surprised when Corey

woke her up at eight o'clock on Saturday and told her that he wanted to take her to the South Fulton Free Health Clinic, one of the few local STD clinics open on the weekends, for her to be tested. Sierra hardly ever got up before eleven o'clock on Saturdays, and by the loud snores still coming from her best friend, she guessed that LaToya didn't either. Slightly stirring LaToya from her sleep, Sierra explained to her friend that she was going out with Corey for a few minutes and, in her disoriented state, LaToya mumbled a few incomprehensible words before falling back asleep.

Sierra was nervous when they walked into the building, but began to calm when Corey assured her that everything would be all right and that he was with her. When a male doctor approached them and handed both of them the forms they needed to fill out, Sierra looked at Corey in confusion. *What does he need one for?* she thought.

"Never can be too safe." Corey shrugged when he saw her watching him fill out his papers.

It took ten minutes for them to complete the forms, and then they waited another fifteen before they were called back into separate rooms to be tested. Sierra was taken to a room at the far end of the hall. As she walked down the corridor, she pulled her coat closer to her body, hoping to get rid of the sudden chill that ran through her.

The doctor left her in the room after she asked for some time alone. She took off her coat and looked around the room at the few posters that lined the walls. *Abstinence is the key.* Sierra laughed dryly at the poster that was taped closest to the window. She thought about God. She really didn't know if she believed in someone she couldn't see, but she wondered if He could be the answer to her problem. She remembered when she lived with her aunt. They prayed together a lot, and Sierra wondered if the God they'd prayed to then was still up there now.

"Couldn't hurt," she said as she got on her knees and looked toward heaven. "God, I really don't know what to say. I just don't want AIDS. I don't think I would be able to live if I had it. So, if you could please spare me this once, I'll try to do better. Amen." As she got up off of her knees, she couldn't believe she had just done that, but she knew it was worth a shot.

"Are you ready?" the doctor, whose name she couldn't remember, asked as he opened the door slightly.

"Yes," Sierra said as she sat on the stool next to a tray with one needle and a few cotton swabs.

"Sierra Monroe. Age seventeen. One hundred and thirty pounds," he said as he read over her chart. "Here for a standard HIV examination?" he asked for confirmation.

"Ye-yes," she stammered.

"Okay," he said as he put on gloves and pushed the left sleeve of Sierra's sweater up her arm. When he picked up the needle, Sierra jumped slightly. "I'm going to need for you to be as still as possible," he said as he searched her arm for a vein before wrapping a large rubber band around her arm and tying it in place.

The band didn't hurt, but Sierra was very aware that it was the prelude to something that would. She'd hated needles since she was a child, but Sierra nodded to the doctor's earlier request and kept her eyes glued to the sharp instrument that was about to go through her arm. Just before the needle touched her, Sierra closed her eyes and felt the tip of it prick her skin. Once the vial was full, the doctor removed it and began wiping her arm with a cotton swab. Only then did Sierra open her eyes and begin breathing freely.

"We should have your results in one to three weeks, depending on the outcome of your test," he explained while placing a bandage over the sore spot. "We'll call you to let you know when they are ready, and you'll have to come here to get them. We can't mail the results to you, nor can we tell you the information over the phone." It sounded like a practiced speech.

"Okay," she said quietly.

As Sierra put on her jacket, she sighed and prayed that things would go in her favor. When she walked out into the waiting room, Corey was already waiting for her.

"How'd it go?" he asked as she walked into his arms for a much needed hug.

"As good as it could, I guess," she replied.

Leaving the clinic, they stopped at Burger King for a quick lunch then headed back to his house, where she would wait.

"What store do you want to go into next?" LaToya said, breaking into Sierra's thoughts.

"I'm hungry. Let's stop at the food court," Sierra said as they walked back to the north end of the mall. "I'm in the mood for hot wings."

After they got their food, they found a table for two and sat down to enjoy their meals.

"Don't look now, but you have a bugaboo alert at three o'clock," LaToya said, trying not to laugh.

Sierra turned her head slightly in the direction that LaToya was looking. She spotted the grungy-looking guy staring at her from across the room like she was a piece of meat. When he smiled, he revealed a mouth full of platinum teeth.

"Definitely not my type," Sierra said as she turned back around to finish her food before she lost her appetite.

"Well, he must think he is, since he is coming over here." LaToya laughed as her friend began to pack her food.

"I'm taking this to go," Sierra said, but before she could leave, the platinum-toothed guy was standing over her like a slave master.

"W'at up?" he said, nodding his head at Sierra.

"Nothing much," she said without looking at him.

"What's your name?" he asked.

Sierra looked at him and smiled slightly. "Cherrie."

"Cherrie," he said smoothly, licking his lips. "I'm Raheem. I'm 'bout to go see this movie. You wanna roll?"

"Sorry, we were just about to leave," Sierra said.

"Well, not without giving me your number, I hope," he said, pulling at the crotch of his baggy pants.

"Tell you what." Sierra stepped so close to him, she could smell his foul breath. "Why don't you give me *your* number and I'll call you."

"Oh, fo' sho'," the guy said while pulling a napkin off the table. "Got a pen?"

"Here," LaToya said, handing him a pen from her purse while trying to keep a straight face.

"Oh, 'preciate it," he said, looking as if he hadn't even noticed LaToya standing there prior to that moment.

He wrote down the number and handed the piece

of paper to Sierra, rubbing her hand in the process. "Holla at me, a'ight?"

"Okay, bye," Sierra said, winking at him as she and LaToya grabbed their food and walked toward the other end of the mall.

"Are you really going to call him?" LaToya asked.

"Girl, you know me much better than that," Sierra said as she balled up the napkin and threw it in a nearby trash bin. "Hand sanitizer, please."

"I was wondering when you were going to ask." LaToya laughed as she pulled a small bottle out of her purse.

The girls exited the mall and jumped into Sierra's Mazda.

"My dad is going to kill me when he sees all these clothes," LaToya said with a laugh as they rode. "No, he is going to bury me alive when he sees the bill."

"Well, my dad's not even gonna notice," Sierra mumbled.

LaToya looked at her friend as they cruised down the interstate. LaToya knew parts of the story behind Christopher's partial absence in his daughter's life, but she never knew how much animosity Sierra had against him for it. She wanted to get her friend to open up to her, but after what happened Friday night, she wasn't sure if Sierra would want to. After Sierra's statement gave way to a five-minute silence, LaToya decided to let the issue go for now.

When they got off the highway, Sierra turned up the radio and tapped her fingers on the steering wheel to the beat of Pussycat Dolls' "Stickwitu." The song made her think of Corey. Friday had been the most wonderful night of her life, and as non-sexual as it was, it was more satisfying than any sexual experience she had ever had. He never really said it, but she knew they would be starting a relationship very soon. She still hadn't told her friend about the talk she and Corey had on Friday night.

Although LaToya was her best friend, Sierra knew that it would take a lot to convince her that she really liked her brother and that she was not sleeping with him. LaToya was like Corey's protective mother, although she was two years younger than him.

"Hey, Toya," Sierra said, trying to get her friend's attention. But when LaToya continued to sing off-key, Sierra turned down the radio.

"Girl, what is you doin'?" LaToya said with her head cocked to the side. "You know that's my song."

"Please. Anything with a good beat is *your song*." Sierra laughed, and then suddenly became serious. "But for real, though, I have to tell you something."

"What?" LaToya asked, hoping Sierra was ready to talk about her father.

"I think I like your brother," Sierra spoke hurriedly.

"What?" LaToya laughed. "For real, what do you need to tell me?"

"That was it."

By the look on LaToya's face, Sierra knew she was not ecstatic with the news.

"Did you sleep with him?" LaToya asked quietly.

"What does that have to do with me liking him?"

" 'Cause to me, when you like somebody, it is usually 'cause you have slept with them or are about to. So, did you sleep with my brother?"

"I tried, but he wouldn't let me," Sierra admitted. "He told me that he did not want it to be like the other relationships I'd had."

"When did this happen?" LaToya asked, clearly feeling as if she was missing something.

"Friday night." Sierra hoped that LaToya would keep her cool. "When you called me over to your house, I really only accepted because I knew Corey would be there."

LaToya listened and looked on as Sierra told her all the embarrassing details of how she came on to Corey and he'd rejected her.

"He wasn't mean about it or anything," Sierra quickly added. "As a matter of fact, he was great. We talked for half the night. Then yesterday he took me to this clinic to get an HIV test." Sierra drove in silence while she waited for LaToya to respond.

"Is that what you were trying to tell me yesterday morning?" LaToya asked, trying to remember the incident.

Sierra nodded.

"So, why would you do that? You know, get tested?" LaToya questioned.

"It was Corey's idea. He got tested too. But I guess it is better to know. So, are you cool with this?"

"Well, as long as you ain't using him for your personal pleasures, I guess it's cool," LaToya said. "But don't go breaking my brother's heart."

"Girl, you know I won't," Sierra said, pulling into LaToya's driveway. "So, what's for dinner?" she asked, changing the subject as they grabbed the bags from the back seat of the car.

"Didn't you just eat?" LaToya laughed as she unlocked the front door.

"Umm, did you forget that my dinner was interrupted by a certain someone with B.O. problems?"

As they walked into the house, their laughter was cut short by the smell of baked chicken that greeted them in the foyer.

"Shoot, I wouldn't mind eating again either," La-

Toya said as Corey came out of the kitchen with an apron tied around his waist. "Since when do you cook, Mr. Emeril?"

"Just a li'l somthin'-somthin' I learned last summer at Aunt Whitney's," Corey said with a grin. "When did y'all leave this morning? I tried getting y'all up at nine for church, but y'all was knocked out cold," he said, looking at them for an answer.

LaToya looked at Sierra and burst into laughter. "Boy, first of all, nobody in this house gets up before eleven on weekends except Daddy, and that is just to go to work. Second, nobody in this house goes to church, never has. Since when do *you* go?"

"Been going for a minute now, and I got saved about six months ago. You didn't know?"

"Are you serious?" LaToya asked when she noticed the sincere look on her brother's face. "Is that why you're so different than you were the last time you came for a visit?"

"I guess," he said, grinning at the compliment as he walked back to the kitchen. "C'mon before the food gets cold."

So, that must be what kept him from sleeping with me, Sierra thought as she and LaToya washed their hands in the downstairs bathroom then took their places at the dining room table. The aroma of chicken, mashed potatoes, and corn entered the room before the actual food did. When Corey set the plates in front of them and bowed his head to bless the food, they were still surprised, but followed his lead when he began to pray.

"Lord, I just thank You for this meal that me and my family are about to eat," Corey prayed. "I pray that anything unclean will be cleansed and used for Your good works. In Your name I pray, Amen." When he lifted his head, both girls were staring at him. "What?"

"Nothing," they said as they began eating their food.

After a few moments of silence, LaToya asked, "Why did you get saved?"

Corey looked at her in confusion. "What?" he asked.

"You know, what made you want to change your life like that?" she said, playing with the corn on her plate.

Corey wiped his mouth with a napkin and cleared his throat. "Well, for one, college is full of trouble that I wasn't even tryin' to get into. Every party I went to, there was beer, sex, and drugs. Now, I am not saying I never got into the mix, but after a while, it got kinda boring." He sipped some of his lemonade. "I was looking for some extracurricular activities, you know, something besides studying in the library," he said with a laugh.

"Then one day, while I was in the library, this guy comes up to me and asks me if I was a Christian. I had no idea where he had come from, asking me questions like he was. Then he sat me down and explained to me that he was recruiting people to join C4C, that's Crusaders 4 Christ. After talking about it for 'bout an hour, I added my name to the list of recruits and told him I'd be at the next meeting. I started going to the meetings, and every Sunday we'd go to a church near campus. From then on, I was hooked." He shrugged.

Sierra stared at him as if he had grown a third eye.

"What?" Corey laughed. "Y'all still don't believe me?"

"No, it's just that . . ." Sierra shook her head. "Never mind."

"What? Go on and say it," he urged.

"Christians are supposed to be like virgins, right?" she asked.

"Not necessarily," he said, not getting what she was trying to say. "There are married Christians who do sleep with each other." He chuckled.

"No, I know that," Sierra said, trying to find another way to ask the question. "I mean, aren't unmarried Christians supposed to be virgins?"

Corey still didn't understand the question. "Some unmarried Christians are and some aren't. It depends on how they lived their lives before they got saved, and how they choose to live their lives after they have accepted Christ—by God's commandments or by their own desires."

"Well, umm . . . are you a virgin?" Sierra asked as LaToya looked at Corey, waiting to hear an answer also.

Corey took another sip of his drink and looked at Sierra. "No."

"Well, if Christians don't have to be virgins, aren't they at least supposed to practice abstinence?"

"Yeah."

"So, why did you need that test yesterday?" Sierra questioned.

"Because before I got saved, I was having sex, and I had never been tested before," Corey answered.

"So did your *religion* have anything to do with you rejecting me Friday night?" Sierra asked the question calmly, but her tone was harsh.

"*Okay*," LaToya said as she gathered her plate. "I'm going to finish this upstairs."

Corey looked at Sierra as if she'd lost her mind. "Why would you ask me something like that?" he said as soon as he thought his sister was upstairs and out of listening range.

"Because I really want to know," Sierra said, sitting back and folding her arms across her chest.

"I did not reject you, Sierra," he said, looking into her eyes. "I thought we already talked about this. I thought you wanted to change."

"I do." She released a lungful of air. "It's just that you are the first guy to ever decline my offer, twice," she said, referring to the time when they were younger.

"Well, if it will make you feel better," he said as he got up and walked to the other side of the table, taking her hands. "It took God and all of my religious convictions to turn you down."

She smiled as he kissed her cheek. "Well, I guess I better get with the program if I'm going to be your girl." Her eyes questioned him.

"For you to truly be my girl, it's going to take more than that. We have to be equally yoked in every way. But I ain't sweatin' it. I already know it's already done."

Sierra didn't quite know what he meant, but it sounded like a "yes" to her.

Chapter 15

"Nevaeh?" Imani said as she opened the door to her sister's room.

"Please leave me alone," Nevaeh said over Trey Songz's *Hatin' Love*.

Imani reluctantly closed the door and went back to her room. "She's still in her room, crying," she said into the phone.

"Ronald's been in his room, too," Nicole said. "He won't talk to nobody, unless it's to yell at anybody who bothers him. Girl, he nearly jumped on Jeremy yesterday because he asked if he would take him to get some shoes."

"Something is definitely wrong," Imani said. "You see she didn't even go to church with us yesterday? That's not like her. I love your brother and all, but if he did something to my sister, it's on."

"Girl, I feel the same way." Imani heard Nicole's mother calling her name. "Well, I gotta go. My mom needs help with dinner."

"Okay, call me later."

"Bye," Nicole said.

"Bye." Imani hung up the phone and sighed.

Nevaeh had been cooped up in her room for the past two days, crying. Everyone had tried talking to her, trying to find out what was wrong, but no one could get an answer. Imani's best guess was that she and Ronald had broken up and Nevaeh was taking it hard.

Nevaeh's phone rang nonstop Saturday night and Sunday afternoon, but she never answered it. Imani answered it once and told Ronald that her sister was not available to speak to him at the moment. He asked if she would tell Nevaeh that he loved her and that he was really, really sorry. Imani never gave her sister the message, thinking it would only make her more miserable.

Looking through her phone book, Imani dialed her sister's best friend's number.

"Hello?" Shimone answered.

"Hi, Shimone, it's me, Imani," Imani spoke into the phone.

"Hey, what's goin' on?"

"Have you heard from Nevaeh in the last two days?" Imani asked, hoping the answer was yes. She knew if her sister had called Shimone, at least someone would know what was going on.

"Actually, I haven't talked to her since before her date Saturday. Why? Is something wrong?" Shimone suddenly went into hysterics. "Is she missing? Did she run away or something?"

"No, but she's been in her room since Saturday night, crying," Imani informed her. "I think it has something to do with Ronald. I was wondering, could you . . . ?"

"I'll be there in twenty minutes," Shimone said, hanging up before Imani could say goodbye.

Imani hung up the phone and kneeled by the side of her bed. "Lord, please let my sister be okay. Heal her broken heart and help her to move on with her life. Show her Your plan for her life. Let her see that everything happens for a reason. Maybe she just needs time away from Ronald to see Your purpose for her life. I just thank You for Your love and protection. In your Son's name I pray. Amen."

After reading her Bible for directions that could help her help Nevaeh, Imani ran downstairs to see if her mother was okay. Ever since Saturday, Michelle had been solemn also. She had barely said anything to Imani or James. This whole situation was starting to affect their family.

"Come in," Michelle said after Imani knocked on the door of her bedroom.

"Hey, Ma, I was just coming to see how you were doing," Imani said as she plopped down on her parents' king-sized bed.

"I'm fine. How is your sister?" Michelle said, closing the novel she was reading.

"Still in her room, probably still crying, too. I talked to Nikki. She said Ron is doing the same, except he's yelling at everybody instead of crying."

"Well, I guess all we can do is pray that their hearts will heal," Michelle said, taking off her reading glasses.

"I already have," Imani said, making her mother smile. "And I called Shimone. Maybe she can help."

"Let's hope so," Michelle said, hearing the doorbell ring.

"That's probably her," Imani said, getting off of the bed. "I'll get it."

Imani ran to the door. Shimone walked in with a grocery bag and a backpack.

"Hey, where is she?" Shimone asked, ready to be the shoulder her friend needed.

"In her room," Imani said, pointing upstairs.

Shimone walked up the stairs and into Nevaeh's bedroom without knocking, with Imani right behind her. She placed the bag of groceries on the floor by the television and dropped her backpack in a corner by the bed. Walking over to the stereo, she turned off the song that had been playing repeatedly for hours.

"Nevaeh Keion Madison, get up right now!" Shimone commanded.

Nevaeh lifted her head off of her pillow and looked up at her best friend as if she was out of her mind. "Shimone, I am not in the mood." She buried her head back into the pillow. "And Imani, get out!"

"Fine, I was just trying to help." Imani walked out of the room, shutting the door behind her.

"Oh, honey, I am not that easy to get rid of," Shimone said, sitting on the bed. "So, either you can tell me what's going on or I'm gonna eat this container of rocky road ice cream all by myself," Shimone said, pulling the small carton out of the bag.

"Go ahead," Nevaeh's muffled voice said. "I don't care."

"Oh, I bet you'd care if I ate all this *butter pecan*," Shimone said, pulling another carton out of the grocery bag. "And you know I can and will do it. I'm eatin' for two, remember?"

"You better not," Nevaeh said, jumping from the bed.

Shimone rolled over in laughter. "I knew that one would get you up."

"You make me sick," Nevaeh said, sitting on the side of her bed. "You know I love butter pecan ice cream."

Shimone looked at Nevaeh and turned away. "Girl, have you not come out of this room since Saturday night?"

"Why?"

"Because you need a shower," Shimone said, fanning her nose.

"Whatever." Nevaeh smelled herself. "Okay, so maybe I need to shower."

"Well, while you take one, I think I'll have a scoop of some ice cream," Shimone said, taking spoons out of the bag.

"You better not even open that butter pecan," Nevaeh said as she gathered some clothes to take a shower.

"Just go take your bath, stanky."

While Nevaeh was in the shower, Shimone flipped through the channels of the television. She stopped when she saw a rerun of *Girlfriends*. The show reminded her of her relationship with Nevaeh. Whatever they went through, they went through it together. And whenever they had disagreements, they knew they'd still be girls in the end. Shimone prayed that she would be able to help her friend though this trial. As the shows credits began to run, Nevaeh came back into the room wearing a huge Douglass High Astros Cheerleader T-shirt.

"That's more like it." Shimone laughed.

"Shut up and pass me some ice cream," Nevaeh said.

They sat in silence as *One on One's* theme song began to play on the television. The relationship between the main characters, Breanna and Arnaz, made Nevaeh feel a sense of loss. She missed Ronald so much that it was starting to make her physically ill. She had thrown up twice yesterday while her family was at church. Seeing how the couple interacted so lovingly made Nevaeh run out of the room. Vomiting in the toilet, she cried heavily.

"Are you okay?" Shimone asked as she pulled a wad of tissue from the roll and handed it to her friend.

"I miss him so much," Nevaeh said as she wiped her tears and her mouth before flushing the paper down the toilet.

"Oh, girl, come here," Shimone said, opening her arms for Nevaeh to receive the hug that she'd needed for the past two days. "Do you want to talk about it?" Shimone asked once they got back into the bedroom.

"I just can't believe it. One minute we were dancing, then he was on top of me, and my shirt was off and—" Nevaeh started.

"Wait, did y'all . . . ?"

"Almost, but then I heard this voice and a man was in the corner," Nevaeh rambled. "Girl, I promise I saw Jesus in that room. He looked dead at me and was shaking His head."

"Wait, there was a man in the house while y'all was 'bout to get y'all's groove on?"

"No, not a real man. He disappeared, and that's when I pushed Ronald off of me." Nevaeh sat on the bed with new tears beginning to cloud her vision. "Then we started arguing about our commitment to practice abstinence, and he was getting mad 'cause he was still a virgin. He had the nerve to tell me that he couldn't stick to a commitment like that, especially when he got girls trying to get with him and take my place."

"No, he didn't," Shimone said with her hands on her hips.

"Yes, he did," Nevaeh assured her. "Then he tried to apologize, but I was already mad at myself for letting it go that far, so I told him to take me home. Then when we got here, I told him I was through with him because we weren't in the same place in our lives." Nevaeh released all of her emotions onto her friend's shoulder.

"Girl, it's gonna be okay," Shimone consoled. "He is not even worth the tears."

"Three years, Shimone," Nevaeh cried. "Do you know what I could have been doing for myself? I *should* have been focusing on my relationship with God for one." Her sadness quickly turned into anger. "I just feel like callin' him and tellin' him how I wasted my time with his sorry behind."

"Then why not do it?" Shimone said, picking up the phone and handing it to Nevaeh.

"Because," Nevaeh placed the phone back on the hook, "I wouldn't be able to say a word of what I just said to you, to him."

"Girl, you are in love," Shimone said through a laugh that was so brief that it was hardly noticeable. "So, you and Ronald are really over, huh?"

"I guess so," Nevaeh said, drying her eyes. "I've been so sick that I feel like telling him I changed my mind, just so my stomach will feel better."

"Girl, please. It's probably just stress," Shimone said, waving her hand in the air. "You'll get over it as soon as you get over him. Now," she said, grabbing the carton of melting butter pecan ice cream, "do you need help finishing this?"

"Girl, you are too much. I'll be right back,"

Nevaeh said as she walked across the hall to her sister's room and knocked on the door.

"Come in," Imani said.

"Hey." Nevaeh entered her sister's bedroom and sat on the edge of Imani's bed. "I'm sorry about the way I've been treating you the past couple of days."

"It's cool." Imani shrugged. "As long as you're okay. Are you?"

"I will be." Nevaeh hoped she was right. "Why don't you come and watch a movie with me and Shimone?"

"Okay."

They walked back into Nevaeh's room and watched *Honey*, one of Imani's favorites. Nevaeh's eyes were fixed on the screen, but she wondered what Ronald was doing.

"Ronald?" Angelica McAfee yelled up the stairs. "Boy, I know you hear me! Get your butt down here, now!"

Five minutes had passed since her first call, and Ronald still had not been seen.

"Malcolm, please go get your son, and tell him I said to come here," Angelica said to her husband as they sat at the dinner table.

"Angel, baby, what do you want me to do?" Malcolm complained as he ate his dinner. "The boy has not come out of his room since we came home Saturday."

"I want you to go up there and tell him that he is eating with this family tonight!" Angelica said near angry tears. "I don't know what is going on with him, but as long as he lives here, he is going to follow our rules," she said as her other two children listened and ate in silence. "Eating with this family is one of those rules!"

Malcolm sighed, laid his fork on his plate, and went up the stairs. After knocking on his son's door three times, he barged into the room.

"Ronald, boy, I know you heard your mother calling you. Get your behind up right now!" Malcolm said, pulling the sheets off of Ronald's head.

"Dad, can't you leave me alone? You see I don't feel like coming down. I ain't hungry, and if I was, I wouldn't eat no way," Ronald said, pulling the comforter back over his head.

"Fine, wallow in misery," Malcolm said, throwing up his hands and storming out of the room, rejoining his family at the kitchen table.

"Well?" Angelica said once Malcolm was back at the kitchen table.

"The boy is not hungry," he replied.

When Malcolm said nothing else, Angelica sat at the table and began to eat her food. She just couldn't understand why her son was acting so strangely. Ronald had always come to her when he had a problem, and she couldn't figure out why this time would be any different. Nicole told her that Nevaeh had been in the same mood since Saturday also, so it made Angelica wonder what could have happened to make her son so depressed.

When it came to who her son dated, Angelica had always been picky. But when she met Nevaeh, she fell in love with the girl and treated her like her own daughter. It hurt her to see her son hurting, and she wondered what or *who* could have caused his pain. Nevaeh didn't seem like the type to be unfaithful, but she knew girls these days could be very sneaky. She also knew how aggressive Ronald could be, and wondered if he was the cause of his own turmoil.

"Jeremy, I need you to go check on your brother for me, please," Angelica said, looking with pleading eyes toward her youngest child.

"Angel, why don't you leave the boy alone?" Malcolm sighed.

Angelica ignored her husband and repeated her request.

"But Mama," Jeremy began to object, "he drew back his fist like he was gonna hit me yesterday just 'cause I wanted some shoes." Jeremy saw the look of authority in his mother's eyes. "Okay," he mumbled as he got up from the table and made his way up to his big brother's bedroom.

"Boy, don't you know how to knock?" Ronald yelled as soon as Jeremy barged into his room. "What do you want?"

"Mama sent me to check on you," Jeremy said, standing in the doorway. "Why is it so dark in here?" he asked as he turned on the lights.

"Man, what are you doing?" Ronald screamed as he shielded his eyes from the brightness.

"When's the last time you shaved?" Jeremy said, getting in Ronald's face. "Eww . . . or brushed yo' teeth and took a bath?"

"Why don't you go back downstairs and leave me alone," Ronald said as he all of a sudden realized how bad his body odor had gotten.

"C'mon," Jeremy said, picking up the phone. "I bet if I called Nevaeh, she could make you get up and take a shower." He laughed.

"Not that it's any of your business," Ronald said,

taking the phone from his brother, "but me and Nevaeh ain't really talking right now."

"Why?" Jeremy asked with interest in his older brother's life.

"She's kinda mad at me," Ronald simply stated.

"Why?"

" 'Cause, man," Ronald said, getting annoyed with the interrogation. "She just is."

"There must be a reason for you to be up here all stank instead of out with her right now," Jeremy said, sounding much older than his actual age. "Did you hit her? My friend, Megan, said that if a boy hits a girl, that makes him a sissy."

"No, I didn't hit her!" Ronald said. "And any guy who hits a girl *is* a sissy."

"Then what's wrong?" Jeremy said, not understanding the problem.

Ronald really didn't want to go into the details with an eight-year-old, but desperately needing someone to talk to, he blurted the words before he could stop them. "She is mad 'cause I want to have sex, okay!"

"Ewwwwww . . . that's nasty!" Jeremy said, covering his ears. "Sorry I asked," he said, walking out of the room, shutting the door behind him.

So much for havin' someone to talk to, Ronald thought.

"Well, at least it got rid of him," he mumbled, turning over in his bed and pulling the covers up over his head.

While Nicole was helping Angelica clean the kitchen, Jeremy walked in.

"You were up there for a while," Angelica said, hoping for some information that would explain her son's mood. "What did he say?"

"He said Nevaeh is mad at him because he wanted sex," Jeremy responded like it was a practiced speech.

Angelica and Nicole stood by the sink with their mouths open, not believing they'd heard clearly the words that had just come out of Jeremy's mouth.

Chapter 16

Christmas Eve

"Hey, Mama," Nevaeh said, walking into the kitchen.

"Morning, angel," Michelle said, glad that her daughter was out of her bedroom. "How are you?"

"Okay, I guess," Nevaeh responded. "I've stopped worrying, and I haven't thrown up in three days. And I've showered every day since Shimone dragged me out of my bed, holding her breath." She laughed at her own quip.

"Well, I'm glad you are doing better." Michelle smiled. "You know your father was about to drive over to Ronald's house Saturday when I told him you were crying."

"What for?"

"To kill him; what else?"

Nevaeh laughed, but she knew if her mother had not been there, her father probably would have killed Ronald, or at least made him wish he were dead. Part of her almost wished her father *would* go knock some sense into Ronald's head.

"Baby, I am just glad that you came to yourself before you did something you'd regret," Michelle said as she motioned for Nevaeh to sit. "I know how hard it can be to abstain, especially in today's world. But you have God and me and your daddy as your support system."

"I know," Nevaeh said, giving her mother a hug. "Thank you."

"You're welcome. But I wish you would have come to church on Sunday. Elder Matthews preached on abstinence to the teens."

"I wish I would have gone, too, instead of being all depressed." Nevaeh sighed.

"You know, I think your dad may have gotten a recording of the sermon," Michelle said, walking out of the kitchen.

While her mother searched for a copy of the CD, Nevaeh walked over to the stove and stirred the collards that Michelle was preparing for the next day's holiday meal. She lifted the tops to the rice, lima beans, collard greens, black-eyed peas, and dressing. Then she opened the oven door and the smell of chicken, turkey, and ham, which her mother had cooked the day before, escaped and mixed in the air, causing Nevaeh's stomach to growl.

When she reached in to sample a piece of turkey, Michelle swatted her on the behind with a dish towel.

"Girl, that's for Christmas," Michelle said, laughing at the puppy dog expression on her daughter's face. "Okay, one piece."

"Thanks, Mama," Nevaeh said, reaching to retrieve the slice of turkey. It tasted as juicy and tender as it looked.

"Here's that CD," Michelle said, handing it to her. "Why don't you go listen to it?"

"Okay," she said.

She kissed Michelle on the cheek before heading upstairs to her room. Closing the door behind her, Nevaeh hoped that Elder Matthews had the word she'd been praying for since Shimone left her house on Tuesday morning. She placed the CD into her stereo, pressed play, and lay back on her bed with her Bible in her hand, ready to follow along.

"The Word says that an unmarried man concerns himself with the affairs of the Lord, but the married man focuses on how he can please his wife," Elder Matthews' voice spoke. "The same goes with a virgin woman who only involves herself with the Lord's business, while a married woman lives to please her husband. The key words here are *married* and *unmarried*."

"Young men and women, if you have yet to marry, do not be concerned with physical pleasures. Focus on your relationship with the Lord. You cannot have a healthy relationship with one of God's own if you have yet to have a healthy relationship with your Heavenly Father."

This is just what Nevaeh needed to hear. She sat up on her bed as she continued to intently listen to Elder Matthews' recorded sermon.

"Hebrews 13:4 says, 'Marriage is honorable, and the bed undefiled, but fornicators and adulterers, God will judge.' I don't know what goes through your mind when you lay down to pleasure yourself with someone who is not your husband or your wife, but just imagine God up in heaven looking down on you and frowning in condemnation. Not a pretty nor a pleasing sight, is it?"

Nevaeh's mind traveled back to Saturday night. She cringed at the thought of what she had almost done. She let temptation take temporary control of her relationship. Then seeing Jesus, or a vision of Him, in the corner of that room had made her shudder with regret. She realized that that temporary moment could have cost her a lifetime of guilt.

"The Word also tells us that the body is not meant for sexual immorality, but for the Lord, and the Lord for the body. 'Do you not understand that your bodies are members of Christ himself?'"

Nevaeh could imagine Elder Matthews pausing to see if someone would respond, and then continuing with his message.

"God tells us to run from sexual immorality because you are committing sin against you own body! God's body."

She heard a thud and guessed that he was hitting his hand against the podium as he usually did when trying to get his point across.

"Preach, pastor!" she could hear a few people shout.

"We have become a sex-crazed world. Virginity is no longer as important as it used to be. Celibacy is no longer a part of the morals and values we teach our children. People were once proud to be pure, knowing that one day they would be able to give their husband or wife something that no one else had ever had. Now it's all about 'gettin' down,' 'doin' the 'wild thang' and 'knockin' boots.'

"Why is it that every song I hear on the radio is about having sex with anybody you think looks de-

cent enough to do it with? I remember the old
school love songs, but now I don't know what is going
on in the world. And it's hard to find someone having
sex with a person they're actually in a relationship
with. Oh no, it's all about sexual partners. Sometimes
even two or three at the same time."

"Jeeeeesus!" several members shouted.

"Guys, why sleep with any nice pair of legs or pretty
face that comes your way?" Elder Matthews paused
again as if waiting for an answer. "And young ladies . . .
mmm . . . mmm . . . mmm. Why give yourself to these
little boys who don't care a penny on the dollar about
you? Then you end up pregnant or with some type of
disease, and he *really* don't want nothing to do with
you then."

"Have mercy on us, Lord!" Nevaeh heard women
in the church bellow.

"I Corinthians 6:9 tells you straight out that the
sexually immoral will not enter the kingdom of
heaven. And you don't just have to have sexual inter-
course," he explained. "Say something impure about
a woman or a man. Or don't even say anything. Just
look at the person in a sinful, desirous manner. Lust
is lust! You are still committing adultery! And it is still
displeasing to God."

Elder Matthews briefly turned back to the scripture. "'So I will cast her on a bed of suffering, and I
will make those who commit adultery with her suffer
intensely, unless they repent of her ways.' Plain as
day," he said emphatically. "Repent of your adulter-
ous ways and you are this much closer to being with
God in the end. What else do I need to tell you? I
know everyone in this building wants to hear God
say, 'Well done, My good and faithful servant.' Am I
right?"

"Amen," several members of the congregation shouted.

"So why not wait?" he asked. "Honor your body. Honor yourself. Honor *God.*"

Nevaeh stopped the CD, kneeled beside her bed, and wept as she prayed, "Lord, I ask for Your forgiveness. I repent before You today. I want to honor my body and live according to Your will for my life. I ask that You heal my heart so that I may be able to move on with my life. I fully give myself to You. This is Your temple, so do with it as You please. In Your name, Amen."

She got up and wiped the tears from her face. For the first time, she felt all cried out, and it was time to move on, this time, without Ronald holding her back.

"Imani, get down here so we can open the gifts," Nevaeh shouted up the stairs.

"I'm coming, I'm coming," Imani said as she bounced down the steps that separated her from the rest of the family.

It was a Madison tradition to open one gift on Christmas Eve. It was also a special time for each of them to express their feelings and to give thanks for something that happened in the past year or something they hoped would happen in the years to come. This year, Shimone and Misty joined them.

The Madisons and the Johnsons sat in a semicircle around the Christmas tree that was decorated with angels, silver and gold ribbons and ornaments.

Also as was traditional, James opened in prayer. "Lord, we give thanks for the opportunity to gather on this occasion one more year. We thank You for sending Your Son to be an example to us all, and we praise You for all that You have done. We hope and pray that everyone here will be blessed by You and we will live to serve You in return. Amen."

"Amen," they all said together.

"Okay, first let's go around the room and tell what we are thankful for," Michelle said.

"I'll go first," James volunteered. "I am just thankful to have family and friends who have a strong belief in God. And I'm thankful that this year, I exceeded the number of sales at the dealership." They all laughed.

"I am thankful to have life and to be able to tell all of you how much I love you," Michelle said. "And I am thankful that my babies are still able to survive in this tough world."

"I am thankful that I passed all of my finals, and that I have people who love me," Imani said.

Shimone rubbed her stomach and said, "I have a lot of regrets from the past year, but I am thankful for the new addition to our family, and I am thankful that God is able and willing to forgive me and to take me in as His child." She smiled as she wiped away moisture that had gathered in the corners of her eyes.

Misty rubbed her daughter's back as she said, "I am thankful also for the new addition to our family, and I am thankful for the growing that my daughter has done over the past month. I am also thankful to you all for your support in this time of our lives."

"I am just thankful that I was able to fight the temptation that took over my body a few days ago. I hope that in the future I will be able to live my life fully, in the absence of a few people, and pleasingly to God," Nevaeh said as her father hugged her shoulders.

Michelle handed each person one gift that had been purchased by another person in the room.

"This is from James and me, for the baby," Michelle said to Shimone.

"Thank you," Shimone said as she took the gift. She took her time opening it, trying not to ruin the wrapping paper.

"Girl, c'mon," Imani said. "We'd like to see it *before* the baby is born."

"Let her take her time," James said.

Finally, Shimone opened the box and found a collection of necessary goodies, all with a Winnie the Pooh theme. There was a small stuffed Winnie the Pooh, bibs, bottles, a diaper bag, diapers, a baby rattle and a musical box with a dancing Winnie the Pooh.

"Oh, it's so cute," Shimone said, hugging Nevaeh's parents. "Thank you!"

"You are quite welcome," James said.

"Here is your gift, Imani," Michelle said. "It is from your sister."

Imani took the gift and shook the box from side to side.

"Stop before you break it," Nevaeh laughed.

"Oh . . . what is it?" Imani said aloud as she tore off the gift wrapper. Opening the box, she gasped as she took the bubble wrap from around the glass heart. "Oh my goodness," she said. "This is beautiful."

"What does the inscription say?" Shimone asked as she leaned over to get a better look.

Imani read the words aloud. "Whatever you go through, I'm by your side. Whatever your trials, I'll help make it all right. Believe in yourself as I believe in you. Always be true to yourself for you are a one-of-a-kind you. I love you, Nevaeh."

"That is beautiful," Misty said. "Did you write that?"

"Yes, ma'am," Nevaeh answered.

Imani reached across her mother to hug her sister. "Thank you, Nev. That was so nice."

"You're welcome," Nevaeh said, returning the embrace.

"Okay, James, this is from Imani," Michelle said, handing him the gift.

"Oh, I wonder what this could be," James said, taking the bag, filled with tissue paper, from his wife. "I wonder if it's the stationery I've been hinting for. Or could it be a watch?"

"Daddy, could you just open it?" Imani laughed.

"Okay, okay." James chuckled as he opened the bag and removed all of the tissue paper. "Oh . . . thank you, princess. I can't wait to use it," he said as he looked through the beige pages of the personalized stationery.

"You're welcome," Imani said. "I was going to get the watch, but I didn't have enough," she said in disappointment.

"That's okay, baby," James said, hugging her. "This is good enough."

"Now, Misty," Michelle said, handing Misty her present, "here is yours from your precious one over there."

Misty looked at her daughter and wondered what she could have gotten her. Shimone was always so caught up in getting herself something new that Misty hardly ever got anything from her.

"Go on, Mama," Shimone said, knowing what Misty was thinking. "Open it."

Misty took the silver wrapping paper from the gift

and set it aside. She opened the heavy box and was surprised to see a sewing kit, complete with needles, thread, and rolls of fabric.

"I thought you could make some of the baby's first clothes." Shimone smiled.

"Shimone, I haven't sewn since you were a little girl," Misty said, fingering the plastic bag that held all the pieces to the set.

"I know, but I thought you might like it," Shimone said.

"Honey, I love it," Misty said, placing the gift back into the box. "And I would love to make my grand-baby's clothes." She leaned over and kissed Shimone on the cheek. "Guess I need to dust off the sewing machine when we get home," she said with a laugh.

"Mama, here's your gift from Daddy," Imani said, handing Michelle the biggest box under the tree.

"James, what in the world is this?" Michelle asked while taking the box from her daughter.

"Just open it, woman," James said, still admiring his stationery.

Michelle tore the wrapper and threw it to the side of the room. She opened the box only to find another box inside. She gave her husband a quizzical look, and he just shrugged. She opened that box, and the box that was inside of that, and the box that was inside of that one.

"James, this is not funny," Michelle whined as her husband laughed. "I'm serious. What is with all the boxes?"

"I think that's the last one, sweetheart," James said, still laughing.

Michelle opened what she hoped was really the last box. Inside was a blue velvet box. She opened it slowly and pulled out the diamond tennis bracelet that lay inside. "Oh, honey," she sang as she held it up for the rest to see. "It's gorgeous. I love it! Put it on me, put it on me," she said as she held her hand out in his direction.

"It took me every lunch hour for the past few months to find the perfect gift," he said as he fastened the bracelet around her wrist. "When I saw this, I knew it was for you." He kissed the back of his wife's hand.

"Well, I love it and I love you," she said, leaning forward to kiss him.

"Okay, okay," Imani said, giving her parents a sickened look. "Nevaeh, you're the last person. I think this one is for you from . . ." she looked at the sticker positioned on the gift, "Ms. Misty," she said, passing the box to her sister.

"Thank you, Ms. Misty," Nevaeh said, taking the box. "But you didn't have to get me anything."

"Well, you've been a wonderful friend to my daughter, and I just wanted to get you something that shows how thankful I am for all you've done," Misty said to Nevaeh.

Nevaeh opened the gift box. Inside was a journal decorated with purple flowers and a set of matching pens.

"Thank you, Ms. Misty. I really love it," Nevaeh said as she hugged her.

"I just thought you could use it when you really need to talk to God. You could write your prayers and thoughts about situations you or someone else may be going through. You know . . . anything that may be on your mind," Misty told her.

"Thank you," Nevaeh said again.

"You're welcome, baby," Misty said.

"Okay, who's ready to eat?" Michelle asked, standing to go into the kitchen.

She laughed when everyone jumped to their feet and raced into the dining room.

After sharing a light meal with her family and seeing Shimone and Misty off, Nevaeh went upstairs for some quiet time in her room. She reminisced about the day's events and doubted that Christmas could top it all.

Feeling the joy of the Christmas season and the rejuvenation from the recorded message from earlier in the day, Nevaeh pulled out her new journal and began to write. The matching pen glided across the page as her thoughts turned into words.

December 24th—Christmas Eve

I want to start this journal out by saying that everything I write in it is for God. This is something I was given to use as an instrument to communicate with God in whatever way I chose to. This is my journal of prayers, poems, thoughts, and dreams.

It has been seven days since I have talked to or seen Ronald Jaheem McAfee. Breaking up with him was the hardest thing I ever had to do. I love him so much that it hurts. I don't think I will ever stop loving him. He has my heart, and it is not going to be easy getting it back.

Lord, I know it was You in that house, shaking Your head at me. You scared me half to death, but I thank You for Your divine intervention. I just ask that You heal my heart and let all the pain go away.

I always thought me and Ron would be together forever. But it has been apparent that we are not heading in the same direction. He wants something I am not willing or ready to give, and I guess he is tired of waiting for me.

He knows how I feel about him. At least I think he does. But I guess he would rather have me show him instead of just telling him. Come to think of it, I have shown him my love. I have sung to him, I've written poetry, and I have been supportive in all that he does. But I guess it was not enough.

I still don't understand how we can go from being all lovey-dovey on Friday to an emotional break-up on Saturday. I guess it was not God's will for us to be together. I wish I would have seen that before I fell in love with him, though.

God, I just hope that You can make my life feel complete without Ronald. I want to be able to watch romantic movies and read romance novels without throwing up. This body is not mine, it is Yours, and I give You complete control over it. I want to give myself totally to You, and that cannot happen if I am still hung up on him. So please, if this is Your will, remove him from my heart. I love You. Amen.

Chapter 17

Christmas morning brought no joy to Ronald, who had not been seen since his shower the night before. When his mother came into his room earlier that morning, she pulled back the black curtains that had prevented any signs of daylight from making themselves known, and told him that he was going to come out of his room whether he wanted to or not. Without verbally responding or even looking at her, Ronald pulled the covers over his head to block the sunlight she'd just invited in, and went back to sleep.

Not even an hour later, another member of his family burst into his bedroom without knocking. This time it was Nicole.

"Boy, get your tail out the bed and stop actin' like the world has ended," she said, pulling the covers off her brother's head.

Ronald looked at her like she was out of her mind. "Girl, you better stop talkin' to me like you Mama, 'cause you ain't. And you need to knock before walkin' up in here like you own it. So before you make me hit you, you might wanna get out," he warned before hiding himself under the covers again.

"Pah-leez!" Nicole showed no signs of fear as she stood with her left hand on her hip and her right one in his face. "I wish you *would* hit me! All I want to know is how do you expect Nevaeh to give you another chance if you won't even come out of this room?" She peeled the covers back once more. "Nevaeh was out of her room on Monday night and spent Christmas Eve with her family. But what are you doin'? Sittin' in this room, crying over something so stupid. All you need to do is go to her house and beg, not ask, but *beg*, for her forgiveness.

"I still cannot even believe that you are mad at her 'cause she ain't being one of them hoochies who just give it up to any and everybody," Nicole continued. "Why are you being so ignorant to the fact that she is, or at least was, saving herself for *you*?" Nicole walked to the other side of Ronald's bed so that she would be able to see his face.

"You always told me, since before you and Nevaeh even started going together, that you were going to marry her. Before you started worrying about what those stupid football players were saying, you said you would always be committed to making her happy." Nicole saw a hint of annoyance on Ronald's face, but she knew her words were sinking in, so she continued. "Well, let me be the first to tell you, *Ron*, she is not a happy person right now. She is healing, but she sho' ain't happy."

Ronald shut his eyes as hard as he could in order to stop himself from breaking down in front of his little sister. But the more she talked, the worse he felt. He had not cried since the whole incident occurred, but now all of his emotions were starting to build up, and with each word Nicole said, they were becoming harder to hold in.

"Ronald, I don't know how love feels," Nicole said, softening her voice when she saw a tear roll down her brother's face. "I have never experienced the kind of love that you and Nevaeh share. I want to." She held her hands in the air. "But I can't if you don't have that love anymore. I know I pick on y'all all the time for being so lovesick, but I would really like to have that feeling someday. Not now, but when I get to be your age, I want to feel what you guys feel for each other; to know that someone loves me like you love her and she loves you. But I can't keep my hopes up if I see you like this. I don't want to fall in love and then get hurt. I don't ever want to be in the position that you and Nevaeh are in right now." She looked at him with worry filling her eyes. "I hate seeing you like this. I've never seen you cry before," she said, lowering her voice to a whisper.

She kneeled by his bedside. "Ronald, I love you. You're my big brother and you've always been there for me. But seeing you like this . . ." She shook her head. "You need to go see Nevaeh and at least apologize. And make it sincere, not one of those stupid 'Baby, I'm sorry' apologies, but a *real* apology, so she knows that you do regret what happened. Don't make it a mission to get her to come back to you. Do it because you need to for yourself." Nicole brought her brother's head into her chest and hugged him. She stood up to walk out of the room, but turned around when Ronald called her name.

"Tell Mama I'll be down in a minute," Ronald spoke. For the first time, he smiled. It was more of a half-smile, but it was enough for Nicole to see.

After his sister left the room and closed the door

behind her, Ronald climbed out of the bed and took a look at himself in the mirror that hung on the wall over his dresser. He had not shaved since Saturday night, right before the date. A shadow covered half of his face. His usually neat goatee was in need of a good trimming, and so was his hair. *I definitely got Dad's genes*, he thought, noticing how fast his hair had grown.

He ran his hands along his five o'clock shadow and through his hair. *Time to clean up my act*, he thought. Ronald knew he needed a haircut, but he really wanted to clean up his life. Not only had he disappointed Nevaeh with his actions, but he had disappointed God. He remembered telling Nevaeh that he only made the promise to remain celibate to her, but he knew that he'd made it to God, also.

What Ronald regretted most was telling Nevaeh that he was basically wasting his time with her when there were other girls who would give anything to spend time with him. The look of anger, pain, and shock that crossed her face made him wish he had a time machine that would let him take back those last few seconds. When she picked up her things and told him to take her home, he wouldn't have guessed that he would end up on her front porch listening as she told him that she no longer wanted a relationship with him.

Nicole was right. He had been sulking for too long, and it was time to make things right. But he couldn't go to Nevaeh looking like he had been living out of a cardboard box on the streets with nowhere to go. Although doing so might make her feel sorry for him, Ronald didn't want to make things worse by trying to make her feel guilty. He needed her forgiveness, not her pity. He knew everything about that night was wrong, and he didn't have any viable excuses that would justify any of his actions.

Ronald picked up his phone to call Marques, hoping he'd get an answer despite the fact that his friend might be spending time with his family.

"Hello?" Marques answered right before the call went to voicemail.

"What's up?" Ronald said. "It's Ron."

"What's up, stranger?" Marques said. The cheery sound of his voice said he was glad to hear from his friend.

"Nothin' much. I was just calling to see if you could trim me up a bit."

"Not today, man. We 'bout to head over to Shimone's for Christmas dinner," Marques said. "How come you ain't tell me how good Ms. Misty cooks? She gon' make a brotha move in," he said with a laugh.

"I know." Ronald chuckled, remembering a time when he and Nevaeh went to Shimone's for dinner. "Well, when can you do it?"

"I don't know." Marques paused. "What's up with you? Why you need a trim?"

"Man, I need more of a shave than a trim. My head look to' up," Ronald said, running his fingers through his hair. "I can 'bout braid this mess. If you can do it anytime before the New Year, I guess that'll be cool. I got some business to take care of, and I can't do it looking like this."

"I hope that business has something to do with Ms. Madison, 'cause I'm tired of hearing my girl dog you, man."

"Man, you act like I care what Shimone be sayin'. I know she's your girl, but she's always talkin' junk. Only reason why I don't even mess with her is 'cause I'm scared she gonna jump on me." Ronald laughed.

"Yeah, I know she crazy, but I love her," Marques said, laughing with Ronald.

"Man, I ain't never heard you say something like that about a girl before."

"I know, and it kinda scares me, you know?"

"Yeah, I know all about it," Ronald said, remembering how he felt when he first fell in love with Nevaeh.

"Well, I got to go," Marques said after hearing his dad call his name. "But I think I can tighten you up on Friday."

"Okay, cool. I'll be there at two," Ronald said right before hanging up.

I get my hair cut Friday, and on Saturday, New Year's Eve, I get my lady back.

"Come in," Misty said as she opened the door for her guests. "The food is already on the table."

"Great, let's eat," Robert said as he walked through the house with several gifts in his hands.

"Robert Anderson, if you don't stop actin' like you didn't just eat before we came over here," Shundra said, walking into the house behind her husband and carrying about as many wrapped presents as he was. "Hey, Misty," she said as Misty helped her put the gifts by the tree.

"Hey, Shun. Where is that child of yours?" Misty asked.

"Right here," Marques said, walking through the door with his arms open for a hug. "Is it time to eat?" he asked as Misty accepted his embrace.

"You just ate too, Marq," Shundra said with her head cocked to the side.

"I know, but that was just a warm-up," Marques replied, rubbing his palms together.

"The food is ready." Misty laughed. "You mind getting Shimone for dinner?" Marques looked at her hesitantly. "Go'n child," Misty said as she pushed him toward the stairs. "If you crazy enough to do something while I'm in this house, then you not as smart as I thought. I'm sure you know where her room is," she added, causing his face to turn red.

Marques took his time walking up the staircase. When he got to Shimone's closed door, he knocked lightly.

"Come in, Mama," Shimone said. "I'm almost ready."

"Okay, but I ain't your mama," he said, walking into the room and startling her.

Shimone was dressed in a black, floor-length jean dress that she was having a hard time zipping.

"Here, let me get it," Marques said, walking over to the full-length mirror that she was standing in front of.

"My mama actually let you come up here?" she asked as he zipped her dress.

"I know. I was as surprised as you are." He chuckled as he took the gold heart necklace she handed him and placed it around her neck. "There, you look beautiful."

"Thank you," she said, staring at their reflections in the mirror.

He put his hands on her growing stomach and rubbed it slightly. "Hey, li'l man. It's Daddy." He laughed at the expression on Shimone's face. "What?"

"When I have a girl, you're gonna feel so stupid," she said as he kissed her neck.

"Well, if we have a girl, I'll do anything you want," he said, leaning his head on her shoulder.

She turned around to look him in the face as she put her arms around his neck. "If we have a girl, you have to pamper me for two weeks after I get out of the hospital."

"But what if we have a boy?"

"If we have a boy, *I'll* pamper *you*."

"Mmm . . . I like the sound of that. Gettin' my back and my feet rubbed, being fed my favorite meals delivered straight from your hand, and your undivided attention." Marques smiled. "But we have to wait until the baby is born," he said, "so if either of us asks about the gender, the deal is off."

"I can't wait to have this baby so I can be treated like a queen," Shimone said as she rubbed her hand across Marques' clean-shaven head.

"Baby, whether we have a girl or not, you will *always* be my queen," he said as she stood on the tips of her toes to kiss him.

"Marques and Shimone, y'all better get down here before Robert eats all the food," Shundra yelled from downstairs.

"Oh . . . let's go," Marques said, pulling a laughing Shimone out of the room.

When they got to the bottom of the stairs, Shundra was waiting for them. "What took y'all so long?" she asked.

"Just talkin'," Marques said as they walked into the kitchen.

"Uh-huh," she said, following them.

Shundra hit Robert's hand just as he was about to grab a piece of fried chicken. "Why don't you lead us in grace?" she said to her husband.

He laughed and bowed his head. "Lord, we just thank You for allowing us to be here amongst family today, and just for letting us see another Christmas holiday so that we may celebrate the birth of Your Son, Jesus. We would just like to bless this food and the hands that prepared it. I already know it is delicious, but I ask that You let us use this food as energy we need to serve You. In Your name. Amen."

"Amen," the others responded.

As soon as the prayer was done, Marques and Robert grabbed bowls of anything they could get their hands on. Shundra hung her head and tried her best not to let her embarrassment show.

"Mama, stop actin' like you all shame," Marques said as he put three hefty spoons of mashed potatoes on his plate.

"Shimone, I hope you can cook like your mama, 'cause you see how he is acting, right?" Shundra said to Shimone, who was shaking her head at her boyfriend's manners.

"Don't worry, Shun," Misty chimed in. "Shimone has been cooking since she was thirteen."

"Good, then I'll have something good to eat while we're at college," Marques said as he stuffed macaroni into his mouth. "But in the meantime," he said with his mouth still full, "I think I'll come over here every day for my dinner."

They all laughed.

As they continued to eat the Christmas feast, they shared laughter and took trips down memory lane.

"Rob, do you remember when Marq first started walking and he would walk around the house naked after we'd give him a bath and powder him up?" Shundra laughed.

"Yeah, we'd be chasing him around the house and he would run until he got tired," Robert said, laughing at the expression on his son's face. "I remember one time he ran outside trying to chase the dog."

"Now, I know y'all making that up, 'cause I would not run outside naked," Marques said, looking at his parents in suspicion.

"Oh, you don't believe us?" Shundra said, getting up from the table and walking into the living room.

"Ma, what are you doing?" he asked, hoping his mother was not about to do something that would embarrass him, like she usually did when they would gather with their family for special occasions.

Shundra came back into the kitchen, carrying a small photo album, which she'd brought with her in her large purse. She sat at the table and flipped through the pictures so that Shimone could see the embarrassing photos.

"Oh, no you didn't," Marques said, trying to take the album from his mother.

"Look," Shundra said, moving it out of his reach. "Here he is running after the dog . . . butt naked."

Shimone laughed so hard that her face began to turn red. "Marq, look at you! Oh my goodness! You look so cute." She looked at him and noticed he wasn't laughing. "Don't be mad. It's not like you're running the streets naked now."

"Oh, you would love to see that, wouldn't you?" Marques smiled.

"Oh, and look at this, cuddled with your little teddy bear," Shimone cooed, pointing at a picture of Marques sleeping with his thumb in his mouth.

"Okay, that's enough," he said, taking the pictures from Shimone. "Dad, did you know about this?"

"Son, I am just as surprised as you are." Robert

laughed. "But those were some funny pictures. I haven't seen those in a while."

"If you want to see some cute pictures, I have some of Shimone in the room," Misty said, getting up from the table.

"Yeah, bring 'em out," Marques said as he bit into a chicken leg.

"Mama, don't," Shimone whined.

"You're right." Misty sat back down. "I think I'll save them for another time," she said to Marques' disappointment.

When they finally finished eating, they all went into the living room, where Misty sat at the piano in the corner of the room.

"Baby, come sing a song," Misty said, holding her hand out to her daughter.

"Mama, no," Shimone complained as if she didn't love to perform.

"I want to hear you sing," Robert said, with Shundra nodding in agreement.

"Okay," she said, getting up from her space on the couch.

Shimone walked over to the piano and told her mother she was going to sing "Silent Night." As Misty began to play, Shimone closed her eyes and imagined God was the only person in the room. She whispered a prayer that she knew only God could hear, and began to sing.

The words flowed from her mouth as she sang from the depths of her soul and hit every note perfectly. Deep down in her heart, Shimone knew God had forgiven her. She had prayed every night to be forgiven of her sins, and she knew that God had shown His grace on her. Each word was sung with such a passion she never knew she possessed. Hitting the final note of the last stanza, she knew what she wanted to do with her life: sing God's praises unto his people.

As the song came to an end and Shimone opened her eyes, the first thing she noticed was a tear streaming down her mother's face. Marques and his parents were giving her a standing ovation as they hooted and hollered. Marques was the last to sit down, and when he did, he was still screaming Shimone's name like he was in a stadium full of people who were doing the same.

"Girl, I didn't know you could blow like that," Shundra said.

"You need to cut a CD with that kind of talent," Robert said. "I know somebody who could help you out if that's what you want."

Shimone was surprised. She had just decided on her career choice, and she was already being recommended to someone. This must have been what God wanted her to do.

"For real?" Shimone said with excitement. "I would love it. I was just thinking about making singing my profession."

"Baby, you definitely could do it," Marques said, putting his arm around her shoulder as she sat on the sofa next to him.

"Shimone, you undeniably have a gift. You always have," Misty said. "But I don't know where you got it from, 'cause it sure didn't come from me."

Despite what she'd just said, Misty knew exactly where Shimone's talent had come from. Shimone's dad sang to Misty on many occasions. Misty remembered thinking that he had the sweetest voice she'd ever heard. She always thought she would have a future with the father of her baby, but her dreams never came true. Every time Shimone opened her mouth to sing, tears welled to Misty's eyes. She shook her head to clear away the thoughts of the past, and tried her best to stay focused on the present.

"Okay, everybody," she said, getting up from the piano. "Let's get these gifts opened."

Following Misty's lead, they all crowded around the tree and eagerly passed around the gifts.

Chapter 18

Sierra was once again on her way to the Thomas'
home for Christmas. Her father was out on another date, letting her know his whereabouts through
another note taped on the refrigerator. She had
planned on telling him about going to get tested for
AIDS. She wanted him to be there for support when
she got the results back, but when she woke up this
morning, she found the note saying he would be
back later that evening.

Sierra was glad when her best friend called just to
check on her. During their casual conversation, La-
Toya invited her over for Christmas, and Sierra immediately accepted. She hopped into her car and
drove down the road at fifty miles per hour. As soon
as she pulled into the driveway, the door flew open.
Sierra took the gifts out of the back seat and ran to
her friend, who was laughing while waiting on the
porch.

"Did I miss something?" Sierra asked as they
walked into the house.

"Just my daddy trying to do these St. Louis dances that Corey is trying to teach him," LaToya explained through her laughter.

Sierra walked into the living room and heard the music blasting from the stereo. Corey was doing the original version of one of the latest Midwestern dances. Alonzo Thomas was standing in front of his son, trying to mimic the dance, but he could not seem to get his feet in sync with his arms.

"Wassup, Sierra?" Alonzo said, still trying to get the dance right.

"Hey, Mr. Thomas." Sierra laughed.

"Sierra, why don't you come over here and teach my dad how to do this thing?" Corey said, still dancing to the beat of the music.

Sierra looked at LaToya, who shook her head and said, "Show him how we do it down here in A-town."

Sierra laughed as she placed her purse and gifts on the sofa. She went into the middle of the room and danced with her back to Corey. She moved to the beat of the song as she mimicked the dance that Corey was doing, adding her own Southern flavor to it. She dropped low to the floor, got back up, and moved her hips to the music.

"Girl, I ain't know you had it like that," Corey said as she started dancing with him.

The upbeat song ended, and a soothing, slow ballad began to play.

LaToya accepted the invitation to dance with her father as "Angel of Mine" flowed through the stereo's speakers. Sierra placed her palms on Corey's broad chest as he held her waist lightly and began to rock from side to side. The look in his eyes said exactly what the lyrics to the song did. Sierra knew she wanted to be his angel for as long as he wanted her to be.

She knew all about his decision to become a Christian. They had talked about it for hours on Sunday, but she didn't know if she was ready to make that type of change in her life. The last time she stepped inside of a church was when she was living with her aunt during her father's rehabilitation. After returning home with her father, church was never even mentioned. Christopher spent most of his time trying to gain his daughter's trust, but quickly lost it once he began dating again.

Sierra wanted so badly for Corey to love her. She knew that what they had could potentially turn into something that would last forever. Their relationship was built on their emotions, not like her other relationships that had been built on shallow physical attractions. Sierra felt like her heart was moving faster than her head, and she was falling deeper and deeper in something she had never experienced before.

When the song ended, Corey and Sierra stood in the middle of the room and stared in each other's eyes, knowing the music had ended, but not wanting to break their connection.

Alonzo coughed. "Umm, I think we should eat now," he said.

"Oh . . . yeah," Corey said, refusing to break their gaze. "I'll go . . . umm . . . heat up . . . the food," he said, hesitantly pulling away from Sierra, who wasn't eager to let go either.

"Sierra, can I see you upstairs please?" LaToya said, grabbing her friend by her forearm and dragging her up the staircase.

"What is wrong with you?" Sierra asked when La-Toya pulled her into her bedroom and shut the door.

"You love him," LaToya said with a wide grin on her face.

"What?" Sierra feigned ignorance. "I don't know what you are talking about," she said, sitting on La-Toya's bed.

"Oh, don't even try lying." LaToya pointed an accusing finger at Sierra. "Look, you're already biting your nails. Now I *know* you're lying."

"I really don't know what you are talking about," Sierra said, forcing the nail of her thumb out of her mouth.

"Well, let me explain it to you. Dancing all slow. Looking into each other's eyes. Just standing in the middle of the living room, with no music, gawking at each other." LaToya rolled her neck with each statement.

"You and your dad were dancing, too," Sierra tried to defend.

"Not like *that.*"

"Okay, maybe I do *think* I love him," Sierra admitted after LaToya stared her down for the truth.

"I knew it." LaToya smiled in victory.

"But I don't want him to know, at least not until I am sure about my feelings."

"Why? He might love you too," LaToya suggested. "I have never seen him look at a girl like he was just looking at you." She paused and thought for a moment. "Actually, I have never seen him look at girls in a suggestive kind of way. I was starting to get a little worried, if you know what I mean."

Sierra fell back on the bed, laughing. "Girl, you know you are wrong. There is no way you thought Corey Thomas was . . . There is just no way," Sierra said, shaking her head. "Maybe he had a girlfriend on campus, back at home at one time. You can't just say 'cause you never saw him look at a girl like he wanted her that he's not interested in the opposite sex. Maybe he was reserved."

LaToya shrugged. "I don't know what it was, but I'm glad that y'all are together, 'cause if he was gay, I don't know how I would be able to take it."

"Toya, Sierra," Alonzo yelled up the stairs. "Y'all come eat."

The girls went into the bathroom to wash their hands.

"You better not tell Corey what I said," LaToya said as she made good use of one of the hand towels. "You know he will kill me if he knew I thought he wasn't straight."

"Girl, don't worry," Sierra said, drying her hands on the same towel. "I am not gonna tell nobody. I don't want people thinking that about my man."

They laughed at the thought of it, and were still giggling when they walked into the kitchen. Corey was the first to address their giddiness.

"What is so funny?" Corey asked while he set plates on the table.

"Nothing," Sierra said, sitting in the chair he pulled out for her. "Thank you."

"Thanks," LaToya said as she sat in the seat her brother offered her.

"Dad, why don't we bless the food first?" Corey said to his father, who'd begun to eat before he even sat in his seat.

"Uh . . . sure," Alonzo said awkwardly, following suit as his children bowed their heads and Corey led them in prayer.

"Dear Lord, we thank You for allowing us to be here today with family and friends. Thank You for this special day that You have given us so that we may honor the birth of Your Son. Thank You for keeping Your love and protection over this household. We bless this food that we are about to eat, so that it may be good for our bodies. In Your Name we pray."

"Amen," they all said.

They dug into the food on their plates. There was a little something for every taste imaginable; turkey, ham, dressing, macaroni and cheese, rice, greens, and peas. There were even pig's feet, chitterlings, and gizzards. Sierra looked at her best friend in disgust when LaToya placed a forkful of chitterlings in her mouth. She looked at Alonzo and Corey and gave them the same look she just afforded LaToya, when they did the same.

"What?" they asked, sounding like a chorale.

"How can y'all eat those stanky things?" Sierra asked, pushing the ones on her plate to the side.

"What?" LaToya asked, holding her plate in front of Sierra's face. "The pig's feet or the chitterlings?"

"Eww, move it from in front of my face," Sierra said, pushing the plate away.

"C'mon," Alonzo said, "you at least have to like gizzards."

"I don't know." Sierra shrugged. "I've never had any of it."

"Wait a minute," Corey said. "How you gonna say you don't like something if you ain't ever tried it? This is a Southern dish, you know, and you are from the South."

"I've never tried them because they stank," Sierra said, turning her nose up at the smell coming from her own plate. "And just 'cause I'm from the South don't mean I have to eat everything Southerners eat."

"Well, if you don't want 'em, pass 'em on over here," Alonzo said, holding his plate out.

Sierra tried not to laugh. Alonzo's accent was much more distinct than Corey's. LaToya was the only one who did not have the ever popular St. Louis accent, and that was only because she had moved to Atlanta at a very young age.

"Please take them." Sierra pushed all the unwanted meats that were on her plate onto Alonzo's.

"See, baby girl, all you got to do is add a li'l hot sauce," he said, demonstrating by drowning them in the spicy sauce, "and you good to go."

Sierra shook her head and continued to eat the food that was on her plate. She could feel Corey staring into the side of her face. She turned to face him and questioned him with her eyes.

"I just can't believe that you didn't even try it before giving it to my dad," Corey said.

"I'm sure there is something that you don't want to eat that you haven't even tried yet." Her stare challenged him.

"Actually, I've tried all kinds of food, like Jamaican, which I love, Mexican, Chinese and Italian. I like those too. I've even tried Japanese food. I am not very picky about foods. I like just about everything." He paused. "Except okra and Brussels sprouts."

"Have you tried them?" she asked.

"It's not like I had a choice," he said. "Someone practically shoved them down my throat when I was little," he said, turning toward his father, who was still stuffing his face with chitterlings.

Alonzo shrugged and said, "The only way you would eat them was if I fed them to you."

"So," Corey said, turning his attention back to Sierra, "if I asked you to, would you try at least one of them?"

Sierra looked at him like he had something growing out of his forehead. "Corey, I don't know," she stated apprehensively.

"Please?" he said, giving her his best puppy-dog face.

Sierra thought for a moment. *What could it hurt?* "Okay," she said, "but only a little."

Corey picked up a gizzard, dipped it in a little hot sauce and fed it to Sierra, who was holding her nose. She chewed slowly and swallowed.

"So . . . ?" Corey asked as Alonzo and LaToya waited for her to critique.

"It was okay. Not totally disgusting," Sierra admitted. "But I wouldn't eat it regularly."

"Well, what about these?" Corey asked, feeding Sierra a chitterling.

She tasted the piece and abruptly spit it into a napkin. "Yuck, no, no, no," she said, wiping her tongue with a napkin.

Corey laughed at her expression and picked up one of his pig's feet. Sierra immediately began to shake her head. "No way. I said one, and I let you do two," she said. "I refuse to eat something that a pig once walked on. No."

"Okay," he said, leaning in her direction. "What about this?" Corey allowed his lips to caress Sierra's.

"Okay," LaToya announced, waving her hands in the air. "Parent and sibling in the room."

Ignoring her comment, their kiss deepened.

"Now, I know y'all need some air," LaToya said, looking at them in disbelief.

"Now *that* was *very* appetizing," Sierra said once they'd finally separated.

Corey grinned and rubbed his goatee. "Most definitely."

Alonzo shook his head at his son. He knew it was too late to advise him on not falling in love too soon. "If *you* guys are done here, then I think we should go into the living room and see what's under that tree," Alonzo said, rising from the table.

Once the table was cleared of their soiled dishes, the four of them went into the living room. Sierra and Corey sat on the loveseat across from Alonzo, who rested on the couch. LaToya sat on the floor by the tree and took the initiative to pass the gifts to the receivers, making sure to announce who each gift was from.

By the time all the gifts had been passed around, Sierra found herself anxiously awaiting Corey's gift. From LaToya, Sierra had received a silver bear charm to add to the charm bracelet she had received many Christmases ago. Alonzo had given her an autographed copy of one of her favorite authors' newest novels. Sierra had also given LaToya a charm for her bracelet, and she had given Alonzo a "#1 DAD" mug and T-shirt because he had been there for her through her toughest times, just like a father should.

It had taken Sierra a while to find the perfect gift for Corey. She really didn't know what he liked or disliked. She went to many stores, but could hardly find anything she wanted to give him. Then, while driving one day, she happened upon a small Christian bookstore near a shopping center she frequently visited. Sierra found just what she had been looking for, and really didn't know it until she'd knocked it off the shelf while looking at another item.

It was a devotional Bible for college students that helped with daily issues such as sexual temptation and peer pressure. She also found a gold bookmark with his name on it, and a gold cross necklace. While at the store, Sierra picked up a devotional Bible for herself before making her way to the checkout counter.

As LaToya gathered all of the torn wrapping paper and went into the kitchen to throw it away, Alonzo went into his office to prepare to head back to work the next day, or even that night in case any type of emergency should arise.

Corey admired the gold chain around his neck and the Bible in his lap with the bookmark sticking out of it.

"Sierra, this is really nice," he said.

"I'm glad you like it," Sierra responded, looking into his light brown eyes.

They sat in silence for a moment, and Sierra began to grow impatient. She didn't want it to seem like all she wanted was her gift, but she knew he had one, and the suspense was killing her. LaToya came out of the kitchen and placed the garbage bag by the garage door to be taken out later that night. When she walked past them, she looked at Corey and he nodded. She ran up the stairs, and Sierra saw a lighter in her hands.

Sierra looked at Corey. "What is going on?" she asked him.

Corey shrugged. "Who knows?"

Another few minutes passed before Corey got up from the couch and started toward the stairs. "I need to go to the bathroom," he said. "Stay right here," he stressed before running up the stairs and disappearing behind one of the doors.

"Something is definitely going on," Sierra mumbled to herself. She sat back against the cushions on the loveseat and waited as she was told.

She had been sitting downstairs for more than ten minutes, and she finally grew tired of waiting. Sierra got up and walked up the stairs, taking one slow step at a time. The closer she got to the top, the more she thought she heard music. Walking down the corridor, she noticed that no one was in the bathroom. She stopped in front of her best friend's door; no music or any other sounds came from the room. Walking faster now, she came to Corey's room. The soft jazz that played the night she walked to his room only two weeks earlier, was playing now. She knocked softly and opened the door.

"Oh my . . ." she gasped and covered her mouth. "It's so beautiful."

The room was lit with vanilla-scented candles. There was an aisle of white rose petals leading to the right side of the room, which was decorated in white. Small stands were positioned a few feet before the makeshift archway that stood parallel to Corey's bed, which had also been decorated to fit the color scheme. Corey, who had changed out of his jeans and T-shirt and was now wearing a white polo shirt and a pair of white trousers, was standing under the arch, waiting for Sierra to join him.

She looked down at her blue jeans and icy blue sweater.

"You look fine," he said, noticing her hesitation.

Sierra walked down the aisle as if she were at her wedding. She took slow, graceful steps and was blinded by emerging tears by the time she reached the person she hoped she would spend the rest of her life loving. When she stood by Corey's side, the volume of the music was lowered, and she noticed LaToya sitting in the corner by the stereo, smiling as her brother took her best friend's hand.

"I did all of this just to *officially* ask you to be my girl." Corey laughed. "You are probably wondering why I didn't just ask you like other guys do. Well, number one, I'm not like other guys, and number two, it is a *little* more intimate than that."

Corey pulled a small red velvet box out of his pocket and took her hand. Sierra looked at LaToya, who was still smiling, and was tempted to pull her hand away. *What is he doing?* she thought. *Proposing? I am only seventeen. What am I going to say?* Millions of questions ran through her head as Corey's mouth opened and asked her the question she wasn't sure she was ready to answer.

"I know you want to be with me," he said. It was a statement, but his eyes questioned her.

She silently nodded, afraid that if she said anything, her quiet, cute cry would turn uncontrollable and ugly.

"And you know how I feel about sex before marriage." He paused.

Sierra's mind raced at the speed of light. *Oh God, oh God, oh God!*

"Would you do me the honor of . . ." he looked directly into her brown eyes, ". . . practicing abstinence with me?"

What! Sierra's jaw dropped in surprise and relief. It wasn't a proposal. At least not the one she feared. This one was much better, and one that couldn't have come at a better time. She broke into a smile.

"Yes," she said as he took the gold band covered in

small diamonds out of the box and slipped it on her right ring finger.

Sierra wrapped her arms around his neck, kissed him, and gave him a hug while admiring the ring that symbolized a vow she knew she was now ready to keep.

Chapter 19

New Year's morning

Nevaeh lay across her bed, admiring the gold locket Ronald had given her last night. She still could not believe he had stopped by, not knowing if her dad was home. She knew James would want to say something to Ronald, particularly since he knew everything that had happened on the night of their break-up. But Ronald took the risk anyway.

She and her family were getting ready for the annual Watch Night Service at their church, and the last thing she needed was for them to come outside and see him on the porch. She was thankful it was Imani who'd answered the door.

"Hey," Ronald said when Nevaeh came to the door.

"Hi." Nevaeh's reply had no emotion attached.

"Could we just talk for a minute?" he asked. "Please, just ten minutes," he added when he saw the hesitation in her eyes.

She walked outside and closed the door behind her. Standing across from him on the porch, Nevaeh purposely averted her eyes so she would not fall into another one of his traps. Ronald's freshly trimmed hair and goatee made it very difficult for her to continue staring at the ground. They stood in silence for several minutes, but when Ronald noticed that his ten minutes had dwindled to five, he began to speak.

"Nevaeh, I am really, really sorry," he said, taking a step toward her. Ronald was surprised and a little offended when she took a step back. He sighed. "I don't know what else to say. I apologize for how things went down at my house. I'll admit I had it all planned out." He shook his head, ashamed at his own antics to get her alone with him. "After my parents went out, I made Nikki call and ask to stay over here, and I sent Jeremy to his friend's house. All so we could be alone. And I am sorry."

Nevaeh finally had the courage to look him in his eyes. She remembered wanting to see what his mysterious eyes held that night, but now, as she looked into them, she saw no mystery. They seemed to resemble endless black holes with no secrets, only lost hope.

"I am not upset with you for setting me up," Nevaeh said as she put her hand up to stop his defense. "That is exactly what it was, Ronald, a set-up, and you know it. A huge set-up to get me to go against my commitment to you and to God. But I forgive you for that because, although I was not in on your plan, I was a part of the sin.

"I forgive you for everything you did and said that night," Nevaeh continued, "even about the girls you said would kill to be in my position. And that really hurt me. But I just cannot forgive you for going against your commitment to me and God as if you never promised us anything." Tears began to pool in her eyes.

"When we first got together, I told you that I was a virgin and I was going to stay that way until I found the husband God was saving for me. You told me you felt the same way." The first tear fell. "We made a pact a month after I said I would be your girl that we would be in this whole celibacy thing together. Me, you, and God.

"What happened, Ron? Why are we not together in that commitment?" She wiped the stream of tears that clouded her vision. "Why am I out here crying and you are not consoling me?"

Ronald took a step toward her, and again, she backed away.

"No." She shook her head. "It's too late. I don't want you to touch me. Every time I think of you touching me, I think of that night; that night when you cared nothing about my feelings on the issue. You sat there and said you never made any promises to God. And I cannot forgive you for that."

Ronald looked in Nevaeh's eyes and remembered a time when he'd see her, and her eyes would be as bright as the sun. But now as he looked into them, he saw no happiness, and he knew there was no one to blame but himself.

"Nevaeh, I know I hurt you," Ronald said. "But it is really hard for me. It's like I'm with you, but I'm not *with you.* I love you so much that I am willing to do anything for you. I wish I could take back that night, but I can't, and I don't want you not to be able to forgive me for something that I said in the midst of an argument."

"You know," Nevaeh said, as if she were talking to

herself and hadn't heard a word he'd just said, "I probably would have gone all the way with you if I had not seen that man in the house."

Ronald was confused. "What are you talking about? There was no one in the house but you and me."

"No, Ronald," she said, looking him directly in his eyes. "We were not the only ones in that house. Jesus was standing in the corner of that room looking at me and shaking His head." She wiped more tears.

"Nevaeh, what are you talking about?" Ronald repeated, starting to think she was crazy. "We were the only ones there. *No one* saw us doing anything."

"You still don't get it, do you?" she said, her voice rising. "God *sees* all. He *knows* all, Ronald. He was there. He saw it all. And I saw Him," she said, bringing her voice to a whisper.

"Okay, I know God sees everything. But I also know He has already forgiven me for that night." Ronald looked at Nevaeh with sadness in his eyes. "Why can't you?"

Nevaeh lowered her head to avoid seeing his pain. She knew he was sorry; she could see it in his eyes. She saw it the night he'd stood on her porch and apologized, also. *Why can't you just forgive him?* her heart asked. She shook her head. *I need time,* she thought.

"I just need some time," she voiced her thoughts aloud. "I need to spend time with God and see what *His* desire is for my future. I need to be certain of whether or not that future includes you." By the time she said the last sentence, her eyes had met his again.

Ronald took the box out of his pocket that held the Christmas gift he'd bought for Nevaeh a week before the incident occurred. He held it in the palm of his hand and stretched his arm out toward her and said, "For you. While you think and pray about our future."

Nevaeh looked at the box and shook her head. "I can't," she whispered.

Ronald stepped forward, and his eyes showed more pain when she froze as he gently took her hand and placed the box in her palm. "Take it," he said, "even if you don't take me." He leaned forward, and she inhaled deeply as he kissed her on the cheek.

As he backed away from the porch, a fresh tear escaped from her eye.

"I love you," Ronald said softly.

He got into his car and drove away, leaving Nevaeh under the porch light, wondering if she would ever be able to forgive him, or even if she'd ever stop loving him.

Nevaeh sat up on her bed and placed the necklace back in its box on her nightstand. She got up, went to her closet and pulled out the navy blue pinstriped suit she'd chosen to wear to church this morning. Although she had just come from the Watch Night Service earlier that morning, Nevaeh was glad to be going to Sunday service, especially since she had not been able to enjoy the service last Sunday because as it was being held, she was helping to decorate the youth center for her church's annual Christmas reception. She had missed out on going to church altogether the Sunday before.

She went to her sister's room and knocked on the door.

"I'm up," Imani yelled through the closed door.

"Just making sure." Nevaeh knew her sister had a tendency to oversleep on Sundays.

Walking into the bathroom to freshen up, Nevaeh looked at her reflection in the mirror. Not getting much sleep after last night's service had certainly taken effect on her. She had been up half the night, toiling over the situation with Ronald. She'd even written her thoughts in her prayer journal, but sleep eluded her until nearly four o'clock in the morning. The reward for Nevaeh's deprivation came in the form of small bags under her eyes that gave her restlessness away.

She washed her face and brushed her teeth before she returned to her room to begin to get dressed. Moisturizing her body, she massaged her legs to loosen the tension that had caused her discomfort all through the night. Nevaeh put on a pair of stockings and then covered them with the pants she stepped into. She tucked in the silver blouse and placed her suit jacket on top of it, and then slipped into her silver heels.

Nevaeh went into the bathroom to put on makeup, which she hoped would hide the fact that she'd gotten little sleep. After pulling her hair into a blue clip, she applied foundation under her eyes in an effort to hide the weariness. She added a little loose powder to even out the tone of her skin, and put on a light blush to brighten up her face. Looking into the mirror, her eyes still looked restless, but she looked better.

She walked back to her sister's room to make sure Imani was really up and getting ready. They would be leaving in thirty minutes, and Nevaeh did not want to hear all the yelling that would result if her sister was not prepared to leave on time. Nevaeh knocked on the door and Imani opened it, fully dressed in a red blouse and a long black skirt complemented by a pair of red heels.

"I thought I'd start the year off being on time for once," Imani said when she saw the look of astonishment on her big sister's face.

"Well, I guess a new year brings new changes." Nevaeh smiled.

"Speaking of change," Imani said, "are you and Ronald okay?"

Nevaeh wondered what exactly her sister meant. "If you're asking am I doing good in spite of the circumstances, yes. But if you are asking if me and Ron's relationship is back to normal, no."

Imani smiled. "As long as you are okay, that's all I need to know. I need to finish getting ready," she added, walking to the bathroom to style her hair.

Nevaeh walked back into her own room to put on her jewelry. She put on a pair of diamond studs and placed a watch on her wrist. Her eyes fell to her empty neckline. *Should I? He did say I could have it, so I'm sure he expects me to wear it.* She picked up the rectangular box from the nightstand and opened it. Nevaeh took out the locket and held it up against her neck while admiring it in the mirror. She opened it for the first time and read the inscription: *You will always be my heart.*

She closed it and held it against her chest, trying to fight off tears. She was too emotional to wear it today. *Maybe later,* she thought. She needed to start the year on a positive note, and fighting emotions each time someone asked her where she got such a pretty piece of jewelry was not going to help. Putting the necklace back into its case, Nevaeh placed it back on her nightstand. She opted, instead, to wear her favorite gold cross necklace that held a diamond in the center of it. Placing it around her neck, she prayed

that an answer to all of her confusion would come—
and soon.

"Girls, come on," James yelled up the stairs. "If you
are going to eat, you have fifteen minutes."

"Okay, Dad," Nevaeh said.

"Coming!" Imani screamed.

Nevaeh grabbed her purse, coat, and Bible. She
picked up her notebook in case something was said
during the service that she may need to jot down for
remembrance. She and Imani rushed down the stairs
to fix themselves breakfast. Grabbing an apple,
Nevaeh washed it and sat at the table across from
Imani, who had fixed herself a bowl of cereal.

Ten minutes later, the Madison family was making
their way to their van. Riding down the interstate,
Nevaeh and Imani sang along to the songs on Praise
97.5. A few minutes later, James pulled the SUV into
the parking lot of Greater Faith Tabernacle and shut
off the engine.

The church could comfortably hold nine hundred
people, but looking at the full parking lot, Nevaeh
knew that people would either squeeze together and
endure the discomfort or settle for watching the service in the overflow section of the church just to hear
Pastor Gerald McKinley's New Year's message.

They got out of the van and walked up the steps to
the church's entrance. Praise and worship service
was about to begin as the students exited their Sunday school classes. The first person she spotted was
Darnell Parker, one of Ronald's teammates.

"Hey, Nevaeh," Darnell said, pulling her into a
warm embrace.

"Hey, Darnell," she replied. "How are you?"

"Good. What about you?" He searched her eyes.

"You look like you didn't get much sleep after last night's service."

"I didn't," she said, mostly to herself. "But I feel pretty good."

"Well, you certainly look nice in that suit." He grinned as he looked her up and down.

"Thank you." Nevaeh blushed. "You look pretty good yourself," she said as he pulled at the lapels on his charcoal gray suit jacket.

"Are you singing with us today?" Darnell asked as the two of them made their way to the sanctuary.

"What are you guys singing?" she asked.

"Well, 'You Are My Daily Bread,' 'Praise Is What I Do,' and 'Let It Rain' are three of the songs they wanted to sing."

"Who's leading?" Nevaeh asked.

He smiled. "Yours truly," he said to her excitement.

Darnell rarely sang, and unless a church member requested it, he usually kept his talents under wraps.

"They also have 'The Lord is High Above the Heaven' on the list, but no one wants to lead," he said.

"And I guess I am your last hope." Nevaeh smiled, realizing why he brought up the subject.

"Well, no one can sing it like you do," Darnell said, trying to persuade her to join them. "I'll even help you out on parts of the lead vocals."

Nevaeh thought about it and then said, "Sure, why not start my year off giving praises to God?"

"Why not?" He shrugged. "Thanks," he said, hugging her again before he walked to the keyboard to begin praise and worship.

Nevaeh looked at him as he sat at the keyboard and began the process of tuning it. She and Darnell had been good friends since he started coming to Greater Faith after he moved to Atlanta from Florida two years ago. With his talent on the keyboards and his vocal skills, the church members often requested that they, along with Shimone, sing and lead devotional services together.

Darnell had recently begun showing interest in Nevaeh, and she wasn't blind to it. He was a very nice guy who was very strong in his faith. The fact that he was six feet tall, 188 pounds packed in solid muscle, with a light brown skin complexion, was just icing on the cake. In spite of the incentives, Nevaeh knew she wasn't ready to start another relationship, especially since she had yet to get over Ronald. Just because Darnell happened to be available in her time of distress wasn't a reason for her to make a move she wasn't ready for. Plus, Darnell was too good a friend for her to use him like that.

Nevaeh took a seat in the front row, next to Shimone and their friend, Liana. Liana was sixteen, and she went to Douglass also. She was almost six feet tall and was thin like the models in fashion magazines. Liana loved the Lord as much as the next person, but she also loved to gossip, and had no clue when to shut up. On one hand, Liana was sweet, but on the other, she wasn't the one to go to with problems unless there was no problem with them being made public.

"Hey, girl," Liana said when Nevaeh sat down next to her. "Was that Darnell who I just saw hugging on you? Now I know it's not my business, but I know if Ronald was here, he would not like that. Not that Darnell isn't fine and all, but Ronald is just . . . girl, I can't even describe it."

Shimone elbowed Nevaeh in her side to let her friend know she needed to tell this sophomore to stay out of her business. Nevaeh shrugged, and Shimone smacked her lips as Liana continued.

"I don't know how you can keep your claws in a guy that fine. I know plenty of girls who would love to be in your position. And who can blame them for wanting a man as cute and romantic as Ronald? Girl, I remember he got you those lilies and stuff for your birthday last year. What is he going to do this year? I know your birthday is like in April, isn't it? Well, he better get you something huge for the big one-eight." She finally took a breath. "So, how has your break been?"

"It's been okay," Nevaeh said, though just the mere thought of what she'd been through recently had her fighting to keep her emotions in check. "What about yours?" She soon regretted asking.

"It has been cool. I got some good stuff for Christmas. My brother brought home his pregnant girlfriend, and needless to say, my mother had a fit. First of all, we only met the girl once, and you know Mama didn't like her from the jump."

Nevaeh saw Shimone roll her eyes, letting her know that she had heard the story and didn't want to hear it again. Nevaeh smiled as Liana continued.

"So, when Lenny brought Sara home and she looked like she was seven months pregnant, Mom went to praying and speaking in tongues and stuff. Said she was trying to get the evil spirit out of her house. Daddy tried to make Sara feel welcomed, but they ended up leaving earlier than planned 'cause of Mama. Then she and Daddy got into it 'cause he said Mama was being mean to the girl and all kinds of things. Mama just kept saying that the devil just keep on moving no matter what, so she got to keep praying. She finally did apologize to Sara, but that was after Daddy dialed Lenny's number and told him to put Sara on the phone and made Mama apologize. But other than that, everything was good." She smiled.

As soon as Liana finished talking, the praise music began to play, and the youth members were called up to the front to lead the service. They sang two songs that had different tempos to keep the worship service interesting.

When Darnell began to play the introduction to "The Lord is High Above the Heavens," Nevaeh walked up to the microphone and took it off of its stand. The congregation stood and clapped their hands as Nevaeh sang, and she enjoyed getting everyone pumped at the same time. She walked back and forth across the stage as she led the verse over and over again, with Darnell jumping in with his tenor ranges from time to time. When the song ended, Darnell motioned for her to keep the microphone as he began the lead vocals of "Let it Rain." Nevaeh joined in once he nodded toward her. For her, it felt good to be back in church and to be able to give God glory for everything He'd done in her life. When they finished the song, everyone was on their feet in worship.

"Girl, why didn't you tell me you were going to sing today?" Shimone asked once Nevaeh returned to her seat.

"I didn't even know," Nevaeh explained. "Darnell just asked me to lead the song when I got here this morning."

"Well, it sounded like y'all had been practicing for weeks," Shimone complimented.

As Pastor McKinley made his way to the pulpit, the

members of the congregation were still on their feet, praising God. When things finally settled down and everyone was able to take their seats, Pastor McKinley opened his Bible and said a word of prayer.

"Our Heavenly Father," he began, "we come to You right now, humbling our hearts as we prepare ourselves to hear the Word that we know You designed just for us. Lord, only You know who needs to hear this today, and I am glad that You have chosen me to deliver Your message to Your people. I don't know what some of these people may be going through, but You do, Lord. So, I ask that You be with them through all of their trials and tribulations, just like You said You would. Keep us covered in Your blood so that we will never forget who You are and what You have done in our lives. We love You, Lord. In Your name we pray. Let the church say amen."

"Amen," the congregation repeated.

"Open your Bibles to Matthew, chapter eighteen," Pastor McKinley said while turning the pages in his. "I will be reading from the New International Version. Please follow along in whatever version you have. Let's start at verse twenty-one."

The sound of pages turning could be heard throughout the otherwise quiet sanctuary. Once the majority of the congregation had found the Scripture, Pastor McKinley began to read. "'Then Peter came to Jesus and asked, 'Lord, how many times shall I forgive my brother when he sins against me? Up to seven times?' Jesus answered, 'I tell you, not seven times, but seventy-seven times.'" Pastor McKinley said, "You must forgive your brothers," walking from behind the podium. "God forgave you, so why wouldn't you want to do the same for one of His children?

"God told the parable of the unmerciful servant. He'd gone to his king begging for an extension on paying his debts. The king granted him his request, but when the servant came upon one of his fellow servants, he basically jacked him up for the money that servant owed him. The fellow servant got on his knees, much like the other servant had done, and begged for an extension. But instead of being merciful, like the king had been with him, the servant had the fellow servant thrown in jail until he paid all of his debts. When the king heard of this, he got mad. He basically said 'I had mercy on you, so why couldn't you show mercy to your fellow servant?' And he threw the once pardoned servant in jail until he could repay all of his debts."

"Now Matthew 18:35 says that Jesus said to Peter, 'This is how my heavenly Father will treat each of you unless you forgive your brother from your heart.'

"Ephesians 4:31-32 says, 'Get rid of all bitterness, rage and anger, brawling and slander, along with every form of malice. Be kind and compassionate to one another, forgiving each other, just as in Christ, God forgave you.'"

Okay, Lord, I hear what you are trying to say. I need to forgive him, but I just don't know how, Nevaeh thought.

Forgive him with the love that I have placed in your heart.

Nevaeh's head snapped up to see if it was Pastor McKinley who'd just spoken the words, but he was talking about Jesus dying on the cross for the sins of the world. She knew it was the voice of the Lord, and she knew what she had to do, but she didn't know when she would be able to do it.

Thirty minutes later, everyone was on their feet

with their hands raised while Pastor McKinley gave the benediction. Once they'd been officially dismissed, Imani went outside to talk to her friends, and Nevaeh grabbed her belongings, said goodbye to Shimone and Misty, who were headed toward the parking lot, and went into one of the Sunday school rooms to wait for her parents, who had to stay behind for special meetings.

"May I come in?" Darnell said as he eased open the door.

Nevaeh shrugged her shoulders. "Why not? I could use the company."

"You were great this morning," he complimented.

"Thanks," she mumbled.

Darnell sat at the table and looked at Nevaeh, who sat across from him, deep in thought. "Do you want to talk about it?" he asked.

"Talk about what?" she said, trying to mask the fact that she did need someone to talk to.

"Whatever it is that has your mind so preoccupied."

"It's nothing," she said.

"You know you can talk to me." He placed his elbows on the table and rested his chin in his hands.

"I'm not so sure I should talk to you about this," she said apprehensively.

"Does this have anything to do with Ronald?"

Nevaeh was taken aback. "Why would you say that?"

"I was just taking a shot in the dark," Darnell said, "but from your reaction, I must have hit a sore spot."

"Everything is fine," she lied, turning her head away so he wouldn't see the tears burning her eyes.

"If everything is fine," he said, placing his finger

under her chin and turning her to face him, "then why are you crying?"

Nevaeh looked beyond his eyes and saw that he was genuinely concerned. She really did need to talk, but she didn't know where to start. Her head was so crowded with thoughts that she could not gather them to make sense of anything that had occurred over the past couple of weeks.

She had convinced herself that everything was fine. She had prayed and asked God for forgiveness, and she was slowly getting over the break-up, but seeing Ronald yesterday had Nevaeh's heart in overdrive, and she could not control her emotions. She felt love, anger, regret, and a million other emotions that she could not get a handle on. Tears clouded her vision, and she gave into the feeling of Darnell's arms around her, consoling her as she cried.

"I just don't know what to do," she cried. "It's like I want to forgive him, but I can't."

Darnell only knew that "him" was Ronald, but he wanted to know what had happened to make her break down in such a manner. He knew Ronald could be overbearing and aggressive; he was like that on the football field. It was okay to have those characteristics when smashing into a 200-pound linebacker, but when dealing with an emotional woman, a gentler and more caring approach was needed.

Darnell remembered how Ronald had acted at the senior party. When he'd offered to drive his teammate home, it was mainly to keep Nevaeh from having to deal with a drunken fool. The whole drive to Ronald's house was a living nightmare. As Darnell drove, he endured an entire ride of Ronald complaining about how stuck-up Nevaeh was and how she needed to loosen up. Darnell knew it was the liquor talking because the usually sober Ronald talked about how much he loved Nevaeh and how he wanted to be with her until the day he died. That's why Darnell never repeated a word of Ronald's drunken rampage to Nevaeh or anyone else. When he approached Ronald about it the day after the party, Darnell knew his teammate wouldn't remember anything he'd said the night before. Ronald brushed him off and told him that he and Nevaeh were fine, but Darnell wondered if Ronald was as loving behind closed doors as he was in front of all of his peers.

When Nevaeh's tears began to wane, Darnell waited for her to continue speaking. He sat and listened as she told him, in detail, what went on at Ronald's home only two weeks before. After she finished, they sat in silence for a few moments.

"I just don't know what to do," Nevaeh said. "Pastor's message really got to me. And Ronald seemed really compassionate when he came by yesterday. I just can't forget how he looked at me and said that he never made any promises to God." She paused. "But I also can't forget how he looked me dead in my eyes and said that God had forgiven him, so why couldn't I?"

"Why can't you?" Darnell interjected.

"I don't know. I want to, but I just don't want to say it and still be upset. I need to get to a place where when I say it, I will actually mean it and I won't continue to get upset every time I think about it."

"I understand where you are coming from," he said. "But think about it from Ronald's perspective. He is a man, and men have needs. Although I am not supporting his actions," he quickly added when Nevaeh looked at him as if he were insane, "he is still a human first. And if you knew the things that he has to hear in that locker room, you'd probably understand why he did what he did."

Nevaeh rolled her eyes. "Just because you hear a bunch of guys talking about how many girls they get with does not mean you have to go out and do the same. Ronald knows that, and I don't even know why he listens to them," she said. "But my whole reason for getting upset was not because he felt he had to sleep with me to measure up to his teammates. It was the fact that he tricked me into doing something he knew I would not have done had he asked me before he planned the whole thing."

Darnell tried to choose his next words carefully, but he knew there was no careful way to say what was about to come out of his mouth. "Do you really feel that he tricked you?" Nevaeh gave him a look that dared him to continue, and Darnell took the challenge. "Do you honestly think that he tricked you into going into his house and slow dancing? Do you really believe he made you lie on that couch and take off your clothes? Do you believe he had that type of control over you, that he did all of that to you? Or do you think that you played a part in the whole scenario?"

Nevaeh looked at him with anger brewing in her eyes, but reality soon softened her stare. She knew everything Darnell had just said was true, but she didn't want it to be. She told Ronald that she didn't blame him because she had played a role in the sin right along with him, but here she was telling Darnell that it was all Ronald's fault that she ended up half-naked in his living room.

"I know the part I played," Nevaeh admitted. "And I told Ronald that I didn't blame him, but really I do.

I don't want to blame myself, but I knew when I walked into the house that something wasn't right. I let my heart convince me that everything was fine, and it turned out that I let the devil lead me right into the arms of temptation."

"But haven't you asked God to forgive you?" Darnell asked.

"Yes, but—"

"And didn't you hear the message that Pastor McKinley just gave?" he continued.

"Yes, but—"

"So," he interrupted again, "why can't you forgive Ronald for his part? You've asked for forgiveness and received it, Ronald has received forgiveness from God, now all you have to do is forgive him and everything will be all right."

"But I am not sure if I am ready to be with him again. We are on totally different paths, and they are not going in the same direction."

"Who said that you had to take him back? All I am saying is let him know that you have forgiven him."

"I just don't know when I can do that," she spoke softly, shaking her head.

"Well, let me pray with you," Darnell offered, standing and grabbing her hands. "Prayer always makes decision-making easier."

Nevaeh took his hand and closed her eyes.

"Most righteous Father," Darnell began, "Nevaeh and I come to You right now asking that You will help her through her problems. Lord, You know everything that is going through her mind right now, and You know how to take care of Your children. So, we just ask that you take control of the situation and let her know that You are here, holding her and protecting her from the evils of this world.

"I also ask that You keep Your arms around Ronald and show him You are there for him also. Show him Your loving kindness. Let him see Your grace and mercy. Lead him back home, Lord. Lead him back to You. Lord, we love You and we praise Your name. Amen."

Nevaeh released his hands and gave him a thankful hug.

Imani walked into the room and looked from her sister to Darnell. "Daddy said that it's time to go," she said to Nevaeh, but looking up and down at Darnell.

"Hey, Imani," Darnell greeted.

"Hi, Darnell," she said through a forced smile.

Nevaeh picked up her purse and other belongings. "Okay, I am ready," she said walking toward the exit, and then stopping to face Darnell. "Thank you."

"Any time," he replied.

Darnell walked with them to the parking lot, but turned in a different direction as they walked to their van. Finally with a moment alone, Imani eyed Darnell in the distance then looked at her sister.

"What?" Nevaeh said when she noticed her sister was staring at her.

"Are you and Darnell . . . ?" Imani asked suspiciously.

"No! He was just helping me through this whole Ronald situation."

"Sure," Imani said, "but you know he likes you."

"Mind your business," Nevaeh said as they climbed into the SUV.

James pulled out of the parking lot and headed home. Nevaeh sat in the back seat and prayed that she would soon be able to forgive Ronald and get this burden off of her shoulders.

Chapter 20

Ronald walked into his room and pulled off the suit pants he'd worn to church earlier. He folded them and placed them on his bed and put on a pair of jeans. Exchanging his starched dress shirt for an extra large T-shirt, he sank onto the mattress and used the remote to flip through the channels on his television.

Ronald thought going to church with his family this morning would help him with his problems, but he only heard part of the pastor's message because his head was swarming with thoughts of Nevaeh.

Going to Nevaeh's house yesterday seemed like a good idea at the time, but apparently he had been wrong. Ronald had practiced what he was going to say, but he lost all words when he saw her. No matter where she was, who she was with; if she was wearing her cheerleading uniform, a formal gown, a T-shirt and jeans, or the long jean jumper dress she had on when she answered the door, Nevaeh always managed to master beauty.

He hated the look she had on her face when she came to the door. It was like she didn't see him . . . or *wished* she didn't see him. It would not have been as bad had she been angry that he'd shown up at her house unannounced. But the emotionless expression she wore on her face was like a knife being twisted around in his heart. When she couldn't look Ronald directly in his eyes, it made him feel worse. He wanted to hold her, but when he took that first step toward her and she stepped back, he didn't know what to do next. His apology was as genuine as he could make it, but she didn't seem to notice or even care how much he regretted what had happened.

He thought she was hallucinating when she said that she had seen a man in the room with them, but he couldn't deny the fact that he too had felt someone else's presence in the house that night. He just ignored it and the voice that repeated the promises he'd made to Nevaeh once they had gotten back together on the first day of their junior year.

I will spend the rest of my life making you happy. And when temptation enters, we just have to stay on our knees, praying that we do the right thing. I love you, Nevaeh.

Ronald remembered everything he'd told her, and all of it ran through his head while he was fumbling with her bra strap. *We just have to stay on our knees, praying that we'll do the right thing.* It played over and over in his head, and he didn't know why he didn't give in to the voice and stop before he ended up losing the only girl he ever loved.

Ronald saw the love still in Nevaeh's eyes, even when she was yelling at him. He could feel the connection that they'd always shared, but he knew she tried with all her might to hide it. He didn't want to stop loving her, nor did he want her to stop loving him. He wanted—no, he needed—a second chance.

What about your second chance with Me?

Ronald knew he needed to get right with God, but he was more concerned with getting right with Nevaeh. He picked up the phone and dialed Marques' number.

"Hey, man," Ronald said as soon as Marques picked up the phone. "Can you meet me at the court?"

They never played ball in the winter, but Marques answered without asking any questions. "Sure."

"Thanks," Ronald said, and then hung up the phone before pulling off the jeans he'd just put on and replacing them with a pair of Nike basketball sweatpants. He grabbed a hoodie, his ball, and car keys. "Ma, I'm going to the court," he yelled loud enough for her to hear him in his parents' room.

"Take your brother," she yelled back.

"What? Why?" Ronald said the words before he could catch himself. He knew his mother did not tolerate questioning her authority.

Angelica came to the door and opened it in fury. "Because I said so," she said in a low, even tone.

"Yes, ma'am," Ronald said, backing away from the door. "Jeremy, get some clothes on so we can go to the basketball court!" he yelled up the stairs.

"Yayyyy!" Jeremy cheered.

Two minutes later, Jeremy was running down the stairs with his basketball tucked under his arm. They walked out front to the Camry, and Jeremy hopped into the front passenger seat. Turning on the car, Ronald cranked up Kevon Edmond's "No Love" as he backed out of the driveway.

"Why are you listening to this stuff?" Jeremy asked

with his face crumpled in disgust. "This why you been so sad. You listenin' to all this sad stuff."

"Man, why are you always asking so many questions?" Ronald asked, looking at his brother. "And Mama said I had to take you with me, but she didn't say I had to let you talk me to death," he said. "Dang, you talk like a female. No, I take that back, you talk more than females."

"So? Mama said I just have a lot to say, and one day it is going to make me rich."

"Sure, listen to Mama," Ronald said with a laugh.

They drove into the park, and Ronald pulled his car between two other cars that were parked in the lot. He was not surprised to see Marques sitting in his car only a few feet away, bobbing his head to the beat of a song. He shut off his engine and got out of the car when he noticed Ronald.

"Wassup, Jeremy?" Marques said, pounding fists with the young boy.

"'Sup, Big Marq?" Jeremy answered.

"So, you ready to get whipped?" Marques asked Ronald.

"Man, just 'cause you rule the court at school don't you got an advantage out here."

As they walked to the basketball court, Jeremy waved to one of his friends in the distance. "Can I go play ball with Terrance?" he asked his brother.

"I don't care," Ronald told him. Jeremy ran toward Terrance, who was playing at the end of the court with a few other boys his age. "Stay where I can see you," Ronald instructed.

"Okay," Jeremy yelled without looking back.

Ronald threw the ball to Marques. "First to twenty-one."

They began playing the game, and every aggressive bone in Ronald's body came out on the court. Fast on his feet, Ronald scored the first five baskets. Marques quickly answered with two three-pointers and shot a lay-up to try to catch up with his friend. Ronald was playing like he was at the state championship, and Marques could tell something was bothering him, but he didn't pry. He knew Ronald would talk when the time was right. But when Ronald went for a three-pointer, elbowing Marques in the ribs, sending his friend onto the ground in pain, Marques decided Ronald needed to go ahead and get whatever it was off his chest before they ended up fighting.

"Man, what is your problem?" Marques asked as he held his abdomen.

"My bad," Ronald said, helping him to his feet.

Marques walked over to one of the empty bleachers that were usually filled with cheering girls during the spring and summer, when large groups of guys gathered at the park to play rounds of basketball. Ronald followed and sat next to his friend. He sighed, remembering the times Nevaeh would come out, sit in the exact same spot he was in, and cheer for him when they held the spring competitions.

"What's up?" Marques asked again.

"Man, it's this whole Nevaeh thing," Ronald said, watching his brother play ball at the kiddy court across the playground. "She is really trippin' off of that night."

"Well, can you blame her?" Marques asked. "You know how into her faith she is. I thought you were into the whole celibacy thing too."

"I'm done with that mess. You know how many females be tryin' to get with me?" Ronald said. He noticed that he was starting to make that his personal motto. "I don't have time to wait until I get married. Shoot, I love Nevaeh to death. I'll kill somebody for her, but this abstinence thing is getting tired, for real."

"I'm just gettin' used to the fact that Shimone ain't down with us *being together* anymore. I thought you could help me out, but here you are tryin' to get rid of your virginity."

"Shimone ain't gettin' with you no more?" Ronald asked in surprise. "Man, I thought she would be the last person on earth to practice abstinence. No, scratch that," he added after a moment's thought. "There *is* one other girl I can't imagine practicing abstinence."

"Who?" Marques wondered aloud.

"Sierra Monroe." Ronald laughed as he rubbed his goatee.

Marques saw something strange in his friend's eyes. He hoped Ronald was not thinking what he thought he was thinking. Marques knew Sierra could be tempting, but not even he had tried to hook up with her. "Man, don't tell me you gonna try to get with that," Marques said, eyeing his friend.

Ronald looked at Marques and laughed. "Are you crazy? That would most definitely set Nevaeh off. Why would I do something like that when I am trying to get my girl back? I am *not* you."

"Watch yourself!" Marques said defensively. "I ain't me no more either."

"Yeah, you right. Shimone has definitely got you whipped."

"No," Marques corrected, "but she does have me

thinkin' 'bout a future with her. I told our families that we are gonna get an apartment off-campus when we go off to college."

"For real?" Ronald was shocked. "I can't even believe that you and Shimone are going to be living in the same house and y'all are going to be celibate."

"See, that's what I've been thinking about," Marques said. "I think I'ma let her have the apartment and I'm gonna live on campus, especially since her mom doesn't really believe in—what do you call it—shacking up? I don't want Ms. Misty to feel like we are always doing something."

"That's a good way to think about it," Ronald agreed.

Marques sat back on the bench and waved at Jeremy, who was arrogantly bragging to his friends about how he just beat the other boy in a game of one on one. Once his bragging session was complete, Jeremy walked over to where his brother sat.

"Did you just see that? I dunked it over his head," he said, imitating the move.

"That's good, Li'l man," Ronald said, rubbing his little brother's head.

"You tryin' to be like me?" Marques teased.

"That ain't so bad," Jeremy said, shooting a pretend ball in the air.

"We 'bout to leave in a few minutes, so go'n and play for a little while longer," Ronald said.

"Okay," Jeremy said, running back to the other side of the playground. "I guess I have time to whip him once more."

"So, what you gonna do about this whole Nevaeh thing?" Marques asked after a brief moment of silence.

"I don't know," Ronald said solemnly. "Sit, pray,

and wait, I guess. She has to at least forgive me, even if she won't take me back."

"Well, I wish you the best, my brotha."

"Ball up," Ronald said.

They got off the bench, and Ronald caught the ball that was tossed to him.

Chapter 21

Nevaeh had decided against riding to school with Ronald. Against her better judgment, she'd spoken with him the night before and he said it wouldn't be a problem for him to pick her up as usual. She just didn't feel up to trying to avoid the awkward silence that was sure to occur if she were to take him up on his offer. Since she knew Shimone would be riding to school with Marques and not with her, Nevaeh, beyond a doubt, did not want to be in the car alone with Ronald.

She looked once more in the mirror, straightening out her boot cut jeans and lavender top, and made sure her hair was in place. Everyone was sure to know about her and Ronald's break-up by the end of the day. *If I am going to go to school and be talked about, I'm at least going to look like it doesn't affect me.*

She looked outside of her window and noticed a blue Mustang pull into her driveway. *What is he doing here?* she wondered as the uninvited guest got out of his car and rang the doorbell.

"I got it!" Nevaeh yelled, not wanting anyone to know who was on the other side of the door, especially not her sister. She raced down the stairs with her purse dangling off her shoulders. When she got to the door, she was literally out of breath. She stopped and calmed herself before opening it.

"Hi!" Darnell said, as if she should have been expecting him.

"What are you doing here?" Nevaeh asked in a low, harsh tone.

"I thought you could use a ride, considering the circumstances," he said, "but if I was wrong, I can head to school." He began to back off of the porch.

"No." Nevaeh softened her voice. "It's just that I was thinking of taking the bus."

"Girl, seniors don't ride the bus," Darnell said, laughing.

"I know, but I don't want people to get the wrong idea. As soon as we pull up, they are going to know that me and Ronald broke up, and they are gonna think I'm with you."

"Who cares what *they* think?" Darnell said, shrugging his shoulders. "So, are you coming or are you taking the *bus*?" he asked, making a disgusted face.

This was one of the many times she wished she had her own car. Being that her dad was an automobile dealership owner, one would think she'd have her own vehicle by now, but James was not dropping a set of keys into his daughter's hands until after she graduated from high school, and even then, she had to graduate with honors or she'd be bumming a ride once she got to college.

Darnell waited for a response. Nevaeh thought about declining and walking to the bus stop. She definitely didn't want anyone spreading lies about her. *Who cares?* her conscience said. *If they have nothing better to do with their lives than to talk about you, then consider it a compliment.*

"Okay, I guess it would be cool," she said, walking out of the house and locking the door.

Darnell helped her into the passenger side and waited until she was situated to close the door. He jogged around to the driver's side and got in, then he reached for the knob to turn down the music as it blasted through the speakers after he'd started the engine.

"Sorry about that," he apologized.

"No," Nevaeh said, grabbing his hand before it could reach the knob. "I like this CD."

"Really?" he said, looking down at her hand that was still holding his.

Nevaeh bashfully released his hand and rested her palm in her lap. He looked at her and smiled. Noticing that he was making her uneasy, Darnell turned away and backed out of her driveway.

The ride was quiet for the first few minutes, but when "Faith" by LaShell Griffin began to blast through the speakers, Darnell immediately began to sing the male's part. Nevaeh was always amazed by his vocal talents. In church, he rarely sang unless someone asked him to, otherwise he was best known as an expert on the keyboard.

Without thinking, Nevaeh jumped in when LaShell began to sing the second verse. Their voices blended perfectly in praise. Nevaeh hit all the high notes, while Darnell went as low as his tenor voice would allow. Forgetting where she was and who she was with, Nevaeh closed her eyes and enjoyed singing the words that described the depth of her faith in God.

When the song ended, Darnell tossed a look at Nevaeh. "Girl, you can really sing," he said, glancing in her direction and then back at the road again. "We should do this song next Sunday."

"Sure," Nevaeh said without thought.

She didn't know what it was, but with Darnell, she didn't have to think about anything. Everything was so natural, not forced. Not that Ronald forced her to not be herself or receptive toward him; it was just that she and Darnell were on the same level spiritually, and it seemed as if they had this undeniable spiritual connection.

They pulled up at Douglass and parked in the student parking area. Darnell got out of the car and ran around to the other side to help Nevaeh out. Several upperclassmen who knew her noticed Nevaeh exiting a car that was not Ronald's, and they began to whisper like professional gossipers while they walked toward the building.

"Don't worry about them," Darnell said, waving his hand in the direction of the onlookers.

"I'll try," she responded, walking to the front doors.

Although Nevaeh knew that gossip was a part of everyday life, she knew today would be anything but normal.

Marques left Shimone's side and rushed to find his best friend, but everywhere he looked, Ronald was nowhere to be found. He'd just heard a few seniors talking about Nevaeh shamelessly cheating on Ronald. Although he knew the cheating part was not true, Marques couldn't deny the fact that Nevaeh might have found someone else and had killed Ronald's dream of ever being reunited with her. He ran through the building, hoping to find Ronald before the first bell rang.

"Marques, don't you think you should slow down before you hurt someone?" the varsity basketball coach said. Then he made his real concern known. "Especially yourself," he specified. "I need you this season."

"My bad, Coach," Marques said, slowing his run to a fast-paced walk.

As soon as he was out of his coach's sight, Marques began sprinting again. Without thinking, he ran toward the gym. When he walked through the doors, he noticed that all the freshmen and sophomores were waiting to be dismissed to their first block of classes. He walked across the court, trying to ignore the intrigued stares of the younger girls who sat closest to the basketball court. Walking into the boys' locker room, he spotted Ronald with a few of the football players. They were laughing about something that, Marques concluded, could not be more important than what he needed to tell his friend.

"Ronald, man, I have to tell you something," Marques said, trying to steady his breathing. "But you gotta stay cool."

"Man, you the one running in here breathing all hard." Ronald laughed along with some of the other football players. "Maybe you should sit," he suggested, continuing to laugh.

"You laughin' now, but when you hear what I just heard, you won't be."

Ronald's face quickly became serious. "What's up?"

Marques calmed himself before saying, "I just heard a few seniors say that Nevaeh has been hanging around Darnell Parker *all* morning. They think she is cheating on you 'cause she rode to school with him and everything. Now, I know she ain't cheatin' 'cause y'all not together, but he might be her new man."

"Ronald, man, you ain't tell us that you and Miss Lady broke up," Mac, the 200-pound halfback on the team, said.

"That's 'cause it ain't your business," Ronald said with a clenched jaw. "Who'd you hear this from?" he asked Marques.

"Man, it's a lot of people talkin' 'bout it."

"Let's go," Ronald said, leading the pack out of the locker room, into the gym full of students.

"Where they goin'?" one of the freshman girls asked as the boys ran past them.

"I don't know, but the dark one in front is cute," another girl said.

Ronald, Marques, and the other guys rushed down the hall toward the commons area where the juniors, seniors, and a few underclassmen who thought they were too cool to sit in the gym with their age groups, waited for the first bell. The boys were like magnets as several students from the gym followed them.

It seemed as if everyone in the commons was talking about Nevaeh and Ronald because as soon as he walked in, almost everyone's conversation came to a halt. He stood in the middle of the commons, searching the area. He spotted Nevaeh at a back table, talking to Shimone and a few of the cheerleaders and dancers.

"C'mon," Ronald said to the boys who were still standing behind him.

Nevaeh saw him and rolled her eyes toward heaven. *Lord, please; not early this morning,* she thought.

"Hey, Ronald," the group of girls said.

"Dang," Mac growled. "I guess y'all don't see a brotha standin' here."

"Hey, Mac," a few of the cheerleaders greeted him.

"Nevaeh, I need to talk to you," Ronald said, walking closer to her.

Shimone quickly got in his face. "Uh, I really don't think there is *anything* you have to say to her that you have not said in the past two weeks."

"Shimone, I really don't have time for your lip," Ronald said as calmly as he could, out of respect for his friend who was standing to the left of him. "So, you really need to get out of my face."

"Boy, who—"

"Shimone, I can handle it," Nevaeh said, cutting off her friend.

"Fine," Shimone said, stepping aside.

"Shimone, you need to sit down," Marques said, pulling her into a chair. "You are in no position to be trying to get in someone's face and causing yourself so much stress, if you know what I mean," he whispered, hinting at the fact that she was about to enter her fourth month of pregnancy.

Although no one had said anything, Shimone knew that her peers were not stupid. They could spot a pregnant classmate a mile away. But maybe they just thought she was gaining weight. Either way, the truth would be revealed sooner or later.

"I know," Shimone said, sitting in the chair.

"Nevaeh, we *really* need to talk," Ronald said, as the rest of the onlookers continued to be nosy.

Nevaeh stood toe to toe with her ex-boyfriend and stared him in his once mystifying dark eyes. "Ronald, there is really nothing for us to discuss. I told you I needed time, and you gave it to me. I appreciate that," she said. "But you running up on me with all these people behind you like you're ready to fight some-body is not going to change the fact that we are no longer together." She paused for effect and breath. "I have forgiven you, and it was all the praying I did that got me to this point, but I have not gotten over the fact that we want two different things."

"Well, why are you running around here with Dar-nell?" he asked abrasively. "If you can find somebody that quick, then maybe it just wasn't that night that made you rethink our relationship."

"What exactly are you trying to say, Ronald?" Nevaeh asked, on the verge of losing her composure.

"Maybe you wanted to be with him, so you found something you disliked about our relationship so you could drop me."

"Ronald McAfee, you know that is not my style. I loved you. I still do, but I don't want to be with some-one who gets mad at me because I want to follow God's commandments."

"If you don't want to be with me, then why are you wearing the locket?" he asked, pointing to her chest.

Nevaeh looked down and held the locket between her fingers. She'd decided to wear it because she thought she could handle it, even though she knew Ronald would be around to see her with it on. But with him standing in her face pointing it out, she knew she should have thought her decision through before taking it out of its box this morning.

"I wore it . . . I put it on because . . ." She thought for a moment. "Because you said you wanted me to have it. Your words were, and I am not paraphrasing here, 'Take it, even if you don't take me.'"

Suddenly, Darnell appeared at Nevaeh's side. Ronald looked as if he wanted to rip his teammate's face off. But Darnell was not fazed by Ronald's threatening look. He looked him dead in his eyes and returned the stare.

"Is there a problem?" Darnell asked, speaking to Nevaeh but looking menacingly at Ronald.

"Everything is fine," Nevaeh said, trying to avoid a confrontation. The last thing she needed was someone getting suspended for fighting because of her.

"I don't think so," Ronald said, stepping closer to Darnell. "You, of all people. We 'posed to be teammates. How you gonna try and take my girl like that?"

"Ronald, I am not your girl!" Nevaeh screamed in his face, surprising him and everyone else who was listening. "Don't you get that?" she said, softening her voice. "We are no longer together."

Nevaeh slowly unlatched the locket from around her neck and handed it to Ronald. She grabbed her possessions and walked off with Shimone trailing behind, leaving Ronald looking at the locket in his hands.

When Ronald finally walked off with his teammates behind him, the noise level in the cafeteria raised to a level higher than it had been before the confrontation began. Everyone was talking about what had just transpired. No one could believe that Ronald and Nevaeh had broken up. People who knew them as a couple knew that whatever had happened between them over the short vacation was serious, because this break-up definitely seemed to be the end.

Chapter 22

Sierra was in her third block Advanced Placement Biology class, and she was having a hard time concentrating. All of her thoughts were on Corey. She hadn't seen him since Saturday when he'd left Hartsfield-Jackson International Airport on Flight 376 going to St. Louis, Missouri. She really wanted to spend the New Year with him, but if he had missed any classes, it would be a nightmare trying to make up for lost time.

Sierra looked at her right ring finger and smiled. She still couldn't believe she had committed herself to celibacy. *I guess love can make you do things you never thought you'd do*, she thought. Twisting the ring around her finger, she marveled at how the diamonds caught the sunlight shining through the window.

"Ms. Monroe," Mrs. Robinson said, standing over Sierra, her large frame blocking the sunlight. "Would you like to join the class and come out of whatever daydream that you are having?"

Sierra looked at the woman and smiled. No one,

not even her least favorite teacher, was going to take away her joy. When Mrs. Robinson turned around and headed back toward the overhead projector, Wanda Younge, a varsity cheerleader, passed a note to her. Sierra opened the note and read its contents. The first sentence caught her off guard.

Ronald and Nevaeh broke up.

She looked across the classroom at Nevaeh. Sierra noticed that she didn't look as happy as she usually did, and that she was barely paying attention to anything Mrs. Robinson was saying. Sierra turned around and finished reading the note.

> *It happened this morning in the commons. Girl, Nevaeh told his behind off! Something happened over the break. Everybody is talking about it! People are saying he cheated; some say she cheated. But from what I overheard between Marques and Ronald, he wanted some and she wasn't offering none! I guess it's fate. Out with the old, in with the new: that means YOU! Go for it, girl!*
>
> *P.S. Shimone is pregnant. Got that from my little eavesdropping moment, too.*

Sierra looked at the note and then looked at Wanda. "So?" Sierra mouthed.

Wanda gave her an *I thought you'd be happy . . . no, ecstatic* look. Sierra refolded the note and placed it in her binder. Wanda continued to look at her friend in disbelief. Everyone knew Sierra wanted Ronald. What had changed? Apparently, the holiday break had changed a lot of things.

Sierra looked at Wanda and held up her right hand. Wanda's mouth dropped in surprise. "We'll talk after class," Sierra mouthed.

Sierra turned around in her seat and faced the front of the classroom, where Mrs. Robinson had begun to lecture the class about disciplinary issues; something that definitely had nothing to do with biology.

Sierra suddenly reopened the note and reread the last part.

P.S. Shimone is pregnant.

Not a surprise to Sierra. When it came to sex, Shimone was almost as bad as Sierra . . . or as bad as Sierra *used* to be. The only difference was that Shimone slept with guys she was in a relationship with. Sierra slept with any guy who wanted her. *But not anymore*, she thought, gazing at the ring again.

Sierra looked toward the clock situated over the chalkboard in front of the class. The bell would ring in a few seconds. She couldn't wait to get out of the classroom. Science was her least favorite subject, especially since she'd never passed a science course with anything higher than a C.

She could not figure out why she was in an advanced placement class since she was not, nor had she ever been, an advanced student. The fact that it was an A.P. science class baffled her even more. There were a handful of seniors who had a science class, and that was only so they could receive college credit. Other than that, many of the seniors used it as a free period to hang out in the library, or take an extra class for more graduation credits. Sierra assumed that her counselor had given her the course so it would look good on college applications, but at the rate she was going, a college would have to be stupid to let her in their school with a grade point average of 2.75.

She'd made a New Year's resolution, though. She was going to try her best to do better this semester. She really wanted to go to a fashion design school in the Midwest so she could be closer to the guy she'd grown to love over the past weeks. But in order to do that, she had to get a scholarship, and to get one, she needed better grades.

"Read chapter twelve for homework," Mrs. Robinson was saying.

The bell rang, and students jumped out of their seats and headed for the door. Sierra gathered her books and walked out of the classroom. She waited for Wanda at the door.

"So what is *this* all about?" Wanda said, holding Sierra's hand in the air.

"I got a *man*," Sierra said proudly. "And not just a minute man. I'm talkin' 'bout a real relationship with a *man* who is committed to me and me only!"

"Who is it?" Wanda asked as they walked down the hall. "And why you keep stressin' the word 'man'? Is he old or something?"

"No, he is not old," Sierra said, placing her hands on her hips. "But he is a man. He is a sophomore at Missouri College. And he is sweet, nice, loving, and *all mine*!"

"Okay, I understand the whole boyfriend part, but what's with the ring? Y'all did just meet, right? Why would he give you a ring so early in the relationship? Sounds a little *Fatal Attraction*-ish if you ask me."

"Number one," Sierra held one French manicured finger in the air, "we did not just meet. I have known him since I was seven years old. Number two, he gave me this ring because . . ." She stopped. She was not sure if she should tell Wanda about her commitment. Sierra was known for being promiscuous, but she didn't want to be for the rest of her high school life. She also did not want to have everybody know her personal business, like with Ronald and Nevaeh.

"Because what?" Wanda asked impatiently.

"You have to promise that you will keep this between us," Sierra said, looking at Wanda in apprehension.

"Dang, is it that serious?"

"Yes, now promise."

"I promise," Wanda said as they came to a stop in front of Sierra's next class.

"He gave it to me as a promise to practice celibacy with him."

"What!" Wanda screamed, drawing attention to their conversation.

"See, that's why I didn't want to tell you," Sierra said, looking at the people who were still trying to figure out what the girls were talking about. "Don't y'all got somewhere to be?" she asked them.

"Not really!" someone in the crowd said while a few others laughed.

Sierra looked at the boy who was audacious enough to respond to her rhetorical question. Her look was threatening enough to cause most of the students to leave and make their way to their separate classrooms. A few were bold enough to stay where they were, but they were smart enough to pretend to be no longer interested in the girls' conversation.

"I cannot believe you made a promise you know you can't keep," Wanda said, pulling her micro braids over her shoulder. "You know how you are. You see

something you like and you go after it, like a predator
on the hunt, and once you get what you want from it,
you throw it away like a defective toy. So, I don't understand why you'd make a promise like that if you
knew, number one, he was all the way in the Midwest
where he didn't know if you'd be keeping your promise
or not. Number two, you have all these fine boys here
who would stand in line for a chance to be with you,
but you choose someone who wants to be *celibate*."
She said the word like it was poisoning. "And number three, there is temptation *all around* us," Wanda
said, looking up as Kevin Pierce, a football and basketball player and wrestler, passed by them in the hall.

"Hey, ladies," he said, walking into the class across
from them.

"Hi, Kevin," Wanda said as she waved while Sierra
barely acknowledged him.

"I can and I will keep this promise," Sierra replied
defensively.

"Okay," Wanda said, looking at her watch. "Do
what you do. I got to go before I get caught in the
hall sweep. Bye," she said as she ran down the corridor.

Sierra walked into her Calculus class just as the
late bell rang. She slid into her seat on the second row.
Her teacher gave her a stern look, reminding her that
she should not just be walking into class. Sierra gave
him an apologetic grin.

Calculus was her favorite subject, and Mr. G, as the
students called him, was her favorite teacher. He ini-
tially became her favorite instructor because of his
smooth skin, light brown eyes, and gorgeous smile,
but as she got to know him, it was his personality and
great teaching methods that awarded him her admiration. He was one of the younger teachers, fresh out

of college, and he was a great instructor, mostly because he could relate to his students on their level. But no matter how much she liked Mr. G, he could not keep her attention because Wanda's words would not get out of her head.

I cannot believe you made a promise you know you cannot keep . . . temptation is all around us.

Sierra knew why Wanda would have her doubts. Anyone who knew about her commitment would probably say the same thing. But she was determined to prove them all wrong. She could do this. At least she hoped she could.

Shimone sat in her Family Consumer Science class and wondered why in the world Wanda Younge was staring at her. She tried her best to stay focused on her class-work, but with Wanda's eyes burning into the side of her face, she couldn't concentrate.

The day had already been hectic. After running from the commons this morning, she and Nevaeh spent much of their first block in the girls' restroom. Nevaeh cried about how much she wanted to kill Ronald for making a scene in front of all of those people. Especially all of her squad, girls who waited for the day Ronald and Nevaeh would no longer be an item.

"Girl, you shouldn't be embarrassed," Shimone had consoled her. "You cut him right in front of his teammates. It's not like *he* told *you* off in front of half the senior class. It was the other way around. He should be the one in a bathroom crying, not you."

"Shimone, I just don't know what to do," Nevaeh cried.

Shimone never thought anything like this would

happen to her best friend. Nevaeh was the nicest person she'd ever met. She definitely did not deserve to be in the position she was in. Ronald should be the one all torn up and upset. Although he probably was, the situation couldn't be affecting him like it was affecting Nevaeh. For Nevaeh, the day had gotten off to a bad start.

It hadn't been an easy morning for Shimone either. After being picked up by Marques, they headed to the nearest McDonald's because Shimone had been craving burgers all night. Being that it was breakfast, Shimone had to settle for a sausage, egg, and cheese biscuit. As soon as she got to school, she ran into the bathroom and threw up in one of the stalls. When she came out of the bathroom, Marques had a look on his face that said he didn't want to know. He did ask her if she was okay, though, and she tried to convince him and herself that she was fine. They talked in the hall for a while, mostly about the baby. That had been the focus of their conversations lately.

Shimone was glad when Marques told her he thought it was best for her to live in the apartment while he lived on campus. She hadn't wanted to say anything before, but she knew she would not be comfortable sleeping in the same house, even in different beds, with Marques. If she was going to get back on track with God, she needed to do it without any temptation standing in the way. Their parents had been right all along.

Shimone felt another episode of morning sickness coming on, and she was glad when Marques said he needed to find Ronald. She didn't want him to have to see her running back into the stall again. After assuring him she was fine by herself, she ran into the restroom and threw up the remainder of her breakfast. When she came out of the stall for the second time, Wanda and Zoë, a dance team member, were in front of the mirror applying makeup to their already flawless faces.

"Are you okay?" Zoë asked, feeling concerned about her captain. "I hope you are not coming down with something. We are going to need you for the upcoming basketball season."

"I'm fine," Shimone said, wiping her mouth with tissue. "But I am not trying out this season."

"Why not?" Zoë asked, pulling a brush through her blonde tresses. "Girl, no one can take your place as captain and I know you wanna be out there dancing for Marques." She smiled.

Shimone looked at Wanda, who seemed not to care about anything except her newly braided hair. "I just don't feel up to it," Shimone simply stated. "I'll see you later," she said just before walking out of the bathroom.

As Shimone tried to listen to what her teacher was talking about, she wondered if Wanda knew about her pregnancy. It was clearly obvious that Shimone was gaining weight, but could Wanda know that it was not from eating?

Shimone wasn't quite ready for everyone to know just yet, but if Wanda knew, she knew she could just kiss goodbye the hope of her pregnancy remaining under wraps. She didn't really care what anyone thought of her, but she hated when people would listen to silly gossip and talk about her behind her back. The least they could do was gather enough nerve to ask her themselves or be bold enough to say what they thought to her face.

"Do you need help with something?" Shimone finally asked Wanda, getting tired of her constant stares.

"As a matter of fact, there is something I need to ask you," Wanda said. Apparently, she had no problem with boldness. "Are you pregnant?" she asked in an exaggerated whisper.

Shimone was not surprised at Wanda's bluntness, but she at least thought the girl had enough class not to ask her in a room full of nosy students.

"Why . . ." Shimone cleared her suddenly dry throat. "Why would you ask me that?"

"I don't know," Wanda shrugged, "maybe the fact that you have clearly gained weight or the fact that you threw up twice this morning." She paused for dramatization. "Or it could be that I overheard your boy talking about it with Ronald this morning."

Shimone felt like she was going to be sick again. How could Marques possibly talk about something like this in public with so many people around? Didn't he know that Douglass' halls were magnets for rumors? Was he not aware that if this got back to her dance coach or his basketball coach, they'd both be in serious trouble? She knew she couldn't be upset with him, though, because she'd talked about their unborn child with him this morning in the very same hallways. The only people who were supposed to know were she, Marques, their best friends, and their parents. Now that Wanda knew, the entire school would too.

Shimone raised her hand just as the teacher turned around. Getting her attention, she covered her mouth, noting she had to go to the restroom. The teacher gave her approval, and Shimone raced out of the room while the entire class looked at her in bewilderment.

She ran down the hall and into the nearest restroom. Barely making it in time, she hunched over a stall that hung from the wall and vomited.

"Hey, girl," a male voice said. "What are you doin' in here?"

Oh my gosh! I can't believe this, she thought as she noticed what type of toilet she was standing over. She came out of the stall and faced the voice that had let her know she'd come into the wrong restroom. She was even more embarrassed when she realized it was Ronald who had seen her.

"Shimone, are you okay?" he asked sincerely.

"I'm fine," she said harshly, trying not to show her embarrassment. She walked over to the paper towel dispenser and pulled out a couple of paper towels to wipe her mouth.

"Do you need to go to the counseling center or attendance office to call somebody?" he asked.

"I said I was fine," she said, turning to walk out of the bathroom. "I don't need any help, especially from you."

Ronald followed her into the hall. "Shimone?"

"What!" Shimone spun around to face the person who'd made her friend's life, in recent days, a living nightmare.

"Could you please talk to her for me?"

Shimone saw the regret, love, sadness, and loneliness in his eyes. And for the first time, she noticed that he'd been crying. She looked into his eyes and wondered how her friends' lives had gotten so messed up. She wanted to hug him, and she knew he needed one, but she kept her stance. But Ronald's eyes softened her heart toward him, and Shimone knew that he was just as torn up as Nevaeh.

"I'll talk to her," she said softly.

Ronald walked to her, taking slow, cautious steps, and she welcomed the embrace. He stepped back and looked in her eyes. "Thanks," he said. "Are you sure you're okay?" he asked her again.

"Yeah, just a little morning sickness," she assured him. "Don't go worrying Marq about it."

"Okay," he said, heading back to his class.

Shimone turned and walked in the direction of the commons area. A security guard was at the other end of the quarters, making sure no one was where they weren't supposed to be. She walked past him without even being asked for a pass, and headed to her classroom.

With a minute left before the last bell rang, she walked as slowly as she could to avoid getting back too early and having to endure the stares of her classmates. As soon as she turned the corner, the bell sounded throughout the building. Students charged out of their classrooms, glad that the day had come to an end.

Shimone walked into the classroom and nearly bumped into Wanda, who had a smirk on her face. *How could someone rejoice during someone else's pain?* she thought.

"Shimone, are you okay?" her teacher asked when she walked into the classroom.

"Yes, Ms. Bradley. Have a nice day," Shimone said, grabbing her books and heading for the exit. She stopped by the gym and told Marques she'd call her mother for a ride instead of waiting for him to finish basketball practice.

"I need to lie down," she explained.

"Okay, make sure you feed my baby." Marques smiled and rubbed her stomach.

Even the thought of food right now turned her

stomach, but she managed a weak smile and a soft, "Okay," as he kissed her on the lips.

Leaving the gym, she used her cell phone to call her mother. She walked outside and sat on the bench as she waited for her ride to arrive.

Shimone began to cry as she thought about her baby. Although she was glad she was having the baby and keeping it, she didn't know how much longer she could endure the sickness that came along with it. It had started soon after she found out she was pregnant. And with five months of carrying this baby left, she didn't know how much she could take. She'd read the brochures on pregnancy that Dr. Anther had given her. Back pains. Bloating. Swollen feet. It all sounded horrible, but the vomiting seemed like the worst.

"God, please be with me during this time in my life," she prayed aloud.

When her mother pulled up a few minutes later, she got off the bench and walked to the car. Before climbing in, she looked toward heaven and saw a bird's feather falling. She held out her hand, and it landed in her open palm. She took it as a sign.

"Thank you, Father," she said, getting into the vehicle.

Chapter 23

Nevaeh walked into her house at six o'clock that evening. She was drained both mentally and physically. All of the drama from that morning still weighed heavily on her mind. The fact that Ronald caused a scene at school, something that she'd prayed would not happen, made everything worse.

After crying in the bathroom, she had gone to her Trigonometry class without an excused tardy. Seeing her red eyes, her teacher didn't ask any questions. Unable to concentrate, Nevaeh zoned out and didn't take her usual notes. She had no idea how to do the day's lesson, so she decided to take the book home and look over the chapter.

All of her other classes seemed to go by painfully slow. She paid little attention in A.P. Biology. In Literature, she'd been distracted because of Ronald's presence in the seat next her. She had even dazed out in Creative Writing, her favorite class. She knew Mr. Lowell talked about writing from experience, and for homework she was to write a poem from any recent experiences. *I could write a whole novel with everything that has happened in my life,* she thought.

To top everything off, Nevaeh had to stay after school for cheerleading practice. Being in the mental state that she was in made her want to just quit, but Coach Jennings had placed her in charge of practice, and she barely made it through all the whispers.

She'd heard the rumors all day, and she was tired of hearing "She cheated," or "He cheated." There was also the scandalous one that had people saying, "She found out she's pregnant and he's not with it," and the completely fabricated, "Darnell started it. You didn't see them holding hands in the hallway?" And then there were those who whispered the actual truth, "He was ready to give up his virginity, but she didn't want to." Whatever was the chosen saying, Nevaeh was sick of them all.

She got through the first hour of practice before she went off on Wanda, who was steadily talking about their breakup while Nevaeh was standing in front of the girls trying to teach them the new cheer.

"You know what, Wanda," Nevaeh said, getting in the girl's face. "Why don't you just shut up since you have no idea as to what went on over the break? If you don't have anything better to do with your life than to sit around making up lies and gossip about other people, then get a hobby!" she snapped.

Now as she lay sprawled across her bed, Nevaeh wished she could take it all back, every word of her rampage. She had asked God to forgive her while waiting for her mother to pick her up after practice. Now she needed to apologize to Wanda, and she'd made a promise to herself that she would do it tomorrow.

Noticing the familiar blinking light on her phone, Nevaeh picked it up and dialed her voicemail code to hear her messages.

"Nevaeh." Ronald's voice caused her to freeze. "It's me, Ronald. You are probably still at school, practicing. I was just calling to apologize for what happened this morning. I didn't mean to start any commotion, but when Marq told me that you rode to school with Darnell, I just flipped. I hope you'll forgive me . . . again." He paused. "I love you. Bye."

She held the phone to her ear, hoping he'd left another message. She wanted so badly to hear his voice again. Nevaeh saved the message and then pressed the code to hear messages that had been stored before it. The stored message was from Ronald too. This time, listening to it made her cry.

"Now that's a voice I'd love waking up to in the morning," Ronald's voice said. Nevaeh remembered how she sat on her bed and listened to the softness in his voice on the day that he'd originally left it. "Hey, beautiful. I was just calling to see what you have planned tonight. If you are free, I'd love to take you out to dinner. Well, I got to go, so call me when you get this. I love you. Bye."

It was bittersweet. The message brought back the memories of that night as she placed the phone back on its cradle. She wished she could take it all back and have everything be like it was before she stepped into his house. If she could just go back . . . She knew it could never happen, though. She failed the test God had given her. Even after asking for forgiveness, receiving it and forgiving Ronald, she still felt guilty.

"God, please take the pain away," she cried as she lay down on her bed.

Peace be with you, my faithful daughter.

* * *

Ronald dialed Nevaeh's number for the fifth time. He'd left her several messages over the past hour, but she had not called him back. Not that he expected her to forget everything that happened this morning, but even if she called and screamed at him, he'd be satisfied.

He couldn't believe how immature he'd acted. He should have known that Nevaeh wouldn't just start going out with someone else that quickly. But even if she had, he still shouldn't have gotten so upset. After all, he didn't treat her with the respect she deserved, so maybe God was punishing him by allowing him to see Nevaeh with someone who did—Darnell.

Darnell! Just the thought of the name made Ronald's stomach cringe. What he really wanted to do was rip Darnell's face apart. He couldn't understand why his teammate would even offer to bring Nevaeh to school. Ronald knew that Darnell and Nevaeh went to the same church, and she probably went to him with their problem, but why would she come to school with him knowing that everyone would start gossiping about it? And why did Darnell want to get involved in Nevaeh's life all of a sudden? Ronald didn't have the answers, but one thing was for sure, Darnell was not going to take his place.

"Hey, Nevaeh, it's me again," Ronald said into the phone when he got Nevaeh's voicemail. "I really want to talk to you. I need to ask you something, and I don't want to do it over the phone. Please call me. I love you. Bye." He hung up the phone and sat on his bed.

He hadn't prayed in a long time, but it seemed like every time he got on his knees it was to *ask* God for something. He hadn't even thanked Him for anything that had happened.

"Probably because I can't think of anything to be thankful for," he mumbled as he sat on his bed, trying to keep his mind off of Nevaeh. *Impossible*, he thought. *That girl is all I ever think about.* He reached for the phone and quickly dialed her number. *Please pick up.*

"Hello," her voice was soft. "Hello?" she said again when he didn't respond.

"Hi," Ronald said, finding his voice.

Silence.

"Please don't hang up," he said when Nevaeh said nothing. "I really need to talk to you."

Still silence.

"Nevaeh, are you still there?" he asked.

"Yes," she said softly, as if she were crying.

"Are you all right?"

"Yes."

"Did you get my messages?"

"Yes."

He wished she'd say something other than "yes," but at least she was talking to him. "Can you meet me somewhere?" he asked.

Silence was her answer, and he didn't know if she was thinking it over or if she was about to yell at him and tell him she never wanted to see him again.

"Nevaeh?" he called.

"Huh?"

"Can we meet somewhere, please?" It sounded as if he were begging, but he didn't care. "I really need to talk to you."

"I don't know. My mom's not here, and I don't have a ride, and . . ." Her voice trailed off.

"Please? I can pick you up."

"I don't know if that is a good idea," she sniffled.

Ronald hated the fact that she was crying, because he knew it was because of him. It seemed like lately, every time he saw her she was either crying, on the verge of crying, or she was angry, and it always had something to do with him or circumstances surrounding him.

"I just don't know what to do," Nevaeh cried into the phone.

"We can figure it out together." He wanted so badly to hold her, but he couldn't. He was silent for several moments as she wept through the phone. *God, please let me make this right. It's not supposed to be like this.*

Her tears subsided, and she spoke the word he'd been waiting almost five minutes to hear. "Okay."

"Thank you. I'll be over in fifteen minutes," he said, noticeably happy.

"Okay," she said.

"Nevaeh," he said before she could hang up. "I love you."

"Bye, Ronald," she said, hanging up the phone.

Ouch, he thought as he placed the phone on the cradle. Ronald remembered a time when he said those words and he could feel Nevaeh's smile through the phone. Now all he felt was a cold shoulder. *At least she is willing to talk to me.* He tried to search for the bright side.

Jumping from his bed, Ronald put on a pair of Timberlands and grabbed his keys and coat. He let his mother know he would be back in about an hour, and was surprised when she didn't ask any questions and happy when she didn't make him bring Jeremy.

He walked out the front door and got into his car.

During the whole drive to Nevaeh's house, he prayed. He hoped that she would hear him out and be open-minded to taking him back. It was hard not being able to talk to her and see her smiling face every day.

He pulled into her driveway and was glad to see that she was waiting for him outside. She stood on the porch and paced with nervousness. Even in her cheerleading sweat suit and her hair pulled into a ponytail, she still looked gorgeous.

Ronald got out of the car and walked to the porch. Nevaeh looked at him with apprehension, but allowed him to lead her back to his car and help her into the passenger side.

The drive to her neighborhood park was completely quiet. There was no talking, and the space was void of the music that usually streamed from Ronald's stereo. It was not the comfortable silence that used to peacefully rest between them; it was very awkward. Ronald felt the need to say something, but he couldn't find the words. Nevaeh was staring out the window, trying to find something to occupy her mind, but Ronald kept entering her thoughts.

He pulled into the park's parking lot and shut off the engine. The entire park was empty. *Good*, Ronald thought. The last thing he needed was some little kid to interrupt their time of what he hoped would be reconciliation.

Nevaeh climbed out of the vehicle and walked over to a nearby bench. Ronald followed her. They sat next to each other in silence for what seemed like hours, but were only minutes. Ronald finally decided that someone should say something, and since he was the one who practically begged for this meeting, it was only natural that he explain why he needed to see her.

"Nevaeh, I really am sorry," Ronald started. "I don't know if you believe me or not, but I am. I don't know what is going on with me lately. I see something I want and I go after it until I get it. I need to control my emotions, but with you it's like I can't. You are you, and I love that about you. I love you and I don't know if I can really see myself without you in my life. I love you so much that it physically hurts when I can't be near you."

"I don't want you to be upset with me. I want us to go back to how it used to be. And I want to go back to our commitment to remain celibate until our wedding night." He'd caught himself off guard with his own statement, but this time, he meant every word.

He got Nevaeh's full attention. *Could he be serious?* Nevaeh asked herself. Was Ronald really giving up on trying to sleep with her? How could she be sure? After what had happened before, how could she trust him? The look in his eyes said yes, but how did she know he wasn't just using that as a feeble attempt to get her to resolve things with him? She looked in his eyes and tried to find an answer to all of her questions. She only found herself falling deeper in love with him. She didn't know how to handle situations like this. Her heart was telling her to dive in full speed, but her mind was warning her that making things too easy could result in another disappointment, or worse, heartbreak.

"Ronald, I don't know." Nevaeh sighed. "I can't see myself without you either, but how am I supposed to know that you won't change your mind? How do I know you are being sincere? What happens if we end up in a situation like before and I say no again, but you decide you don't want to listen? I don't want to set myself up for something I know will end in disaster. I don't want to end up in your living room with my clothes off and you not seeing anything wrong. I don't want to lie in my bed for three days crying because I know that we may never be together again. I don't want to have any regrets about decisions that I make in our relationship."

"Baby, I promise that as long as we are together, I won't do anything to jeopardize our relationship. If you knew how much I loved you, I think you would understand. I just don't know any other way to put it." He ran his hand over his face. "I don't want you to hate me. I need to know that there is some part of you that still loves me enough to give me a second chance."

"Ron, *every part* of me loves you," she stressed, "but I have given you chance after chance, and my heart is extremely vulnerable when it comes to you. I want to be with you, but the fact that this is the second time we've broken up over this issue makes it hard for me to make any decisions. I just need some time, and if you cannot be patient with me, then this is the end. I want to still be friends with you. I want to be able to come to you if I have a problem. But if every time I see you, you keep badgering me to forgive you, which I have already done, then it is not going to work either way."

"So, are you saying that we can't be together, only friends?"

"I'm saying I need time to think things over, and until I come to a definite conclusion about us, yes, we can only be friends," she responded honestly.

Ronald thought about his options: choose not to just be friends with Nevaeh and tell her that it's all or nothing, or choose to be just friends for the time being and try to charm his way back into her life. His head was leading him toward option one, but then he'd risk the chance of losing her completely. His heart had already chosen option two, but that could mean they'd always be just friends and nothing would ever develop from it. And at the pace they were going, Ronald doubted that they would go back to being a couple any time soon.

Ronald looked at Nevaeh, who was waiting patiently for an answer. *I love this girl too much to risk losing her*, he thought. "Okay, we can be friends." He was glad when a smile spread across her face. "If you take this back," he added, taking the locket out of his pocket and dangling it in her face.

Nevaeh thought about it. "No strings attached?"

"None whatsoever," he said honestly.

She nodded and he unlatched the necklace and placed it around her neck. He stood and pulled her up off of the bench. He looked down into her eyes, and for a moment thought about kissing her, but he pulled her into a warm embrace instead.

Suddenly, Ronald pulled back. "I just need to know one thing," he said.

"What's that?" Nevaeh wondered.

"Are you and Darnell together?"

"I told you we weren't." She sighed. "He was just there when I needed him to be, that's all."

"Well, as a *friend*," Ronald said seriously, but with a hint of sarcasm, "I'm telling you he is feeling you, so be careful."

Nevaeh couldn't help it as she laughed aloud. "Are you saying that because you think he really wants to get with me and you don't think we'd make a good couple, or is it out of jealousy, and you don't want me to go out with anyone but you?"

Ronald pretended to ponder on the question

heavily. "A little of both, but I would lean toward the second reason more so than the first," he said.

"Well, I can assure you that Darnell and I are *just* friends," Nevaeh said then smiled. "For the moment."

Ronald gave her a look that said her joke was not in the least bit funny.

"I'm just playin'," she said, poking him in his side.

Ronald put his arm around her and they quietly headed back to his car.

Chapter 24

Friday afternoon, Shimone and Marques were headed back to Dr. Anther's office for her checkup. Misty and Shundra sat in the back seat of Marques' car, debating over what to name the baby.

"Why not Nia?" Misty said. "It's Shimone's middle name, and it means *purpose.*"

"The child is going to need a sense of identity," Shundra argued. "I say they name her Ebony or Amana, which means *faith.*"

"Oh, I kinda like that, Shun," Misty agreed. "Ebony Amana."

"Why y'all comin' up with all these girl names?" Marques asked from the driver's seat. "How y'all know it ain't a boy? Y'all should be thinking of somethin' like Darrell, Sean, or Marques Tyrone Anderson II," he said proudly.

"Boy, please," Shimone said. "I like Ebony, though. It's pretty."

"Yeah, I like it too," Marques said, "but I refuse to name my son Ebony."

"Child, you are so crazy," Shundra said, hitting him in the back of his head.

They reached the doctor's office ten minutes before their scheduled appointment. Walking into the almost empty waiting room, Marques hoped they'd be seen on time.

"Well, hello, Shimone," Dr. Anther said as she walked into the waiting room.

"Hi," Shimone replied.

"I see you kept your promise and brought your mother," Dr. Anther said, slipping her arm around Shimone's waist and smiling toward Misty. "How are you doing this morning?"

"Good, thank you," Misty replied.

"Doctor Anther," Marques said, "this is my mother, Shundra Anderson."

"Hi, how are you?" Shundra said, stepping forward to accept the doctor's outstretched hand.

"Just fine." Dr. Anther smiled. "Well, this is just fantastic. We have the whole family here for support. Why don't you guys come on back so we can get started?"

They followed her into one of the checkup rooms and helped Shimone get situated on the bed.

"We don't usually give second ultrasounds this early, but I'll make an exception for the sake of the mothers. So, just lay back and relax." Shimone followed Dr. Anther's instructions. Dr. Anther put the gel on Shimone's stomach and allowed everyone to see the baby's movements on the monitor. The baby squirmed around, and they were able to see its arms and legs.

"Oh my," Shimone said, nearing tears. "She is so beautiful."

"Yes, *he* is," Marques corrected.

Dr. Anther looked at the couple and smiled. "You know, if you want, I could tell you what you are having," she proposed.

Shundra and Misty looked at their children, who looked at each other. Marques laughed at the pleading look in Shimone's eyes.

"Remember the deal," he said and laughed again as Shimone rolled her eyes and smacked her teeth.

"What deal?" the women asked at the same time.

"I told Shimone that if we have a girl, I would pamper her for the first two weeks after she gets out of the hospital, and if we have a boy, she'd pamper me," Marques explained. "But if either of us asked what we were having before we had it, the deal was off."

Misty and Shundra laughed, and Dr. Anther shook her head. Shimone lay on the bed with her arms across her chest. Marques continued to laugh at his girlfriend, who was acting like a spoiled, but cute, little brat.

"Well, I guess that answers my question." Dr. Anther smiled as she wiped the gel from Shimone's stomach. "I can tell you that your baby is fine. Its hair is growing a little, and its kidneys are producing urine. As long as you continue to take those vitamins I gave you, you should be fine," Dr. Anther said as she continued to write information about Shimone's progress on the chart. "You have been taking those vitamins, right?"

"Yes, ma'am. Mama makes sure I take them, and she makes me drink a lot of water." Shimone's face became concerned. "But I have been having pains right along here," she said, rubbing her lower abdomen.

"Oh, that is normal. It is called round ligament

pain, and it is caused by the stretching that your muscles and ligaments have been doing in order to support your uterus, which is still growing," Dr. Anther said as Shimone nodded. "You may also notice some dark patches on your face or arms. Don't worry, though. They are called chloasma. This is from the increase in melanin, the substance that colors your skin, hair, and eyes. They may last all through your pregnancy, but they fade shortly after you have your baby," she explained. "Have you and Marques attended the classes I set you up for?" Dr. Anther asked.

"We've been a couple of times, but I've had to work on some weekends, so I was not able to take her to every class," Marques confessed.

"Well, you know, if it's not a problem, one of you could take her," she said to the mothers.

"I don't mind," Misty said, with Shundra agreeing. "As long as I know the schedule, I could take her. I'd have to rearrange some of my classes, but it'll work."

"Also, you need to make sure you stay active," Dr. Anther said to Shimone, sitting on a stool next to her. "And I know you are on the dance team at school, so stick with that and you should do fine."

Shimone looked at her mother, her boyfriend, and his mother before turning her attention back to her doctor. "Umm . . . I was thinking of quitting dance."

"What?" Marques said.

"Shimone, why would you do that?" Misty asked with her hands on her hips.

"Well," Shimone started, "I just didn't want everybody in my face about me being pregnant."

"Girl, don't worry about them children," Shundra said. "You need to make sure that you and this baby stay healthy."

"And the only way to do that is to stay active," Dr. Anther added. "The dance team is a good way to make that happen."

"Look," Marques interjected, "I'll talk to Coach Bullock and let her know what's up. I'm sure she will make sure that you are taken care of during practices."

"Last year, this girl on the dance team got pregnant, and Bullock said she could not participate in the program," Shimone explained. "It's not that I don't want to dance anymore. I love to dance. It's just that I don't want any special treatment because I'm pregnant."

"Well, I will write a note and you take it to your dance coach on Monday," Dr. Anther said as she began to scribble on a sheet of paper. "She will have to let you participate, considering this is doctor's orders. I'll have it typed up and sent to you by tomorrow," she said. "Now, you won't be able to continue dance for too long. After you enter your third trimester, you will need to take it easy for you and your baby."

"Thank you," Shimone said.

Dr. Anther smiled. "Now, I will need to see you back here in four weeks, which is February eleventh, so I can see how well you're progressing."

"Okay," Shimone said, putting on her coat.

"Thank you, Doctor," Marques said.

"You're welcome," she replied. "It was nice seeing you again, Ms. Misty, and nice meeting you, Ms. Shundra."

"You too," both women said.

They walked out of the doctor's office and to Marques' car. Marques helped Shimone into the passenger side seat as their mothers reclaimed their seats in the back of the vehicle. Marques got into the driver's seat and started the car.

"I'm hungry," Shimone said as she rubbed her growling stomach.

"Me too," Marques said as they pulled out of the parking lot. "Ms. Misty, do you have anything to eat at your house?"

"Boy, you don't ask somebody if they got food to feed your greedy behind," Shundra scolded her son.

"Girl, it's okay. I don't have anything to eat today, but if you come to Sunday service with us, I think I can whip up somethin' for after church," Misty offered.

"Okay," Marques said quickly.

Shimone looked at him and smiled. "You are going to church?"

He shrugged. "I don't see why not. Your mom can cook."

"Well, I guess I'll see you on Sunday then," Shundra said to Misty.

"I guess I can endure Mama's food tonight." Marques sighed.

"Boy, don't make me come up there," Shundra warned over the laughter of the others.

Sierra sat nervously in the waiting room of the South Fulton Free Health Clinic. As she had been on her way home from school, she'd received a call on her cell phone from the center, telling her that her results were ready. It had been almost four weeks since she had gone to take the AIDS test with Corey, and she had been wondering what could be taking them so long to get the results back to her. She'd tried not to, but had been thinking about the test since Corey was called to receive his results days before he left for St. Louis. His had come back negative. She wanted to be happy for him, but she couldn't help but worry over her own results.

She'd been happy since returning to school. Corey was her life now, and she didn't know what would happen if she was to lose him all because of her promiscuous past. She was terrified of what the results might be, and had voiced her concerns to him over the phone a few days ago.

"Corey, what if they come back positive?" Sierra asked him.

"Sweetheart, all you have to do is keep on praying. I know everything is going to be all right," he said, trying to cheer her up.

Sierra wanted to believe him, but it was hard. She needed to know that he would be there for her if things didn't turn out the way they wanted. "Corey?" She said his name, afraid to even ask the question.

"Yes?"

"If the test does come back positive, are . . . are you going to leave me?" she asked softly into the phone.

Corey seemed not to know what to say. But when he spoke, his words shocked her. "Baby, I would never leave you just because of something like that. It would be different if we just met and I was not in love with you, but that is not the case."

Sierra couldn't believe what he'd just said. "What did you say?"

"I said that it would be different if I was not in love with you," Corey repeated.

"You're in love with me?" she asked.

"Sierra, I've loved you since you were fifteen. I just couldn't do anything about it because I was seventeen and you were too young for me to be messing with," Corey explained.

"Are you serious?" Sierra was still in shock.

"Why is it so hard to believe?" Corey laughed. "Do I need to say it in a formal way just so you will believe me?" He cleared his throat. "Sierra Celeste Monroe, I love you."

"I love you too, Corey," Sierra whispered.

They sat up for more than three hours, talking about the test results and what they would do in case they didn't turn out the way they prayed they would. After the conversation ended, Sierra felt a little bit better about receiving the results, but she still stressed over the fact that it was highly likely for her to have caught the disease, considering her past carelessness.

She watched the clock on the wall and constantly looked at the door that led to the examination rooms. *What's taking so long?* she thought, looking at the receptionist who offered her a reassuring smile.

"Sierra Monroe?" A man who'd walked from the back said her name as if he wasn't sure he was pronouncing it correctly.

"That's me." Sierra stood abruptly and almost fell back into her seat before she could catch her balance.

The man beckoned for her to follow him to a back room. The walk down the same hall she'd walked before seemed even longer the second time around. Her palms were sweaty and she felt like she was going to be sick, but she made it to the room without passing out as she'd feared.

God, please, please, let this be good. She sat in a chair offered to her by the man.

"Ms. Monroe," the man began, "I know we've taken a long time to get in contact with you, but we like to run several tests on the blood samples to make sure the results are accurate." His face was blank, and she had a hard time trying to determine if he had good news or bad news.

He handed her an envelope, and her hand shook as she reached out to take it. Sierra held the letter in her hand as the man continued to talk.

"Those are just the results on paper, but—"

"Wait," she suddenly interrupted. "I was here with my boyfriend a couple of weeks ago, and you guys didn't give him a letter."

"I know." He sighed. "Your tests results came back positive. I'm sorry," he said.

Sierra sat emotionless. She felt numb, and it seemed as if her heart had stopped beating.

Noticing her blank face, he seemed not to want to continue with the treatment information, but he had to. "But this can be treated. So, I would suggest contacting a physician that specializes in treating HIV patients. We will give you a list of specialists that we recommend. It would also be in your best interest to immediately be tested for other sexually transmitted diseases. You'd also need to inform any previous or current sexual partners," he concluded.

Sierra had heard him, but she wasn't listening. She continued to sit, staring blankly at the envelope in her hands. This couldn't be right. Why would God do this to her? If He really loved her, why would He hand her a death sentence at such a young age? She tightened her grip around the letter, causing it to crumple. She needed to get out now. She stood, signaling to the man that she was ready to end this conversation.

"If you feel that you need any more information, you can call this center or your local AIDS hotline," he informed her.

After walking her to the lobby, he placed a strong hand on Sierra's shoulder and brought his voice level to a whisper. "It's not the end of the world, Ms. Monroe. Trust me, I've been living with this disease for five years, and I'm still very healthy. If you keep God first, everything else will fall into place."

She continued to stare at him blankly, and his words seemed foreign in her ears. She only nodded because she knew he was waiting for a response. She left the building in a hurry, wanting to get as far away from the center as possible, and drove home as quickly as she could. She still hadn't cried. It was as if she couldn't cry because she knew this would be how things would turn out.

She arrived home, but before she could even run up the stairs to her room, she collapsed on the living room floor, next to the sofa. How could this happen to her? Her life was officially over. What was she going to tell her father? He'd probably just yell at her and tell her that she should have been more careful. Who was she to turn to now?

Turn to Me.

Corey, she thought. She felt around for the phone. She quickly dialed what she hoped was his apartment number.

"Hello." a female answered. Her voice seemed groggy.

Sierra was confused. "Hello," she said, trying to calm herself. "Could I speak to Corey?"

"May I ask who is calling?"

No you may not, Sierra thought. *You may get Corey like I asked.* "Sierra," she sniffled.

"Just a minute," the girl spoke.

Sierra heard a door open and the girl said, "Corey, there's somebody named Sierra on the phone for you."

"Can you tell her I'll call her back?" Sierra heard Corey say through the sound of running water.

"Okay," the girl said to him.

"Thanks, sweetie," she heard Corey say.

Sweetie? Sierra thought. *Why is he calling her "sweetie?" And what was he doing that is so important that he can't take a minute and talk to me?*

"I'm sorry, but he is in the shower," the girl said. "I could give him a message if you'd like." She paused for an answer. "Hello?"

Sierra hung up the phone before the girl had a chance to say another word. She should have known better. Why would Corey want some high school girl when he could have any college woman he wanted? She was just someone to hang out with while he was visiting home.

But how could he say he loved her and then turn around and have some girl in his apartment that he probably had been seeing before he even came to Atlanta for the Christmas holiday? How could he do something like that knowing all the pain she'd gone through with guys? He didn't even care. *Christian my foot*, Sierra thought.

She looked down at the unopened letter in her hands and opened it. Her eyes scanned the paper, which said everything the man at the center had already told her. Her fate had been decided for her. She would live the rest of her life in fear of dying. She lay down on the sofa and cried and prayed that all the pain would go away. She cried until she felt like it didn't matter whether she was dead or alive. No one wanted her anyway. Not Corey, her dad, or anyone else. It didn't matter anymore.

Chapter 25

It was 7:30 when Sierra woke up, still on the sofa where she'd drifted off. Hoping it was all a dream, she got up and looked around for any evidence that would contradict her hopes. Seeing the letter on the floor, she picked it up and sank into the sofa cushions. The one word that stood out above all others brought back the harsh reality. *Positive.*

Sierra got up and went to the kitchen. She opened the glass cabinet and pulled out one of her dad's expensive wines. She poured herself a cup and drank it like it was water. She went upstairs with the bottle in her hands, changed her clothes, fixed herself up, and grabbed her car keys off of the nightstand.

Why not have a little fun? she thought as she got into her car and let up the garage door. *I'm dying anyway.* She laughed at the thought. Pulling out of the garage, she took a large gulp of the wine. Sierra drove all over downtown Atlanta, club hopping, using the fake ID that she'd had since she was a junior. She danced with any guy who would buy her a drink. When she got tired and left, she drove from downtown and back into her neighborhood. She looked at the ring on her finger. She took it off and stuffed it in her glove compartment. Before she turned onto her street, she made an illegal U-turn. *Why not share the wealth?* She laughed through her clouded thoughts. She clearly was intoxicated, and had no intentions of going home just yet.

Twenty minutes later, she pulled up to Ronald's house. His car was the only one parked in the driveway. No sign of his parents. *Good*. She clumsily got out of her car and stumbled to the front door. She pressed down on the doorbell as it rang over and over.

"Dang, I'm coming!" Ronald yelled as he walked to the door. On the night everyone in his family decided to go to the movies except him, someone chose to show up at his house, unannounced, and ring the bell like he should be expecting them.

He looked through the peephole. "Sierra?" he said as he opened the door.

"Hey," she said, half walking, half floating into the house.

Ronald could tell that she was clearly out of it. "What are you doing here?"

"Can't I stop by to see a friend?" she cooed, leaning into him.

The strong smell of wine on her breath caused him to pull away quickly. "Sierra, we have never been friends."

"We could be," she said, touching his chest. "If you'd just give me a chance."

"Sorry, I'm not interested."

"You should be, especially since I know Nevaeh is not taking care of business like you want her to."

She had hit a sore spot. Although he and Nevaeh still hung out and even rode to school together on occasion, things hadn't been the same between them. Nevaeh tried to stay away from Ronald when they were alone, and he didn't like this "just friends" agreement at all.

"Look, not that it's any of your business," Ronald said, getting agitated, "but me and Nevaeh are just friends."

"Too bad." Sierra smiled. "Well, all the more reason for you to take this opportunity," she said, unbuttoning her top.

Ronald swallowed as he looked at her open blouse then back at her face. "Sierra, I think you need to go home. Better yet, I'll call somebody," he said, picking up the phone. "You shouldn't be driving in the state you're in."

Sierra walked closer to him and took the phone from his hands. Placing it back on the cradle, she gently pushed him onto the couch. She leaned into his chest and he pushed her away. "Why are you being so stubborn?" she whined, then her tone became seductive. "I promise, I won't bite," she said with a laugh.

She was so close to him that he could smell her perfume. Suddenly, the smell of the liquor was no longer the dominant odor in his nostrils. Sierra smelled like freshly picked flowers . . . just like Nevaeh. Her skin was as soft as rose petals . . . just like Nevaeh's. Her kiss was soft, sweet, and sensual . . . just like Nevaeh's.

Ronald found himself back in his living room. He saw himself holding Nevaeh as she danced with him in the middle of the floor. He saw himself helping her pull her shirt over her head as he kissed her. He saw himself leading her to the couch and laying on top of her as he tried, unsuccessfully, to unlatch her bra.

He heard the words, *I will spend the rest of my life making you happy. And when temptation enters, we just have to stay on our knees, praying that we do the right thing. I love you, Nevaeh.*

Nevaeh.

Nevaeh!

Ronald quickly opened his eyes and saw Sierra lying underneath him, almost completely naked. He realized his own shirt was lying in a pile on top of Sierra's shirt, skirt, and shoes. Getting up, he interrupted her exploration of his muscled arms.

"What's wrong?" Sierra asked.

Ronald didn't say anything until he had put on his shirt. "You have to go," he simply stated.

"What! Why?" She was visibly frustrated.

"Because I said so," he said, handing her the clothes from off of the floor.

Sierra refused to take the clothes as tears began to well in her eyes. "Why does everyone keep denying me? No one cares about me!"

Ronald had no idea what to say, but he really needed to get her out of his house before his family got home. The last thing he needed was for Nicole to see a half-naked, drunken Sierra sitting in the living room and tell Imani, who would tell Nevaeh.

Sierra sat on the couch, crying about her boyfriend cheating on her and how her life was so messed up that she felt like killing herself since she was dying anyway.

"Sierra, I don't know what is going on, or what

you're talking about, but you really need to get home and get some rest," Ronald told her.

Sierra looked at him and growled, "Fine." She fumbled through the process of putting on her clothes and picked up her keys.

"No," Ronald said, blocking the door.

"Ooooh," she cooed. "Changed your mind, fine nigga?"

"No, but you're drunk," he said. "I can't let you drive."

"I'm fine. I know how to hold my liquor, trust me," she assured him, clearly disappointed that he'd not decided to take her up on her offer. "Besides, if you drive me home, my car would still be over here, and you'd have to explain to your family why I was at your house."

Ronald thought about it. Sierra had a good point. He definitely didn't want to explain to his parents why someone's car was parked in their front yard. She'd driven to his house on her own, and she didn't *look* drunk. Sierra seemed clear-headed enough, so he decided she would be okay. "Fine," he said, stepping away from the door.

She walked out of the house, got into her car and drove off. Ronald closed the door and slid to the floor in anguish. How could he do something like that? Why did he always let temptation into his life? Did he want to live alone for the rest of his life? At the rate he was going, he was never going to get Nevaeh back. She'd be livid if she knew Sierra was at his house, in his living room, almost . . . naked. She'd kill him if she knew he'd kissed her and was close to losing his virginity to someone he hardly liked. It seemed like his hormones always took over his body.

He needed to gain control, otherwise he'd be headed for destruction.

"God, please help me!" Ronald screamed so loud that the neighbors probably thought he was being attacked, but he didn't care. He sat in his living room and prayed until he was all prayed out.

Chapter 26

Corey pressed the "snooze" button on his alarm clock for the third time on Monday morning. If he was going to make it to his eight o'clock class, he needed to get up this time. He slowly climbed out of bed and made his way to the bathroom that he and his roommate shared. He turned on the showerhead to its hottest temperature, and then turned it down a little so he would actually be able to tolerate it.

It had been four weeks since he'd gone to the center to receive the results of his AIDS test. Although he was happy to learn that he hadn't contracted the disease, he was worried about Sierra. He was sure she'd called on the day she got her results, so he knew it was to tell him the outcome of her test.

But when Monica told him she was on the phone, he had just gotten into the shower, so he told her to tell Sierra to leave a message and he'd call her back later. When he got out of the shower and Monica said Sierra had hung up without leaving a message, he wondered what would make her do that. He didn't remember doing anything to upset her. He had tried to call her back since then, but every time he called her house, he always received her voicemail. Why was she avoiding him? The only answer he could come up with was that her test, apparently, came back positive.

He wanted to be there for her in her time of need, but how could he if she wouldn't let him? He loved her and he knew she felt the same about him, but why would she shut him out? He had always told her she could come to him if she ever had a problem, but she seemed to be pushing him away.

Corey turned off the shower and wrapped a towel around his waist before walking through the living room and back into his bedroom. He looked at Dustin's closed door and shook his head. Clothes were scattered around the living room floor as if it was the dirty clothes hamper. *How many times do I have to tell him to stop letting his girlfriend leave her clothes all over the floor?* he thought as he stepped over some of Monica's clothes that led to Dustin's bedroom.

Corey loved Monica to death, she was like an older sister to him, but he was getting tired of having to stay in the library for an extra hour just because his friends wanted some "alone time." When Dustin asked Corey to share an apartment with him last summer, he had accepted, but he had no idea that Monica would be in and out of Dustin's room every other night.

He had tried to convince Dustin and Monica to join C4C, but they both refused and said they'd rather spend time with each other instead of a group of holier-than-thou Christians who didn't know how to have fun. Although they continued to refuse his invitation, Corey didn't stop trying because he knew that deep down they had some interest in what Christianity was all about, especially since they often questioned him about his spirituality.

Corey quickly grabbed some clothes and went back into the bathroom to dry off and get dressed. After brushing his teeth and putting on his clothes, he groomed his mustache. He brushed his freshly trimmed fade and looked into the mirror to make sure everything was right. Satisfied with what he saw, he walked out of the bathroom and put on his black Reeboks to match the black C4C T-shirt he'd decided to wear today.

He looked at the telephone and then at the clock. It was 7:47 in the morning, an hour behind Atlanta, and too late to call Sierra. She would be in her first period class right now. He sighed and grabbed his books for his first class. *I guess I'll have to see what's going on with her later*, he thought as he walked out of his room.

Sierra lay in her bed, wide awake. She hadn't gotten much sleep in the past two weeks. Corey had left her multiple messages that she had not even bothered to return. She knew she should talk to him, but she didn't want to hear any lame excuses for why he had a girl in his room.

LaToya had also called several times in the last week and a half. Sierra had decided to answer after noticing LaToya's number on her caller ID for the sixth time in two days. She told her friend that she was fine, but she didn't feel like talking to anyone. LaToya bombarded Sierra with questions, but none of them were answered. Sierra simply told her friend that she didn't feel like being bothered. That hadn't ed LaToya from coming over last Saturday, ough. She stood outside, knocking on Sierra's front door for nearly fifteen minutes while trying to reach her by phone at the same time. Since Sierra's father was out, and, obviously, Sierra was not going to climb out of bed to answer the door herself, LaToya left without being able to see about her friend.

Apparently getting the hint, LaToya had left a message saying, "Sierra, I'm not sure what's going on with you. I do think I have an idea of what could be up, but I'm going to leave you alone until you come to me. You know I'm always here for you. I love you, girl."

The message brought tears to Sierra's eyes, but she couldn't bring herself to return her friend's call.

Sierra's father had not even asked her why she hadn't gone to school in the last two weeks. He was so busy with his work and women that he probably hadn't even noticed that she barely came out of her room since she received the results of her test.

Sierra noticed that he was also working later and later into the evenings. At one time, he would come home around ten o'clock. Now it seemed he didn't leave his office until midnight, and walked into the house at a quarter 'til two in the morning.

Sierra rolled over in her bed and looked at the piece of paper that sat opened on her nightstand. *Positive.* She'd read that word at least a million times in the past couple of weeks and heard the man's words: "Your tests results came back positive. I'm sorry." The reality had just begun to sink in. *I'm dying.* She began to cry into her pillow. She didn't want to die. She knew she had so much to live for.

"God, why me?" she screamed. "Why are You doing this to me?"

She thought about the night she went to Ronald's house after she found out about her test. She knew he was probably agonizing over the fact that he'd almost slept with her. But what he didn't know was that she felt just as guilty. She was so out of it that it took a night's sleep to realize that she could have ruined his life. At the time, she didn't care, and a part of her still didn't, but she knew that had he not come to his senses, she would have handed him his death sentence that night, and he wouldn't have even known.

Sierra looked at the clock and noticed it was 11:25. If she got up now, she would be able to make it to school in time for her lunch period. Even though she wasn't hungry, she just wanted to get out of the house. She climbed out of bed and made her way to the bathroom. Sierra looked at herself in the mirror and almost cried. Her eyes were puffy and red and had heavy bags under them. Her hair was mangled, and her body odor was terrible.

Turning on the shower, Sierra climbed in. She washed herself as well as her weak muscles would allow. Once her bath was complete, she blow-dried her hair, washed her face and brushed her teeth. Sierra pulled a comb through her hair and gathered it into a ponytail before walking back into her room to put on some clothes. Normally, Sierra wore skirts and heels to school, but today she pulled out an old pair of jeans, a sweatshirt, and a pair of old K-Swiss that looked brand new because she rarely wore them. She didn't feel like dressing up today, especially since she was not trying to impress anyone.

She pulled out of her driveway and a few minutes later, she pulled into the student parking lot. Sierra walked into the building and signed in at the front office. When they asked her for an excused absence note for the past two weeks, she said she'd been sick, but never went to the doctor for a note. She could tell they believed her, especially since she looked as if she should be on her death bed.

She walked into the cafeteria and sat at a table alone. Some of her classmates looked at her as if she were a bum off of the street, but she just ignored them. LaToya, looking as if she had just stepped off the runway with her flawless hair and makeup, had been sitting at a nearby table and when she spotted Sierra, she walked over to and sat beside her friend.

"Girl, I've been trying to call you for the past two weeks," LaToya said. "What is going on with you? And why are you ignoring my brother? He's been trying to get in touch with you for the longest. Have you lost weight?" LaToya asked, giving her friend the once-over.

Sierra tried to hold back the tears, but they released themselves anyway. She hated crying in public, particularly because everyone at the nearby tables was staring at her and she couldn't stand that. LaToya pulled her into her arms and let her friend cry. She had tried to go see about her friend, but Sierra refused to let her in at the time. LaToya had many questions, but hardly any answers. All she knew was that Corey had gotten his AIDS test results and they came back negative. By Sierra's unusual behavior in the last two weeks, LaToya could only conclude that her friend had tested HIV positive.

Once Sierra had calmed down, LaToya led her to a back corner in the cafeteria. She needed answers, and she needed them now, before Sierra started crying again.

"Sierra, please tell me what's up?" LaToya asked.

"My test . . . came b-back . . . positive," Sierra said between gasps that sounded like hiccups.

"Oh, sweetie," LaToya consoled. "Everything is going to be okay," she said as she pulled Sierra into a hug.

"No, it's not." Sierra continued to cry. "My life is over. I don't have anyone to talk to, and no one wants me."

"Girl, what are you talking about?" LaToya said, pulling back. "You know I'm always here for you. And Corey is too."

"No, he is not," Sierra said angrily. "He doesn't want me anymore."

"Where are you getting this from?" LaToya asked, confused. "He has been trying to get in touch with you for as long as I have, but you are avoiding him."

"I don't want to talk to him. When I did want to, he was too busy, and some girl answered his phone soundin' like she had just woke up, in his bed, I am sure." Sierra sobbed.

"I don't know what girl you are talking about," LaToya said, wiping Sierra's tears. "But I can assure you that my brother is not cheating on you."

"Well, it doesn't matter. He is not going to want me anyway," she sniffled. "I'm sure he doesn't want some girl with a deadly disease that would ruin his life."

LaToya had no clue how to help her distraught friend. She'd known Sierra since she was five years old, and she had never seen her so distraught. Without really thinking, LaToya looked down at Sierra's finger.

"Where's your ring?" she asked. She prayed Sierra hadn't done something she'd later regret because of her emotional turmoil.

"I took it off after I hung up on that girl," Sierra answered, wiping tears from her eyes. "I figured if he couldn't keep the commitment, then neither should I."

"Sierra, please don't tell me you went out and had sex with somebody," LaToya said, disappointment etched across her face.

"Almost," Sierra whispered. "I went to Ronald's house and we were really close, but he sent me home before we went all the way."

"I can't believe you would even go to Ronald," La-Toya said with her hands on her hips. "You know what happened between him and Nevaeh. And you could have given him the disease. Why would you even do something like that?"

"I was drunk! I didn't know what I was doing." Sierra fell to the floor while everyone looked at her like she was crazy. "God, please help me!"

LaToya joined her friend on the floor of the cafeteria as the bell for the next lunch period rang. La-Toya saw Sierra's counselor across the commons, heading back to her office. "Ms. Patricia," she called

When Patricia Welling saw one of her favorite students on the floor in tears, she dashed across the cafeteria to see what was wrong.

"God, help me," Sierra cried over and over again. "God, please help me."

"I don't know what to do," LaToya said to Patricia.

"Help me bring her to my office," Patricia said.

LaToya and Patricia practically had to carry Sierra to the counseling center. Once they were in the office, Patricia closed the door. Sierra sat in the chair and continued to cry. LaToya was on the verge of tears herself. She hated that she couldn't do anything to stop the river of tears that flowed from her best friend's eyes. Nor could she do anything about the disease that was causing the flood.

"Sierra, sweetie," Patricia said calmly, "I can't help you if you don't calm down. Please tell me what's wrong."

Patricia had been like a mother figure for Sierra since she entered Douglass High as a freshman. Sierra was always able to tell her everything in confidence, and she knew she could share this with Patricia and be assured that it would never leave the office.

"I tested positive for HIV!" Sierra cried.

Just outside the door, Wanda's mouth dropped in astonishment. She couldn't believe she just heard what had come out of Sierra's mouth.

Chapter 27

Nicole and Imani took their places behind the curtains at Greater Faith Tabernacle's auditorium as they got ready to perform their dance routine. They wore black leotards and a matching sheer wrap skirt. Their feet were bare and their hair was pinned in neat buns at the napes of their necks, with gold butterfly clips surrounding them.

The girls had practiced almost every weekend since they were asked to perform in this recital. They knew they were ready.

"Are you nervous?" Imani asked Nicole.

"A little," Nicole responded. "What about you?"

"I'm shaking."

They laughed.

"Let's pray real quick," Nicole suggested.

They took each other's hands and Nicole started, "Lord, we thank You for this opportunity to minister to Your people through our dance. We hope that our energy and passion will flow from our bodies to theirs. We want people to realize that we're not only here to entertain them, but to serve You, also." She squeezed Imani's hands. It was the cue for her friend to take over and Imani did.

"Lord, we pray that we will do well, and hope that every movement is pleasing to You. We know that we are not perfect, but we just hope that in Your eyes You see that we tried to come as close to it as we could, just so we could lift Your name even higher and praise You to the fullest. We love You. In Your name we pray."

"Amen," they said together.

They released hands and moved back into their positions. When the music began to play and the curtains opened, the audience clapped. Their families were in the first row and gave a standing ovation as if the performance was complete already.

Although Nevaeh had seen the routine many times over the past month, it still amazed her to see her little sister on stage, releasing her passion into the audience. Imani had been dancing ever since she could walk. And every time she danced, she'd do it with so much energy that Nevaeh thought it was her way of releasing everything that might be holding her down, and giving it to God. Nicole seemed to be the same way when she danced. Both girls had dreams of becoming famous dancers, and Nevaeh knew if they continued to perform like they were now, they would realize those dreams.

When the music ended and both girls were kneeling on the floor in prayer position facing each other, the audience stood and clapped. Everyone was on their feet. Some of the church members had gotten excited and started shouting without music. Others threw the roses that had been given to them as they walked in onto the stage. Their family members and friends yelled their names as if they were famous artists who had just given the performance of a lifetime.

When the curtains closed, the girls got up from their positions on the floor and hugged each other. They were in tears by the time the curtain opened again for them to take a bow. The other performers joined them on stage and the cheers got louder. They held hands and bowed on accord. When Misty came from behind the curtains, the screams got even louder as the dancers clapped along with the audience. Misty took a bow and took the microphone that was being offered to her by one of the backstage workers.

"I think we should give all of these kids another ovation," she said as a thunderous applause erupted before she could finish her statement. "These kids are so talented, and we all know that it came from God," she said as praises erupted from members of the congregation. "I would just like to thank each and every one of you for taking time out to come and support our children. We really appreciate it. As you can see, parents, your money is not going to waste. These kids are practicing every weekend with determination and perseverance. And it shows out here on the stage. Once again, I thank you. Have a wonderful evening." Applause erupted once more as Misty backed off stage and the curtains closed. "Girls, you were fantabulous!" Misty said, hugging each of them.

"Thank you," they said as they grabbed their things and headed to the front to meet their families.

"Y'all were killin' it up there," Shimone said to

Imani and Nicole once they were out front. "I am going to have to talk to Coach Bullock to see if she can open up a spot for you guys next year. Freshmen don't usually make the dance team, but we can make an exception for you two."

"For real?" Imani said, her eyes bulging. "I always wanted to be an Astro Dancer."

"Well, if you guys keep it up, you will be." Shimone smiled.

"You girls were great," James said, with Michelle nodding in agreement.

"I'm going to have to make sure you stay in that dance school," Malcolm said to Nicole. "I can see that my money is definitely not going to waste."

"In other words," Angelica interjected, "you were wonderful. Both of you were."

"Thank you," the girls said.

As the other members of the church came to congratulate the girls on their performance, Ronald pulled Nevaeh toward the exit. He'd been trying to tell her what happened between him and Sierra three weeks ago, but every time he tried, he either lost his nerve, or someone would interrupt their conversation.

"I really need to talk to you," he said once they were outside.

"About . . . ?" Nevaeh asked.

"I have to tell you something," Ronald said slowly. "But I don't want you to get upset."

Nevaeh placed her hands on her hips. "Ronald, usually when you start a sentence off like that, it means I most likely *will* get upset."

"I know you will," he said, "but I just need to tell you this before I cop out again."

Nevaeh stepped away from the church's entrance.

If Ronald wanted to tell her something that would make her upset or angry enough for her to cry, she didn't want anyone to see it as they walked out of the building.

"What is it?" she asked, bracing herself for the worst.

"A few weeks ago, Sierra came by my house," Ronald started. "She just showed up unannounced and was banging on my door. When she walked in, I knew she had been drinking 'cause she could barely walk straight."

Fear arose in Nevaeh as she said, "Ronald, please don't tell me—"

"Nev, please let me finish," Ronald said and continued after Nevaeh hesitantly nodded. "When she came in the house, she was talking 'bout how me and her should be friends and mess like that. And then she told me that I should get with her since you and me not kickin' it no more. Then she started unbuttoning her top and kissing me. I tried to push her off, but she just kept coming at me," Ronald said as he saw tears forming in the corners of Nevaeh's eyes. He wanted to stop because he knew it was hurting her, but she needed to know.

"Ronald," Nevaeh said quietly, "are . . . are you trying to tell me that you slept with Sierra?" she asked, hoping that wasn't the case.

"Next thing I know, I was on top of her and her clothes were off," he continued without answering her question. That made the tears come faster. "And all I was thinking about was you. I was dreaming that you were the one lying under me, kissing me.

"Then I heard the promise I told you that day we got back together our junior year." Ronald said the words quietly. "I will spend the rest of my life making you happy. And when temptation enters, we just have to stay on our knees, praying that we do the right thing. I love you, Nevaeh," he said, locking his gaze on her tear-soaked eyes.

Nevaeh let the tears roll down her cheeks without bothering to wipe them away. She remembered when Ronald said those words too, and she wanted to hear them again so she would know that he only wanted to be with her.

"When I heard your name in my head, I came to," Ronald continued. "It was like a wake up call before it was too late." He looked into her eyes. "I didn't sleep with Sierra. I'll admit, I kissed her and I helped her out of her clothes, and I regret even touching her or letting her in the house. But I promise you, I didn't sleep with her. I sent her home before anything more happened."

Nevaeh inhaled and exhaled to steady her beating heart. For some reason, she was relieved. But she still needed answers for his actions. "Do you want to be with Sierra? I mean, did you want to sleep with her?" she asked.

"No, no," Ronald said, "I don't want to be with her at all. I have no feelings for her. It was just a temporary lapse in judgment." He stepped closer to her. "I only want to be with you, Nevaeh. I love you."

He was so close to her that she could feel his heartbeat. She could smell his masculine scent. Nevaeh looked in his eyes and noticed a familiar feeling she used to get when he would look into her eyes. She could no longer hold his stare like she had been able to do over the past weeks when they had been just friends. She turned her head to keep from getting lost in his eyes. Ronald placed a finger under her chin and turned her face so she would be looking back into his eyes.

She didn't protest when he leaned down to taste the sweetness of her lips. She placed her arms around his neck as he held her waist.

Nevaeh loved the feeling of being back in his arms. She missed being his girl and him being her man. She had been out with Darnell a few times and Ronald knew that, but Darnell was not Ronald, and her relationship with him was not like her relationship with Ronald. Even Shimone had told Nevaeh that Darnell was not for her. Although they were on the same level spiritually, they did not share the same type of connection that she and Ronald did. Shimone let her know that she and Ronald belonged together and they needed to find a way to resolve their issues and quit acting like this "just friends" agreement was satisfying them, because it wasn't.

Nevaeh loved Ronald, and she knew that was never going to change. Even if they separated after high school, there would always be a part of her that loved him, and she couldn't deny that any longer. She pulled back slightly and looked at him. "I love you, too." She let herself fall deeper. "I don't want to be just friends anymore."

Ronald grinned and let his dimples show. "Neither do I," he said and pulled her into a hug. He inhaled the fresh scent of her hair and thanked God for the second chance . . . or was it the third? Either way, he was thankful.

"Umm . . . excuse me," Imani said, interrupting their moment.

Ronald released Nevaeh and turned around to see Imani and Nicole standing with their hands on their hips, with the rest of their families standing behind them. Everyone was grinning at them as if they already knew what had just happened.

"Malcolm," James whispered to Ronald's father, "do you think that I could talk to your son for a minute?"

"Sure." Malcolm shrugged. "I would like to join you if you don't mind."

"Not at all." James smiled. "Ronald, son, your father and I would like to speak with you."

"Daddy!" Nevaeh whined. She knew her dad was about to give Ronald "the talk." The one on respect, which James thought he'd never have to give him.

"What?" James said. "I just want to talk to the boy."

"Nevaeh, it's fine." Ronald smiled, knowing he needed to hear whatever the men were about to tell him.

Nevaeh sighed as Ronald and their fathers walked to the other side of the building.

"Child, calm down," Misty said to Nevaeh. "Your daddy ain't gon' bite the boy. He just wants to talk to him."

"And from the looks of things," Angelica added, "I think we should talk to you, too."

"I was just about to suggest the same thing," Michelle said. "And since Imani and Nicole are getting older, I think they should hear this, too."

"You too, Shimone," Misty said.

The women walked back into the church and into the auditorium and sat in the empty chairs. They sat in silence as the mothers took in their daughters' appearances.

"You all are beautiful young women who have the rest of your lives to think about getting married and having sexual relations with the person you marry," Michelle started.

"And if you ever feel pressured to do something that you don't want to do," Angelica said, looking directly at Nevaeh, "get out of that relationship, even if it is my son." She smiled.

"If you find yourself in a situation that you can't get out of," Misty said as she looked at her daughter, "get on your knees and start praying that you make the right decision for *all* those involved."

"Don't ever think you can't talk to us," Angelica said. "If my son gets out of line again, call me. And if you think you are in some kind of trouble, please call one of us. If something happens and you can't get in touch with us, get in touch with God. He is always there."

"Never think you are not good enough," Michelle said. "All of you have talents that can be used to glorify the name of Jesus and make you rich both spiritually and physically. You are better than good enough."

"Always let your light shine," Misty added. "If no one sees your light, you are not fulfilling your promise to your Father in heaven. He wants for people to be able to see Him through you, so always let your light shine, no matter where you are."

Each girl gave each woman a hug. When they went back outside, Ronald, James, and Malcolm were waiting for them. Ronald smiled, letting Nevaeh know that everything was okay. She sighed in relief. They each made their way to their separate vehicles and took rejuvenated spirits with them.

Chapter 28

Sierra sat in her Biology class on Friday afternoon and tried to concentrate while everyone in her class periodically stared in her direction. She knew this was bound to happen. Almost everyone in school knew about her being HIV positive, and no one wanted anything to do with her. The only person who stood by her side during all of the stares, whispers, and hard times was LaToya.

All through her meeting with Patricia, Sierra cried. She relived her life's story to her counselor all over again. Although Patricia had heard the story of Christopher not being there for his daughter many times before, she listened intently as Sierra explained how much it hurt her that her father would not pay any attention to her, even after the miscarriage, which he'd caused. He always told Sierra that she would never amount to anything in life, and she had allowed everything he'd said to sink into her soul.

She never let anyone get too close, in fear that

they would walk out of her life. That was the reason she never let LaToya in on anything about her father. Sierra didn't want anyone to know that she had a father who didn't love her like he should. She didn't want anyone to know that he had locked her in her room after he found out she'd gotten pregnant once before her miscarriage. She didn't want people to know that her father would hit her for unknown reasons when he was angry. Sierra didn't want to share with everyone that he would leave for days and not give any hint as to where he had gone. She'd kept it a secret that, even after her father had stopped verbally and physically abusing her, he acted like she was invisible, only speaking to her when necessary. No one knew that that was why Sierra lived her life like she did. She only wanted people to know the glamorous side of her life.

When she and LaToya finally left the counseling center, Sierra felt a little bit better. Although she was still agonizing over her disease, she knew she needed to get her life in order. She decided to start with her relationship.

Sierra called Corey as soon as she got home from school.

"Hello," Corey answered on the second ring.

Sierra was surprised that she did not burst into tears at the sound of his voice. She had missed hearing his soothing tone in the last couple of weeks. But there was no emotion in her voice when she said, "I tested positive." At first there was silence. And before Sierra lost her courage and just hung up the phone in his ear, she repeated herself. "Corey, I tested positive. I have HIV."

"Sierra, I-I," Corey stammered. Then he took a

deep breath and got his words together. "I'm really sorry," is all he could say before he fell silent again.

"I'm sure you are," she replied angrily. "You were so sorry that you couldn't have been there for me when I really needed you to be." She took Corey's silence as him feeling guilty and not having any excuse for his actions, so she continued with her accusations. "Yeah. You were too busy entertaining some girl in your apartment to take a few minutes and talk to me—the girl you claim to be in love with." Her tears began to flow. "Corey, I'm a big girl. If you didn't want to be with me, all you had to do was say so. I don't have time for games. I thought you were different, but I guess not."

Suddenly, Corey's laughter rang throughout the phone line. He was laughing so hard that he could not even speak. Sierra was too shocked to respond to her boyfriend's apathetic outburst. She couldn't even hang up in his face like she wanted to. All she could do was hold the phone against her ear as more tears flooded her eyes.

Apparently, her cries brought Corey out of his laugh fest. He suddenly became serious, though Sierra could clearly tell through his tone that a smile was still on his face.

"Sierra, sweetie, I'm sorry," Corey finally spoke. "It's just funny to me that with the news you just broke that you'd be more concerned about a girl in my apartment than what you have to deal with."

"That's because I love you more than I love myself," Sierra blurted, bringing silence back to Corey's lips.

"Oh, Sierra, and I love you too. That's why everything is going to be okay," he assured her. "That's why I'm going to be here for you no matter what. Testing positive is not a death sentence, it just means that we have to appreciate and not take for granted the time God has blessed us to be together. You're not alone, and I believe that's why God put me in your life when He did, and I'm grateful." Corey listened as Sierra whimpered through the phone. "Look, I didn't mean to bust out laughing like that. It's just funny that you'd actually think I'd have a girl in my apartment."

"Corey, I'm not stupid. The chick answered the phone sounding like she'd just woke up."

Corey allowed a soft chuckle to escape his lips.

Sierra was becoming agitated. "I can't believe that you're sitting here making a joke out of something so serious. The day I called you, Corey, was the day I found out about my test results. That was a time when I really needed you, and you were too busy with that girl to even talk to me."

"Sierra," he called her name softly. "*That girl* is my roommate's girlfriend, Monica. Dustin—that's my roommate—was supposed to be taking her out, and she was waiting for him to finish getting ready."

Sierra, apparently not buying Corey's story, asked, "Why was she answering your phone? Why couldn't you or Dustin answer it?" She knew she sounded like a jealous girlfriend, but at the moment, she was.

"Because, like I said, Dustin was still getting ready for their date," Corey explained, "and I had just come home from a C4C meeting and I had to jump right in the shower before heading out to work."

"Well . . . why'd her voice sound so groggy?" she asked, her voice still harsh as she tried to hide the jealousy she still felt. "She sounded like she had just woke up."

Corey laughed. "Well, I'm not going to lie to you," he started, and Sierra braced herself for the brutal truth. "Monica does spend a lot of nights at the apartment with Dustin, *but*," he quickly added, "that day she was battling a bad cold. Her voice wasn't groggy; it was raspy."

The ice around Sierra's heart was slowly melting. "But you called her sweetie," she pointed out in a gentler tone.

"Sierra, I call a lot of girls sweetie, including my sister. It's an unconscious habit." His voice became soft and full of disappointment. "Baby, I apologize for not being there for you when you really needed me, but I hate that you shut me out like you did because of something you assumed. I love you; I could never cheat on you. Besides, I promised you that I would stick by your side. I'm not going to abandon you in your time of need. I still want to be with you, despite your health status. I hope you feel the same way."

Sierra smiled. "I do," she said softly. Soon guilt taunted her conscience. She'd accused Corey of being unfaithful when he had not been, but she, herself, had fallen during her moment of vulnerability. She decided that it was only fair to tell Corey the complete truth.

"I apologize for assuming such a horrible thing about you, Corey," she began, her voice shaking and her eyes filling with more tears. "I want us to be honest in our relationship with each other."

"So do I," Corey agreed.

"Well, I have a confession to make," she continued. "That night I found out about my test results and that girl answered your phone, I went out partying."

"Sierra—"

"No," Sierra cut in. "Let me finish. By the time I decided to go home, I was so drunk and out of my mind that I drove to this guy's house."

"Sierra—"

"Corey, please," she stopped him again as she wiped a few tears from her eyes. "I've always had a crush on this guy—Ronald. And before you and I got together, I was planning to steal him away from his girlfriend, who I am very jealous of. I just felt like I deserved the love that they shared. So, after I assumed you were cheating on me, I decided that I could do the same. So, I went to Ronald's house and tried to seduce him. It almost worked, but thankfully, he came to his senses." She paused. "I'm really, really sorry."

"Sierra, I can't believe you would—" Corey began, but stopped. "I'm not going to fuss at you because you're not a child. It's apparent that you've realized your mistake and you're taking responsibility for it."

"Corey, you sound like you're trying not to yell at me, and I don't want you to hold back anything you're feeling," she told him, though she was afraid of him losing his temper. "It's better you get it off of your chest now than to hold it in."

"Baby, I'm disappointed in you, but you weren't yourself. You were intoxicated and emotionally unstable. I'm going to forgive you because I love you."

There must be a God, Sierra thought. She knew that the Man upstairs was looking out for her. "I love you, too, Corey, and I promise no more drinks or sexual activity. I'm dedicated to our commitment with each other."

"That's good to hear," he said. "Now, let's pray on it."

"I'd like that," she said with a smile.

They took their relationship to God in prayer, praying that His will would be done in their lives. They also prayed that God would keep His hand over Sierra, and that the path her life would take from then on would be directed by Him.

After talking to Corey, Sierra stayed up until one o'clock in the morning so she could talk to her father once he got home. She greeted him at the door and surprised him with a big hug. When he returned the embrace, she released tears from years past on his shoulder. He sat her down on the sofa in the living room and let her cry. When her tears finally subsided, Christopher apologized to his daughter repeatedly for everything that he had and had not done.

"Baby girl, I am so sorry," he repeated for the tenth time. "After your mother died, I just didn't know what to do. I guess I turned to the first thing I saw—that liquor. And after that, when I stopped spending time with you, and you would do things that didn't seem like things my little girl would do, I'd lash out in the wrong way. I am so, so sorry."

"It's okay, Daddy," Sierra sobbed. "I'm just glad that you are here." She hesitated and then decided it was best to tell him now. "Daddy?"

"Yes, baby girl."

"I started dating LaToya's brother, Corey. He's a sophomore at Missouri College and he is a Christian," she explained. "Well, I told him about how I slept around and stuff, so he took me to get an AIDS test." She started to cry again. "And . . . and it came back p-pos-positive."

Christopher looked at Sierra as she cried in his lap. He could not believe that his little girl had HIV. Even with all that he knew she had done in her short life, her father never thought something like this would happen to her. As hard as he tried not to, Christopher couldn't help but to blame himself. If he had been there like he should have, like he promised, Sierra probably would have never turned to guys she didn't know, love, or care about, trying to find the love she should have been getting from him. He had no idea what to say to make her feel better, so he just held her until she had no tears left.

"Daddy, I don't want to die," she said.

"Don't worry, baby girl," he said, rubbing her back. "We'll get through this, *together* this time. I know we will."

Now, as Sierra sat at her desk, barely listening to what her Biology teacher was saying, she continued to replay the conversation in her head. Ever since their talk, Christopher began to treat Sierra like he used to before he started dating again and before he became abusive. She and her dad had spent time together over the past week, and he'd started coming home earlier to eat dinner with her in the evenings. She and Corey would talk on the phone every other day, just to see how the other was doing. She had also started wearing her ring again, but this time it was to keep herself from any more harm that may occur through sexual contact.

Although everything was back to normal, Sierra still struggled with the reality of her health. She knew what the disease was, and had begun taking medical treatments for it, but it was still hard to come to terms with the fact that she could easily die in the next ten years, or even sooner. Her stress was apparent to all those who came in contact with her, and people could tell she'd had many restless nights. No longer did she come to school dressed to impress.

She now wore whatever was within her reach. Although she would glam up every so often, everyone knew she was not the same Sierra Monroe.

She looked over at Wanda, who had the most menacing smile on her face. Sierra heard through the grapevine that Wanda had been the one to start the gossip about her heath status. How could someone who claimed to be her friend spread her business around school? Sierra didn't know why she even hung out with Wanda. All she ever did was talk about and degrade others. It was always, "She know she don't need to be wearin' those shoes," or "He look like he can't even breathe in them pants," or "You know he 'bout to break up with her to go with that other girl he been messin' 'round with," or "Did you see her with him, actin' like she don't have a boyfriend?" Now that Sierra thought about it, the only thing that ever came out of Wanda's mouth had something to do with what someone else was wearing or doing in their private time.

Once the bell rang, Sierra walked out of the classroom and into the hallway full of students who seemed not to be able to control their eyes as she walked by. She met LaToya in the commons, and they began to proceed to their lockers, but were stopped when they heard someone calling from behind.

"Hey, Sierra," Wanda said, walking toward them.

"What do you want?" Sierra said, already aggravated with her former friend.

"I was just coming to see how you were doing today," Wanda said, and then leaned forward in a theatrical whisper. "Considering your condition and all."

"Why don't you go find something to do with your life?" LaToya snapped.

Sierra was on the verge of tears, but she refused to break down again in front of the entire school.

"What's wrong, Sierra?" Wanda taunted. "Why are you so pale? Don't be ashamed. Everyone knows."

"I don't know what you're talking about," Sierra stated with as much dignity as she could gather.

"Oh, I'm sure you do," Wanda said.

"Wanda, why don't you leave her alone?" Nevaeh said, walking up and standing beside Sierra. Nevaeh had tried to be civilized with Wanda for the sake of pleasing God, but the girl was starting to get on her last nerve.

"Who do you think you are?" Wanda spat angrily.

"Oh, I *know* who I am," Nevaeh said coolly. "But I think that you need to retrace your steps and figure out who *you* are. Or do I need to call Mother Younge and let her remind you?" Nevaeh said, referring to Wanda's grandmother/ guardian, an active member of her church.

Wanda stared at Nevaeh, who returned the stance. After a moment of staring each other down, Wanda walked away, leaving everyone who looked on in shock. Wanda never let anyone talk to her like that, and her walking away showed everyone that she wasn't as tough as she tried to be.

Nevaeh turned and looked at Sierra, who was still trying to hold back her tears. "Are you okay?" she asked Sierra, her voice and face full of concern.

"Yes," Sierra whispered. "Thank you."

"No problem," Nevaeh said and then began to walk away.

"Wait," Sierra said. "Umm . . . I just wanted to apologize for what happened between me and Ronald. I was out of it that night and—"

Nevaeh waved off her apology. "It's cool. Me and Ron worked it out. I'm just glad you got home safely. He never should have let you drive yourself home, but under the circumstances . . ." Nevaeh allowed her sentence to go unfinished, but she smiled when she continued. "Plus, I hear you have yourself a man who loves you."

"Who told you that?"

"*Everybody's* talking about it," Nevaeh exaggerated. "There's a rumor going around that he is here today."

"Are you serious?" Sierra questioned, not believing that Corey was actually at her school. She looked at LaToya, who had a grin on her face, and she wondered if her friend knew something that she didn't.

Nevaeh broke the short silence. "Tall? Light-skinned? Muscular? Fine, with a St. Louis accent? Yeah, he's here. I saw him myself. He was just in the front office." She looked up toward the front of the building as she spoke. "I think that's him right there."

Sierra looked in the direction she was pointing and was surprised to see Corey standing at the center of the hall with her counselor, searching the crowd to see if she was around. She watched as Patricia pointed Corey in her direction. Spotting her, Corey gave the counselor an appreciative smile before making his way through the maze of students.

"What are you doing here?" Sierra asked when he stood next to her.

He leaned down and kissed her and handed her the white lilies he had hidden behind his back.

Sierra's smile was wide as she took the lilies. "Thank you." She kissed him again, and then repeated her earlier question.

"Toya called me," Corey said

Sierra looked at her best friend, who held a sheepish expression.

"I couldn't help myself. You've been looking so sad lately, this was the only way I thought you'd cheer up," LaToya said with a smile.

"What about school? Don't you have classes you should be in right now?" Sierra asked Corey in concern.

"I skipped all my classes today and booked a nonstop flight all the way down here. I'm only staying for the weekend, and then I have to go back." Corey smiled, and then took her hand. "So that means we can make this weekend our first Valentine's together."

"But I have a class to go to in like one minute. Are you going to stay here for almost two hours?"

"No," Corey said, "I have a dinner to prepare. You go to your class and come home with Toya. Everything will be set by then."

"Okay," she said, giggling at the way his accent changed the pronunciation of the word "everything."

He nudged her playfully. "You're gonna have to stop picking on me," he said with a pout.

She smiled, and he leaned down and kissed her one last time before walking toward the exit and leaving the building. Sierra couldn't stop smiling as she made her way to her locker.

"Hey," Nevaeh said. "Take care of yourself, okay?"

"Okay." Sierra smiled.

"I'll see if Coach can open up a spot for you on the squad for basketball season," Nevaeh said. "You need to stay active, and what better way to do it than to do something you are good at and something you love, right? I'll be praying for you."

"Thanks." Sierra never noticed how sincere Nevaeh was. She always thought that Nevaeh was just being nice to everyone for the sake of keeping up her good girl image, but Sierra was starting to realize that Nevaeh was just being herself. She was showing that she could be a good friend, and that was definitely something Sierra could use more of.

After getting their books from their lockers, Sierra and LaToya headed to their last period class. Sierra brought the flowers up to her nose and inhaled. She hadn't been this happy in years and, in spite of the circumstances, she couldn't deny that in the past few months, she'd received so many blessings that she couldn't count them all.

Chapter 29

February 14

Nevaeh looked across the table at Ronald and he smiled. A week ago, she would not have imagined that she would be able to celebrate this day with him; now she was sitting across from him at the Sun Dial Restaurant in downtown Atlanta. The rotating restaurant was one of her favorite places in Atlanta, but she rarely ate there. It gave a great view of the city, but dining there could be quite costly, especially for two high school students.

"Where did you get the money to bring me here?" she asked, sipping her water.

Ronald placed his hand on top of hers. "Don't worry about it. I can pay for everything, so get whatever you want."

Nevaeh smiled and looked away as he stared at her intently. Earlier that day, Ronald had brought a teddy bear, a box of chocolates, and a bouquet of red roses to school to give to her, disregarding the fact that school administrators had warned students all month long that any outside gifts would be confiscated. She accepted the gifts, but quickly took them to her counselor, who promised to hold them in her office for her until the end of the day.

"You look beautiful," he said for the millionth time as he admired her dress.

Nevaeh looked down at her dress and picked imaginary lint off of her sleeve. She had chosen the dress just for this night. She had gone to every store and tried on every dress, but found nothing she liked. When she saw the long-sleeved red dress, she knew she had to have it. The neckline was decorated with small jewels, and the bodice fit her perfectly. The bottom flowed loosely around her feet, which were adorned in red heels.

"Thank you." She smiled.

"And that necklace goes perfectly with it," he said.

"Thank you," she said again while fingering the locket that hung from her neck.

Ronald gazed at her, making her shiver. Nevaeh looked at the menu, in order to keep him from seeing her blush. While letting her eyes roam over the list of dishes, she noticed that the lowest priced meal was twenty-six dollars. *You have got to be kidding me!* She searched the menu again for something she wanted that was not too high. *Please! Everything on this menu is too high*, she thought.

When the waiter approached their table for their orders, Ronald waited for Nevaeh to place hers first.

"Umm," she said as she continued to scan the menu. "I think I'll have the seared Atlantic salmon fillet," she said, hoping that the lowest price printed was not too much for Ronald to pay for.

"What about you, sir?" the waiter asked Ronald.

"I'll have the grilled tenderloin of beef," he said after skimming through the menu.

"I'll have those out momentarily," the waiter said, taking their menus.

Ronald looked at Nevaeh and smiled as she looked away. She focused her gaze on the view. "It's so beautiful," Nevaeh admired.

"*You* are so beautiful," Ronald said, making her blush once again. "Nevaeh, how many times have I thanked you for taking me back?"

"About a trillion times," she said with a smile.

"Well, here's a trillion and one," he said sincerely. "Thank you for giving me another chance. I know you didn't have to, but you did, and I am so grateful."

"Ronald, you don't have to continue to thank me. I don't know what my dad said to you that day after our sisters' recital, but you've been more respectful than you were before."

"Let's just say both of our fathers talked some good sense in my head." Ronald laughed. "Especially my dad. He said, and I quote, 'If you lose her again over something so stupid, I swear I'm gonna knock you over the head so hard, you gonna wonder where your mind went'."

"Well, remind me to thank him." Nevaeh laughed.

When their food arrived, Nevaeh was surprised when Ronald immediately took her hands and began to bless the food. Usually it was Nevaeh who had to lead prayer or remind him that they needed to pray before eating. This was definitely a nice change. When he finished praying, Nevaeh looked at him and smiled.

"What?" he asked as he dug into his beef.

"You are growing, aren't you?"

"I'm trying," Ronald admitted. "And not only for

our sakes, but I really want a better relationship with God. And I'm not gonna stop 'til I get it."

Nevaeh smiled as she used her fork to cut her salmon. Throughout dinner, they talked about the last three years of their relationship, their good times with each other and their bad times. Ronald apologized for so many things that Nevaeh finally told him all was forgiven, even things he had not apologized for already.

After they had finished their food, Ronald paid the check and left a tip for their waiter. They walked arm in arm to the elevator that would lead them to the ground floor. They'd parked one block away, but the fresh outside air did them good. Ronald opened the car door for Nevaeh and started on the drive home. Although the ride was a quiet one, it was not awkward; they felt as comfortable as they had in the past.

Ronald turned on the radio, and Nevaeh began to sing every love song that played. Although she was not looking directly at Ronald, she was singing for his benefit.

Several minutes later, he took her hand as he pulled into her driveway. Looking in her eyes, he repeated his promise to her as he pulled out a rectangular velvet blue box, much like the one her necklace had been in.

"I will spend the rest of my life making you happy. And when temptation enters, we just have to stay on our knees, praying that we do the right thing. This time I mean it," Ronald smiled. "I love you, Nevaeh," he said, taking the bracelet out of the box and fastening it around her wrist.

"Oh my God," Nevaeh said as she admired the small gold hearts that dangled from a chain to form the piece of jewelry identical to the one that was around her neck. "This is really beautiful," she said.

"When I got the necklace, I couldn't afford the bracelet," Ronald said, "so I decided to have them put it on hold until I got the money for it."

"I love it," she said, kissing him.

"I thought you would," he said.

He got out of the car and ran around to the passenger side to open her door. Bringing her home from a date and walking her to her door felt phenomenal. Having lost the privilege before, he didn't take anything for granted anymore. Ronald said a silent prayer of thanks to God for allowing Nevaeh back into his life.

"I had a great time," she said as they stood under the porch light.

"Me too," Ronald said. He leaned down and kissed her on the cheek, much to her surprise. He smiled and shrugged when he noticed the look on her face.

"I'm really starting to like the new Ronald." Nevaeh smiled. "Happy anniversary," she said as she unlocked the door.

"Happy anniversary," Ronald said, touching her chin affectionately.

He waited until she walked into the house and had closed and locked the door before he walked back to his car and drove home, smiling.

Epilogue

Easter Sunday

Greater Faith Tabernacle was packed with over one thousand members and visitors for the annual Easter Celebration Service. Children got up in front of the church and recited practiced speeches. The drama department put on a moving reenactment of Jesus' death and resurrection. The Greater Faith Dancers performed a lively dance to "Your Love" by Fred Hammond. The program was set to make sure everyone participated, whether in front of the congregation or from their seats, as they joined in praise and worship.

Once the main program was finished, Nevaeh and Shimone weren't as surprised as their families and friends were when they heard Pastor McKinley call them to the front to perform a duet. They were fully prepared as they got up and walked toward the front of the church.

"Over the past few months, I have been through

some trying times," Nevaeh started. "I have had my faith tested in ways I couldn't imagine, but I know it was God who helped me get through them."

Agreeable amens came from all throughout the sanctuary.

"As everyone can see," Shimone, now six months pregnant, said, placing her hand on her stomach, "I have been through difficult times too, but I also know the Lord doesn't make mistakes when he brings life into this world, and I thank Him for the grace and mercy He has shone on me in the last few months."

"We would just like to sing a song that describes how we feel at this point in our lives." Nevaeh closed her eyes and began the first words of the song.

Marques sat in the third row from the front, next to Ronald. He watched in amazement as Nevaeh and Shimone sang, in harmony, "Coming Back Home," by BeBe Winans, a cappella. They sounded heavenly as they told of their desire to return to God as His children.

"Dang, I didn't know your girl could sing like that," Marques whispered.

Ronald smiled and nodded as he watched Nevaeh use her gift to glorify God. When they finished, they received a standing ovation. All through the remainder of the service, the song stayed on Ronald's heart. He knew it was time for him to come back home. Living life one apology after the other was not what he wanted. He noticed that he had been living on the promise that God would always forgive him for his sins, and he knew it was not right. He needed to stop letting temptation enter his life. He wanted to always be available to God, not just when it was convenient for him. He needed to make everything right. It was time for him to get his life back on the right track.

At the end of the service, Pastor McKinley opened the altar to anyone who wanted to give their life to Christ or rededicate themselves to the Father. "Jesus died for you and arose on this day, so that you may live in sin no longer," Pastor McKinley said into the microphone. "The Bible says that if you confess with your mouth that Jesus is Lord and believe in your heart that He rose from the dead, you will be saved. Will there be one?"

Ronald got up and was surprised when Nevaeh grabbed his hand and walked to the front with him. Imani and Nicole came from the row behind their siblings and walked toward the front of the church, ready to fully give their lives to the Lord also.

Marques sat quietly in his seat, trying to decide if he should make the walk. He had been coming to church with Shimone's family for more than a month. At first it was just so he could go to Shimone's house and eat Misty's cooking afterwards, but lately he had been feeling like he needed a change in his life. He wanted what Ronald, Nevaeh, and Shimone had. He liked the fact that they didn't pretend to be perfect, and he knew that if he came as he was, God would accept him into the family also. *It's a short walk*, his heart told him. *C'mon.*

He leaned in Shimone's direction. "Shimone, will you go with me up there?"

Shimone smiled and took his hand. "Sure."

As they made their way to the front, Marques was surprised to see LaToya and Sierra walking from the back of the church, both girls on their fathers' arms. Several other members, from small children with their parents guiding them, to teenagers, to middle-aged adults, came to the front to give or rededicate their lives to the Lord.

Sierra cried her prayers to the Lord and asked Him to accept her as His child and forgive her for her past. Marques prayed that God would forgive him and accept him as His child. Ronald prayed that his life would be changed forever, and that he would become a new person and continue down the path that would someday lead him to his heavenly Father. Shimone prayed that as she embarked on this new journey in her life, God would walk with her and carry her through the hard times. Nevaeh prayed that her future would be bright, and that her light would shine everywhere she went, so that people would know she was a child of God.

As they began to repeat the Sinner's Prayer, a sudden peace came over the entire building and swept through the bodies of those who were letting Jesus into their hearts. They knew they would never be the same.

Group Discussion Questions

1. Who was your favorite character and why?

2. Do you believe there were signs Nevaeh could have been aware of that would have indicated Ronald's changing opinion on intimacy in their relationship?

3. Sierra's father's absence throughout her life was clearly illustrated, with him being nearly nonexistent throughout the novel. How do you feel about Christopher's distance?

4. How do you think Sierra's life would have been different if her father had played a more active role?

5. Sierra stated that she did not want to ever ask a guy for anything because she knew she would have to give them something in return. Do you agree with LaToya when she said that Sierra was giving her sexual partners something that she did not want them to have?

6. What was your reaction to Marques' decision to step up and take responsibility for the child he and Shimone had conceived?

7. Marques promised to be faithful to Shimone, even though he had been tempted to hook up with a few of his ex-girlfriends. Do you believe it was because of his love for her, or only for the sake of their unborn child? Do you believe he will be true to his word and stay with Shimone without sharing the physical intimacy that they once had?

8. How did you feel about Corey's proposal to Sierra? Do you think she was using Corey as a substitute for her father's absence, like she had been doing with other guys?

9. What was the significance of Jesus, carrying the cross on His back, appearing to Nevaeh while she was with Ronald?

10. How do you feel about Darnell's interest in Nevaeh? Do you think that it was inappropriate considering her circumstances?

11. What was your reaction to Ronald's apology to Nevaeh after the confrontation at school? Do you believe it was genuine? Do you think that his decision to continue to remain celibate with her was just an attempt to get her to take him back?

12. Sierra's test results sent her into a depressed state for two weeks. Discuss her reaction to her health status and how you would react if you received the same news.

13. Despite the saddening news, do you think that this was what Sierra needed to get her life in order?

14. Evaluate each couple's relationship with each other, and now, with Christ. What do you think the future holds for each of them?

15. The Bible teaches that sex is honored by God only in the confines of marriage. How important do you think it is that parents impart this message of celibacy to their children?